REBELS RISING

NLA Digital, LLC
1732 Wazee Street, Suite 207
Denver, CO 80202

Production Manager: Lori Bennett
Cover art and book design: Angie Hodapp

ISBN 978-1-62051-264-7

REBELS RISING

SHANNA SWENDSON

Also by Shanna Swendson

Rebel Mechanics
Rebel Magisters
Rebels Rising

A Fairy Tale
To Catch a Queen
A Kind of Magic

Enchanted, Inc.
Once Upon Stilettos
Damsel Under Stress
Don't Hex with Texas
Much Ado About Magic
No Quest for the Wicked
Kiss and Spell
Frogs and Kisses
Paint the Town Red (short story)

CONTENTS

In Which My Every Move Is Observed 5
In Which I Engage in Clandestine Correspondence 20
In Which I Volunteer for a Task 37
In Which I Must Avoid Carolers 56
In Which I Must Watch My Words 71
In Which I Am Put on Display 87
In Which I Face the Perils of Christmas Caroling 113
In Which I Set Out on a Very Long Walk 129
In Which We Shed Some Light on the Situation 146
In Which I Have a Startling Revelation 163
In Which I Must Leave the City 180
In Which I Return to the City 195
In Which I Write the Story of a Lifetime 218
In Which I Must Reveal the Truth 235
In Which I Am Reunited with Family 252
In Which I Make Difficult Choices 270
In Which I Visit a New Land 285

AUTHOR'S NOTE

This novel is a work of alternate history. Adding magic to the mix meant that events didn't play out the way they appear in history books. Some things are entirely different, and some things are happening at different times or in different places. Figuring out where the real history might fit in is part of the fun.

NEW YORK CITY 1888

GOVERNMENT ROCKED BY FINANCE SCANDAL WHERE DID THE MONEY GO? PUBLIC CALLS FOR RESIGNATION

BY ELIZABETH SMITH

THERE HAS STILL BEEN NO PUBLIC COMMENT from His Grace the Royal Governor about reports that the New York colony's treasury has been emptied. The approved newspapers have yet to mention the scandal, but sources inside the administration say the governor and his cronies are frantically trying to raise funds to restore the treasury before Crown auditors can arrive to review the accounts.

What has been announced is a possible tax hike. Are colonists now required to pay for their government's poor management, with no say on who makes up that government and not even a vote for the parliamentary representatives who choose the government?

Calls for the resignation of government officials involved with this affair have come from all levels of society. The Lord Mayor of New York City has called for an investigation. Several nobles who wish to remain anonymous say they believe a break with Britain is in order.

SECRET POLITICAL PRISONER ESCAPES TRANSPORT TO ENGLAND

BY LIBERTY JONES

A HIGH-RANKING POLITICAL PRISONER HELD without charges or trial disappeared recently from the holding cells of the West Battery Fort, on the eve of transport to England.

The titled nobleman was arrested on suspicion of treason, but he was never brought before a judge. His family's solicitor was not allowed to see him or speak with any official about his case. Sources say the prisoner was to be sent to England in order to keep his case out of the public eye to avoid scandal being attached to his prominent family.

Military officials are baffled as to how the prisoner managed to escape. Guards found his locked cell empty. No unusual activity was noted at the fort.

If the government is persecuting titled magisters, is a crackdown on other rebel groups imminent? Some members of the magister class see this arrest as evidence that no one is safe. Rebel magisters have begun talks with other rebel groups, including the Rebel Mechanics.

Rebel groups claim no knowledge of the whereabouts of the missing political prisoner.

IN WHICH MY EVERY MOVE IS OBSERVED

I was completely surrounded by the enemy. At least, that was how I felt. It was an odd feeling to have at a ball, but all the other guests were high-ranking magisters, members of the magical ruling class. I was there as a chaperone, so I was more or less invisible, but I couldn't help but wonder what these people would think—or do—if they knew what I really was.

For one thing, I was a magical half-breed, a person whose very existence was illegal. For another, I was affiliated with the Rebel Mechanics, as well as a rebel group among the magisters. I wrote for the unauthorized radical newspaper under a pseudonym. I was a spy who used my position in a magister home to gather intelligence on the government that I passed to the rebels. I'd helped a prisoner accused of treason escape, which meant I would be considered a traitor, as well.

And yet, all these people walked right past me, barely acknowledging my existence, entirely unaware that I was working to bring down their society. I hid my smile behind my fan.

My charge, Lady Flora Lyndon, returned to her seat and gave a not very encouraging smile to her dance partner, who was clever enough to read the signs and leave her be rather than pushing his case. "How much longer do you think we must stay, Miss Newton?" she asked me. "These men are all so very shallow."

A few weeks ago, I'd never have believed that Flora would become my only ally in a situation like this, but she'd taken on the rebel cause with great enthusiasm, and I was beginning to believe that it wasn't merely because she'd met a rebel she found appealing. Now, it was all I could do to stop her from wearing a Rebel Mechanics insignia and shouting revolutionary slogans at society functions.

"Perhaps two more dances would give you an excuse to plead exhaustion," I said. "We really must keep up appearances." That wasn't merely about social status now. Across the room were the two men I'd come to think of as Inspector Stout and Inspector Tall, who'd been watching us ever since Lord Henry Lyndon, my erstwhile employer and Flora's uncle, had disappeared. I saw them outside the house, lurking on a street corner. One of them followed whenever I went out with the children. Now they were at the ball, dressed in military uniforms. There was a third man I thought of as Inspector Nondescript because he did a much better job of blending in. I imagined he was watching the house, ready to catch Henry sneaking home.

Flora paled ever so slightly. I'd managed to keep the younger children from noticing the followers, but Flora was well aware of them. "Of course." She turned a dazzling smile on the next man who passed, and soon she was sweeping around the ballroom in his arms. In order to allay suspicion, we made every effort to behave like carefree girls, which meant that we'd attended far too many balls, luncheons, and tea parties for my taste lately. Even Flora, who usually enjoyed socializing, was wearing out.

"Excuse me, Miss Newton, is it?" I glanced up to see a young man looming over me. He actually knew very well who I was, as he was one of Lord Henry's close friends, Geoffrey, Viscount Hayes. "I don't suppose I could get you to plead my case with Lady Flora."

I had to struggle to keep a straight face because Geoffrey was extremely unlikely to be interested in Flora. "I'm not sure how much good it would do you, as she seldom listens to me," I replied.

"Even so, you have more of an opportunity to talk to her than I do." He took Flora's vacated seat next to me and leaned over to whisper, "Have you heard anything?"

"Nothing," I replied. "But we're being watched, so I've made no effort to get word."

"Ah, I'm afraid I've been doing the same. I must admit to being somewhat worried."

"We surely would have heard if anything had gone amiss."

"I hope you're right. We're still meeting, but we're being very cautious who we let into our circle. We can't risk another betrayal." He stood and bowed slightly. "I appreciate your assistance, Miss Newton."

"Here's Lady Flora now, if you'd care to dance with her," I said, unable to resist the temptation. Flora batted her eyelashes at him and allowed him to lead her to the dance floor. He looked like a man being forced to bite into lemons. I couldn't help but grin. This was the most enjoyment I'd had since I'd said farewell to Henry.

I turned to notice another man standing next to me, Philip Spencer, who was also a part of Henry's circle. "You really must dance with me, Miss Newton," he said with a gallant bow. "I don't consider it a successful ball unless I've danced with every eligible young lady present."

"I'm hardly considered eligible," I demurred.

"Well, you're young and pretty, so you must dance with me."

I suspected that what he really wanted was to talk to me, so I reluctantly acquiesced and took his hand. Just as I thought, as soon as we were dancing, he whispered into my ear, "So, Verity, have you heard anything from our friend?"

"Nothing at all," I murmured. "Which is probably good news."

"Do you think it'll be safe to meet up with your other friends anytime soon? I'm feeling awfully cut off, and we need to get things moving. It's getting interesting in our world."

"It is?"

"Oh, yes, by golly. That news about the missing colonial funds really shook things up. There have been calls for the governor to resign. My father said that it even came up on the floor of the Assembly, and what's really surprising was that my dear father didn't seem to think it was a bad idea. You may have noticed that flock of swine flying over the city."

I wasn't sure whether the governor resigning would be such a good thing for our cause. As it was, he was the grandfather of the children I taught and chaperoned, which gave me access to his inner circle. I'd gained much valuable intelligence from my position. We wanted to topple the government, not merely get new leadership. I said as much to Philip. "What we want is a governor we elect to rule our own nation. It doesn't help if we merely get a new one appointed by the Crown."

"Baby steps, Verity. Get them opposed to this governor, and they get used to the idea of opposing the government. We'll get there someday."

The orchestra ended the song, and we had to stop talking. He escorted me back to my seat, where Flora had already retreated after dancing with Geoffrey. "*Now* may we go?" she asked.

"I believe we have—" A fanfare cut me off. Everyone in the room stood and faced the entrance.

"Oh, bother. That's Grandfather arriving, isn't it?" Flora said. "Now we can't leave. It would look rude, and I'll have to greet him."

Looking rude didn't appear to be a concern for everyone. The applause at the governor's entrance was weaker than I'd ever heard, and as soon as he'd acknowledged it and taken his seat, the crowd on the dance floor thinned dramatically. A good third of the guests departed, none of them paying their respects to the governor before they took their leave. I barely caught myself before I asked Flora who they were, and then I remembered that while she was aware I had rebel connections, she didn't know the full extent of my involvement. All I could hope was that Philip and Geoffrey made note of those who might be potential sympathizers.

As Flora and I made our way across the room to the governor so she could greet her grandfather, I couldn't help but overhear snatches of conversation along the way: "Do you think he's responsible?" "He knows exactly where that money went." "You have to wonder what else is going on that we don't know about." "That's what happens when your officials are accountable to no one." I barely stopped myself from turning around to see who'd made that last statement. It sounded like someone who might harbor revolutionary ideas.

The crowd of well-wishers and sycophants around the governor was smaller than normal. I almost felt sorry for the man. My guilt was somewhat exacerbated by the fact that the intercepted letter that had revealed the whole scandal was currently tucked away in a secret compartment in my desk, and I was the one who had revealed its contents to the world. He'd never been anything but kind to me, and sometimes I had trouble reconciling my beliefs about his position with my feelings for the man.

He looked genuinely glad to see us when we approached, which made me feel even guiltier. "Flora, Miss Newton," he said, rising and moving to greet us. He kissed Flora on both cheeks and nodded to me. "Are you enjoying the ball?"

Flora gave a languid sigh. "I suppose so, though it's not the most stimulating entertainment. We were just about to leave."

"You're starting to sound like your aunt," he said with a hearty laugh. Lady Elinor, the younger sister of the children's late mother, was an invalid who seldom left her bed. Since she'd stepped in as guardian to the children in Henry's absence, I'd learned that she was in perfectly good health, aside from getting a headache at the thought of dealing with society. She played the invalid to avoid having to take on the role of her widowed father's official hostess.

"My aunt can be very wise," Flora said.

"I hope you aren't planning to leave now that I've arrived," the governor said, taking Flora's arm and escorting her to the chair next to his. A footman moved to unobtrusively situate a chair behind hers for me. It seemed that we were trapped for the time being.

Flora being seated next to the governor brought renewed attention from the male guests, and soon she was being escorted to the dance floor, with a plaintive look at me. I wondered how long I needed to wait before I could claim a headache that would make Flora insist she needed to get me home. The governor went to dance with the hostess and some of the higher-ranking ladies, leaving me alone.

Although most of the people who remained at the ball were apparently supporters, not all of them held the governor in good opinion, and they didn't seem to notice me when they talked about him in his absence. I forced myself not to react in any way that might remind them that I could hear what they said as I eavesdropped on the conversations around me.

"I can't believe he's showing his face in public, under the circumstances," one lady said.

"What would you have him do?" a man asked.

"After what happened in the Assembly this week, I must say that I'm shocked, as well," another man said.

"What happened?" the lady asked.

"There was a motion made to call for his resignation."

"And the vote was in favor," a third man said. "It's nonbinding, of course, but it does put the government in an interesting position."

Yet another man said, so softly I had to strain to hear, "It won't matter, as he's going to disband the Assembly."

"He can't!" the woman said.

"The Crown can," the man said. He was behind me, but I imagined him shrugging. "And they wonder why there's talk of revolution. The Assembly is the only voice we have in our governance. Without that, it all comes from the Crown."

"And Parliament," one of the other men said.

"For which we have no vote."

I fanned myself furiously, hoping my face hadn't grown as red as it felt. Disbanding the Assembly? That was huge news, and the best thing was, it would be perfectly safe for me to be the reporter to break it, as it would be the last thing a governess should be expected to learn. I usually had to be careful with what I reported, lest anyone be able to plot my whereabouts against the intelligence reported by my alter ego. The problem would be finding a way to get the news to any of my rebel contacts while I was being closely watched by the authorities.

I scanned the crowd for those I knew to be among the rebel magisters. They might be able to relay word to some of the other rebels. But, alas, I'd already danced with Philip, so he was unlikely to approach me again, and Geoffrey had stayed just long enough after the governor's arrival to avoid the appearance of rudeness.

When Flora returned from the dance floor, she regarded me, then gasped. "Why, Miss Newton, you look quite pale. Are you feeling ill?" Her wink wasn't at all subtle, but no one around seemed to notice.

"It's only a little headache, but I'll be fine. There's no

need for you to interrupt your evening on my behalf," I said, allowing myself to sound weary.

"Nonsense! If you remain much longer, your headache will only grow worse, and then you might not be able to carry out your duties tomorrow." I thought that was a particularly clever touch on her part, as she wasn't known for being overly fond of me. Her concern for me being able to do my job made the charade more believable. She whirled to face her grandfather, who'd just returned from his obligatory dances. "Grandfather, I'm afraid we must leave immediately. Miss Newton is developing a headache, and if she's to be able to work tomorrow, she needs to get home and rest. I hate to abandon you like this."

"There's no need to leave on my account," I said weakly.

"I insist."

"I'm sorry to hear you're unwell, Miss Newton. Flora is correct. You should go home and rest," the governor said, and I was surprised by just how concerned he did look.

Flora helped me to my feet and supported me toward the cloakroom, where we gathered our wraps. Our carriage waited for us in front of the mansion, and Flora assisted me down the steps. Once we were inside the magical horseless carriage and on our way home, Flora burst into a fit of giggles. "I can't believe I kept a straight face through all that, and you played your role perfectly," she said.

"You're becoming quite the clandestine operative," I replied. "You were utterly convincing."

She settled back in her seat. "I believe I can get

Grandfather to believe anything I tell him. He's always favored me, though he doesn't take me at all seriously. He never agreed with Henry's insistence on my being educated. I just hope he doesn't get any ideas about sending me to finishing school abroad now that Henry's away. I could never abide that." Her eyes narrowed and her voice hardened. "I'd run away first."

"I doubt it will come to that," I said. If it did come to revolution, I thought she might be safer abroad, but I doubted she'd see it that way.

"Did any of Henry's friends have news of him?" she asked.

"No. They asked me that same question."

She glared at me. "*Do* you know anything?"

"You don't think I'd have told you? No, we're trying to avoid anything that might link us to his escape, and I'm trying to avoid doing anything that might look like a connection with anyone even suspected of rebel sympathies, so I've tried to stay out of it entirely. It's for his protection."

She sighed in a way that almost sounded like a sob. "I just wish we knew *something*."

"They'd have found a way to let us know if anything had gone wrong, I'm sure. He's probably safe and having the time of his life without having to worry about his position, for once." I started to say that I wouldn't be surprised if he'd gone back to banditry, but then I remembered that she didn't know that her uncle had been the leader of the Masked Bandits, who robbed wealthy magisters and the government to help smaller businesses pay their taxes and to fund Rebel Mechanics inventions.

But even as I'd told her why we could have no contact with the rebels for the time being, I suspected that my news was worthy of breaking the ban. It had been several weeks, and my cover for meeting with my various rebel contacts had always been friendships and daily errands. I had a network of shopgirls I could rely upon to pass messages to the rebels. I felt it was time to call upon that network again.

The next morning, although it was quite cold, I bundled up Rollo and Olive, the two younger children, and we walked with Rollo to school rather than taking the carriage. Olive and I then took care of some errands on the way home, stopping in at shops along the way. Six-year-old Olive enjoyed shopping enough that she didn't seem to notice anything unusual about our outing, and she also didn't seem to have noticed Inspector Stout following us.

"It will be Christmas soon, won't it, Miss Newton?" she asked as she skipped along beside me. "How will we send Uncle his presents?"

"We won't be able to, since we don't know where he is," I said, perhaps more loudly than necessary, but I wanted to make sure Inspector Stout could hear.

"Will he be able to send presents to us?" she asked, her lower lip beginning to tremble.

"I doubt it. But I'm sure he'll be thinking of you."

"It won't be a happy Christmas without Uncle."

"Your aunt and your grandfather will do everything they can to make it happy, I'm certain."

"Might we get extra gifts to make up for it?"

"I don't know. I can't speak for your family."

There were tears in her eyes, and I felt awful for her. It would be my first Christmas away from home, the first since the death of my mother, and I'd been trying not to think about that. It would have been different with Henry around. Without him, and with the cloud hanging over him, it was likely to be a bleak holiday, indeed.

"Don't cry, Olive," I said, squeezing her hand. "Why don't we stop and get some cake?"

"May we? And we don't have to bring any home to Flora?" She smiled through her tears.

"It will be our little secret." I bustled her into a small bakery, where she got to select tiny frosted cakes from a glass display case. Inspector Stout lurked outside, and I hoped he felt awkward watching a little girl cry.

But he didn't come inside the shop—much to my relief, for the girl working behind the counter was one of my contacts. I got Olive settled at one of the tables with her cakes and returned to the counter to select one for myself. The shopgirl leaned over, pointing out the merits of the various flavors. "That does sound good," I said out loud, then whispered, "I need a meeting, as unobtrusive as possible, as I'm being watched. It's critical."

"I'll let them know," she whispered in response.

I selected a cake and paid for our purchase, feeling

lighter with the success of my errand, though my pulse quickened at the thought of how risky my next move would be.

I didn't know how long it would take the message to be relayed. The Rebel Mechanics had technology that allowed messages to be sent as fast as light through a system of wires, so there was a chance that they would already have my news by the time I returned home.

Later that day, while the girls were occupied with music lessons, I set out for an afternoon stroll in Central Park, across the street from the Lyndon mansion. It was a habit for me, so I didn't think my watcher would find anything amiss. Inspector Stout apparently had the afternoon shift in spite of working that morning. I passed him on my way into the park, and I thought I could sense him following me at a discreet distance.

I frequently encountered my Mechanic friends in the park, so there was a good chance they might attempt to meet me there. I walked quickly to keep myself warm—and to make my watcher struggle to keep up. I couldn't hold back a grin when a well-dressed woman wearing a fur-trimmed hat hailed me from a passing magical roadster. "Why, Miss Newton! Fancy meeting you here," she said. "And out walking in this weather!" It was Lizzie Flynn, one of my closest friends in the rebel movement.

"I imagine walking keeps me warmer than sitting in your contraption," I replied.

"It has a heater," said the driver, whom I recognized

beneath his respectable disguise as Lizzie's brother, Colin. "Hop on board and join us for a spin."

Knowing how insanely jealous Flora would be, for she was desperately infatuated with Colin, I stepped up on the running board and squeezed into the space on the seat Lizzie made for me. It was a rather brilliant scheme, as Inspector Stout wouldn't be able to keep up or eavesdrop on us, and the use of the magical roadster would surely keep anyone from suspecting my friends were Rebel Mechanics.

I could only hope that the real owners didn't report it stolen while we were using it.

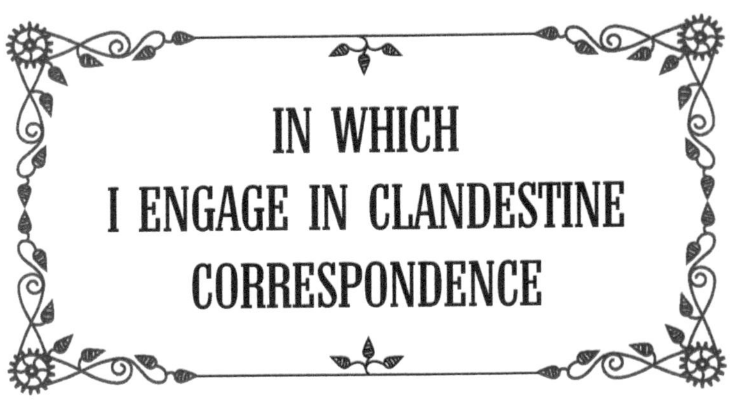

IN WHICH I ENGAGE IN CLANDESTINE CORRESPONDENCE

"I notice you're still being watched," Colin said, glancing in the rear-facing mirror to see Inspector Stout.

"Yes," I said with a weary sigh. "I'd have hoped they'd have given up by now, but I'm afraid they believe watching us is their best chance of finding Henry." I hesitated, hardly daring to ask, but I had to know. "How is he? Is he safe?" I said as softly as I could and still be sure Colin and Lizzie could hear me.

"He's safe," Lizzie said, patting my hand. "And I'm sure he sends his regards."

I felt my cheeks grow warm. Considering the way he'd kissed me when he said farewell, I certainly *hoped* he had regards to send. I'd relived that moment countless times, and I'd finally convinced myself that there might have been earlier evidence I hadn't noticed that he had some feeling for me. How many chances had I missed by not noticing? Not that it mattered much if I never saw him again, I thought bitterly.

"I doubt you asked for a meeting just to learn about Henry," Colin said, jolting me out of my momentary reverie. "Especially when it's still risky for you to do anything out of the ordinary."

"I overheard something at a ball last night," I said. "The governor is going to disband the Assembly. Apparently, some members called for him to resign, and rather than face a vote, he's getting rid of the Assembly entirely. Mind you, I haven't confirmed this, but it's unlikely to be publicly reported when or if it does happen." I slid a folded sheet of paper out of my glove and pressed it into Lizzie's hand. "Here's an article I wrote."

Lizzie hurried to tuck the article into her purse. "That was very dangerous, Verity," she scolded. "Having that article on your person would have been incriminating if you'd been caught."

"They're only following me. I don't think they'd dare demand to search me." I said it with a laugh, but inwardly, I knew Lizzie was right. I had taken a huge risk.

"We've been running the occasional item under your byline, so it shouldn't draw suspicion to you when this appears," Lizzie said. "Would anyone expect you to have had this information?"

"I overheard it when people were talking during a ball, and I don't think they even noticed I was there. Anyone present in the Assembly would be more likely to have this information than I would. They'll suspect one of the dissenters talked to the press."

Colin pounded his hand against the steering wheel. "If they disband the Assembly, we'll have no choice but to act. That's basically a declaration of war against the colonies, removing our last form of representation."

"Not that they ever represented us," Lizzie muttered.

"You're supposed to be magisters out for a spin," I reminded them. "You should probably refrain from revolutionary rhetoric." I forced myself not to look over my shoulder for my follower.

"Aside from being watched and having your employer absent, how are you doing, Verity?" Lizzie asked.

"Well enough, I suppose. You've probably noticed that we've remained in the house rather than having to move into the governor's mansion. The children's Aunt Elinor came to live with us as guardian. She may not be quite as radical as Henry, but she's hardly conventional. She doesn't go out, and she doesn't entertain. I'm not even sure she'd mind my activity, though I still have to be careful because of the servants." Actually, I had a very strong suspicion that Elinor was at least as radical as I was, if not more so, since I believed her to be the mysterious woman in black who helped fund the Mechanics, but I hadn't confirmed it, and I didn't want to reveal her secret if they didn't already know her identity.

I glanced at Colin and grinned. "Really, I'm more

concerned about tempering Flora's newfound radicalism. She's ready to burn down the Assembly Hall and drive the British soldiers into the ocean."

"Ah, a girl after my own heart," Colin said with a grin.

"Yes, well, at the moment I'm trying to avoid looking like that's what we're doing, since they still aren't quite sure we weren't responsible for spiriting Henry out of their custody in the middle of the night." I couldn't resist a slight smirk. "Of course, the fact that we *were* responsible makes that somewhat more challenging."

We'd made a loop of this portion of the park and passed my follower, who'd taken a seat on a bench near the path I'd have to take to return home. I was tempted to wave at him, but reminded myself that I was pretending not to notice him.

Once we'd passed him, I turned to Lizzie. "I just wish there were a way I could safely keep in touch with all of you. Mail is too risky, as I'm sure it's being read before we receive it. The seals always look like they've been tampered with. It's difficult to just bump into the right people at the right time and in the right place, but arranging a meeting means that I might expose one of my contacts, and I never know if one of them is under suspicion. But I hate not knowing what's happening, and I'm still getting valuable intelligence that I need to pass on."

"Our people are working on something that might be useful," Lizzie said. "That's all I can say now, but you'll know when we have it working. Now, should we confound your follower by taking you home?"

"Yes, please," I said.

"I hope you don't mind if we drop you off right away," Colin said. "We only have so long before the owner of this little beauty notices her missing."

When I returned home, I found Flora sitting by a window in the family parlor, painting a watercolor of the park while Olive practiced the piano. I leaned over to inspect Flora's work. "That's very nice," I said. "You've managed to capture the stark beauty of the bare trees, and it looks cold even without snow."

"When will it snow?" Olive asked from the piano.

"Soon, I'm sure. I'm surprised it hasn't already," I replied. When Olive went back to playing, I leaned closer to Flora and whispered, "Henry is well and safe. That's all I know. And Colin sends his regards."

Flora looked up abruptly from her work, her cheeks flushing, then she caught herself and returned her eyes to her easel, though her paintbrush trembled. "You've seen him?" she whispered.

"Colin. Not Henry."

"I should hope not Henry. If he's in the park, he's even more mad than I thought. But you saw Colin?"

"I had news I needed to share, and he and Lizzie met me under cover."

"I wish you'd brought me along."

"If I had, then we'd have had to bring Olive. And I won't be having more meetings with them for the time being, unless events warrant."

I went back to being cut off from the outside world. We got the officially sanctioned newspapers, but one would never have the slightest inkling that anything was wrong from reading them. They'd never mentioned the scandal of the missing funds, and they certainly weren't reporting any unrest within the Assembly. Rebel activity wasn't even acknowledged. I didn't dare purchase the unauthorized newspaper while I was being watched.

For the first time since I'd come to work for the Lyndons, I was functioning as exactly what I appeared to be: a governess and chaperone. I wasn't even working on my magical training, since other magisters could sense magic in use nearby, and Henry had been the only person who knew my secret. I liked and trusted Elinor, but while I suspected she was a rebel, I didn't know where she stood on people with mixed heritage.

I noticed in the next few days that the watchers seemed even more diligent. I wasn't sure if it was because I'd evaded my watcher for the meeting with Colin and Lizzie or if something else had happened to make them concerned. I received a perfectly innocuous letter from Lizzie—well, innocuous to the person who'd obviously opened it. I knew that something odd must be happening, as the letter referred to my flirtation with Alec, one of the other rebels. He'd recruited me as a spy by pretending to woo me, something that was still a bit of a sore spot for me, a fact of which Lizzie was well aware. She must have been laying the groundwork for something by making it look as though I had an admirer. Someone would have had to know me very well to recognize that there was a message lying beneath the words of the letter.

Certain that I was meant to play along, I wrote a response, mentioning my feelings for Alec and asking Lizzie for advice on getting his attention. I was tempted to write the way some of Flora's friends talked about boys, but anyone who'd been watching me as closely as the authorities had would be suspicious if I suddenly began behaving that way. I tried to write a letter in keeping with a responsible governess who also happened to be a seventeen-year-old girl.

Days went by without a reply. I distracted myself with my duties, which were more than enough to keep me busy. Olive was an eager and diligent student, but she was alternately excited about the upcoming Christmas holiday and mournful about not spending it with her beloved uncle. Rollo was even less enthusiastic about school than he usually was, and I had to stand over him to make sure he was doing his homework rather than drawing diagrams of machines. Flora had taken to reading history books and the few works by radical authors that were in the family library. Until recently, I would have been overjoyed that she was reading something other than the gossip pages of the newspaper and fashion plates, but now I worried that she'd be climbing out of her window on a rope made of bedsheets and running off to join the rebels. I didn't disagree with the impulse, but our status was so very precarious at the moment.

Finally, I received a parcel in the post. Either it had been badly wrapped or it had been opened. It turned out to be a vial of what appeared to be perfume, with an atomizer top that allowed it to spray as mist. I gave it a tentative spray once I was alone in my room and was rewarded with the scent of lavender. It was nice, but it didn't seem like the sort of thing Lizzie was likely to send me. The package also contained an elegant pen and a little bottle of ink.

Her letter said that she was certain that Alec would enjoy receiving letters from me, and to encourage me to write, she was sending me a special pen and ink for the correspondence. She suggested giving my notes a hint of scent that would remind him of me. I contemplated her letter and the bottle of scent, then on a whim I sprayed her letter.

Words appeared on the page, around the letter itself. It read, "Isn't this clever? If you write a letter with this ink, the writing will soon disappear, and only reappears when sprayed with the other formula. You can use this to send messages hidden within perfectly innocent correspondence."

I barely restrained the urge to laugh out loud in glee. Now I should feel less cut off from my compatriots, and all right under the noses of those who were watching me.

To test it, I wrote a normal letter to Lizzie, thanking her for the gift and saying I would take her advice and write to Alec. Then, in the spaces between the lines, I used the special ink to add a note letting her know that I'd found her hidden message and understood the instructions. Almost as soon as I wrote the words, they disappeared. Even holding the page up to the light revealed no sign of the secret message.

"You're looking cheerful," Flora noted at dinner that evening.

"I received a letter from a friend," I said, unable to hide my smile.

"Which friend is that?" Elinor teased. Although she'd remained in her room when she was at home, she'd taken to joining us for meals while at the Lyndon home. She'd sworn us to secrecy, for if her father knew she was capable of getting out of bed, it would ruin her ruse.

"The friend I visit every so often," I said.

"Not a young man?"

"No, though she is encouraging me to correspond with a young man I know."

"You should. A governess is allowed to have some fun."

"And you are unlikely to meet someone suitable for you while chaperoning me," Flora said in the haughty tone she'd used to talk to me before we became partners in crime in working to free Henry.

"You also got a present," Olive said. "Was it for Christmas?"

"I'm afraid not," I said. "My friend merely sent me supplies to encourage my correspondence."

"I was thinking that for Christmas, we could go to the country estate," Elinor said. "If there's snow, we could have sleigh rides, and we could cut a Christmas tree. I think it would do us all some good to get away from the city."

That perked Olive up, but I wasn't sure I liked the idea. Being away from the city meant being even farther away from the action. Then again, Henry was away from the city. Was that Elinor's plan, to go somewhere Henry might be able to join us? I studied her face, but her expression revealed nothing. Elinor was good at keeping secrets, and I had a feeling we'd only just begun to discover how many secrets she was keeping.

The rebels didn't waste any time using the new means of communication. In the next afternoon's mail, I received a note from "Alec." The seal was suspiciously loose, but if anyone had read it, they'd have seen nothing more than an invitation to join him for dinner that evening. He would call for me at seven. I suspected there was more to the message than that, but I had to wait until I'd collected Rollo from school and the children were quietly reading or working on homework before I could find out.

The hidden note on the page was terse, saying merely, "If you can get out, we'll take care of it. There's a meeting and you need to be there."

I had to set the note down on my desk because my shaking hands were making it flutter. I couldn't see how this would possibly work. I couldn't attend a rebel meeting while I was being followed, and if I did anything that made it appear that I was trying to lose the follower, it would only make me look worse. Frankly, it might have been easier for me to sneak out, so I was never followed.

But they knew the risk, which meant this meeting was very important, indeed. I went to Elinor's room and found her lounging on a chaise with a book in one hand and a teacup in the other. She glanced up before I had the chance to subtly announce my presence. "Oh, hello, Verity. Did you need something?"

Forcing myself not to clutch and wring my skirt like a nervous child, I said, "A friend has invited me to dinner tonight. Lord Henry didn't usually mind if I went out in the evening, but I wanted to see if you minded."

"The children have had their lessons, and Rollo has been escorted to and from school. It seems to me that your work for the day is done. Go and have fun." She grinned mischievously. "This isn't your gentleman friend, is it?"

"Actually, it is."

She pursed her lips in a way that would have appeared disapproving if her eyes hadn't been so merry. "Hmm, an unattached young lady dining out with a young man? How scandalous! But you are fortunate to be of a class for which that isn't entirely inappropriate, and you will be in public. I know some aren't keen on the idea of ladies dining in restaurants, but it seems to me that it's better than them being behind closed doors at home."

My face flamed at the thought of how much time I'd spent behind closed doors at home with Henry, even though nothing untoward had happened between us. Did she have any idea about us? She teased so much, I could never be certain.

She set her teacup down and gestured for me to take a seat opposite her. "Why don't we have a chat while you're here? We haven't really had the chance to do so since I arrived. We've been so busy with the children, and everything else. Tea?" She bent over the pot on the low table next to her.

"Yes, please," I said. She poured a cup and handed it to me with a couple of fingers of shortbread, then took some more for herself.

"Now, you probably gathered this already, since I gave you no conflicting instructions, but I do want you to continue with the children as you did when Henry was here."

"I was aware that you two saw eye-to-eye about the children's education," I said.

"I also want to assure you that I have no intention of giving anything but the most glowing reports about you to my father. You needn't worry about pleasing me, so long as you continue the way you have been. I also hope that you and I may become better friends, now that we're living under the same roof. That may be the best thing to come out of this difficult situation. You have no idea how I've longed for genial company."

"I was under the impression that you had plenty of callers. You're known for being more aware than almost anyone of what's going on in the city."

She smiled and shook her head. "I'm not getting the same number of callers here as I once did—that may suggest that many of my friends were using me as an excuse to possibly gain an audience with my father—and I could do with a friend. A *real* friend. I enjoyed your visits before, and it seems a shame we haven't taken advantage of the opportunity with me living in the same house."

"Well, we have had a lot going on," I said.

"We have, haven't we?" She sighed. "Henry's absence troubles me. The children seem to be coping, but it's not easy for any of us."

"Olive asked me the other day if she would be receiving a present from her uncle."

"Oh, dear, poor thing. She doesn't understand, does she? And I'm not sure what we could say to help her understand. I'm not even certain *I* understand. I know Henry has ideas, but treason? Disappearing the way he did made him look even guiltier, but I don't suppose he had much choice."

I wasn't sure what she wanted me to say, so I merely sipped my tea. I almost felt as though she was fishing for information, saying things and hoping I'd either elaborate or correct her. Did she want me to confess to my activities?

"Did you suspect he was part of anything that serious?" she asked, breaking a long silence.

"As you said, I knew he had ideas."

"And where do you stand on those ideas?" I must have looked aghast at the question, for she smiled and said, "Truly, Verity, I'm not investigating you. I merely want to know how free I should be to speak in your presence. Things are about to happen around us, and I want to be certain where you stand."

"I agree with Lord Henry on a great many things," I said. As I was fairly certain she knew. If I was right about her, she'd seen me at a number of Rebel Mechanics gatherings.

Raising an eyebrow, she said, "I suppose that's a start. Then I should tell you that I, too, agree with him on a great many things. We can discuss these things, if you like. And don't worry about anything you say getting back to my father. He's a good man, and I love him dearly, but he's a representative of a system that doesn't belong on these shores. What do you think of him?"

If she was weaving a web to entrap me, it was an insidious one. It would take delicate maneuvering to stay out of it without also appearing to disagree with her. "As you say, he seems like a good man. He's always been kind to me, though I hated to see how he upset Lord Henry."

"Oh, that's all bluster. He really did think he should have been guardian of the children when their father died, but he wouldn't have had time to deal with them. They'd have been brought up by nannies and governesses and never would have seen a family member. Henry really was the best guardian for them, though being a guardian wasn't the best thing for Henry."

"I don't think he minded at all," I said, remembering evenings at the dinner table, picnics in the park, and Sunday afternoons in the parlor with the children.

"No, he wouldn't," she said with a fond smile. "Now we must hope he can find a way to sort everything out so he can come home."

"Do you really think that's possible?"

"I think a great many things would have to happen first, but we can hope and pray."

"Yes, we should do that." And more. Bringing down the government Henry opposed would be a good start.

I was as nervous that evening as I would have been if a gentleman caller really had been coming to take me out on the town, but the butterflies in my stomach had nothing to do with romantic feelings. I wasn't sure the Mechanics took my followers seriously enough, so I feared this would be the night when I was caught either consorting with rebels or giving my pursuers the slip.

Alec arrived at seven sharp. Although I was already waiting in the foyer, Mr. Chastain, the butler, opened the door for him and gave him a proper glower before stepping aside to allow me out the door. I wasn't sure if Alec should have properly gone to the servants' entrance instead, but my place in the household was rather nebulous, and I hadn't had the opportunity to tell him to go elsewhere. I took Alec's arm as we went down the front steps. He nodded to Inspector Stout in passing, the way he might have nodded to anyone he saw on the street.

When we were well out of hearing range, I whispered, "That's one of them."

"And they follow you everywhere?"

"As far as I can tell. There are three I've spotted who sometimes work together and sometimes take shifts. Someone always seems to be watching the front of the house. I haven't had a good excuse to check the back. Who knows how many more there might be."

"And they really think that Henry would be stupid enough to just walk up the front steps of his home after escaping Imperial custody?"

"We are talking about Henry, so crazy and reckless is a distinct possibility, though I don't know how they'd know that. But stupid he isn't." I sighed. "Actually, I have no idea what they think. I don't know if they suspect me of helping him escape, if they think he might try to contact the children, if they hope the children might let something slip, if they believe Henry's allies might try to contact us. Or if they're just trying to unnerve us enough that we make a mistake. But then I'm also not sure if they know that I know they're there." I turned to look at him when we paused at a street corner. "And I have no idea how you're going to get me to a meeting without them following and without them knowing I deliberately lost them. If I lose them, they'll know I'm up to something."

"Why, wouldn't any innocent young lady be alarmed to be followed by a strange man and take steps to escape him?"

"I'm not sure most innocent young ladies would even consider the possibility that they were being followed. These men are fairly good at it. It took me a day or two before I was certain."

"Well, you have nothing to worry about. Leave it to me."

IN WHICH I VOLUNTEER FOR A TASK

Alec was perhaps the most levelheaded and reasonable member of the Rebel Mechanics, so if I had to trust anyone to have a serious plan to evade my followers, it would be him. However, I wasn't certain I was willing to take that risk with *anyone.*

I would have felt better if I'd known for certain whether or not I was being followed, but I hadn't dared turn to look. When we reached Third Avenue and were well away from the row of mansions, we entered a more bustling neighborhood where it was easier for us to blend in, and likely more difficult for us to be followed. It was a few weeks before Christmas, so many of the shops were open late, and patrons streamed in and out of them, adding to the chaos on the sidewalk. The taverns were doing a brisk business, as well.

A Father Christmas stood ringing a bell at the next corner, with a group of carolers behind him and a swarm of children in front of him. We had to fight our way through the boisterous mob, and Alec pulled me into a restaurant just around that corner. "Quick, give me your hat," he said.

I reached up to remove the hatpin and pulled my hat off. He took it from me and turned to hand it to a young woman about my size, with similar coloring. She put it on, adjusting the brim so that it shaded the side of her face, and Alec took her arm to lead her to a table.

I was left standing in the back of the restaurant, feeling rather abandoned, but a moment later, a door to the kitchen area opened, and a woman in an apron beckoned to me. "Through here," she said.

I slid through the doorway and followed her through the bustle of the kitchen to a door leading to a basement storeroom. Another door led to a dark flight of stairs. "You'll want this," she said, handing me a bowler hat with what appeared to be a jeweled hatband. I recognized one of the Mechanics' lantern hats and grinned as I put it on. It didn't fit well over my bun, so I took my hair down. That left it a little too large for me and wobbling on my head, but it did light the way down the stairs, as long as I remembered to look in the direction I was going.

When I reached the bottom of the stairs, I found myself in a passageway with a stream of lights flowing down it—people either wearing lantern hats like mine or carrying lanterns. I found a gap in the stream and joined the others as we headed to what turned out to be one of the stations for the Mechanics' underground railway system. It had been built and then abandoned by magisters before the railway was ever implemented, and the Mechanics had adapted it to their own needs with their own technology. This station was barely a cavern hewn out of rock, with no benches or other amenities.

There was a pilot car with a couple of open passenger cars behind it being loaded at the station, but the cars were already almost full. The conductor shouted that they'd be back soon, and the train shot down the tracks. I wondered if everyone was going to the meeting or if rebels were moving around the city for other reasons. The railroad was secret, but it wasn't only used for rebel activities. It also offered a way for poor workers who were involved with the movement to get to and from distant jobs, greatly expanding their opportunities.

Before the train returned, Alec rejoined me, grinning. "It worked," he said.

"Oh?"

"He must have lost us in the crowd, doubled back, saw my friend there with me, realized it wasn't you and that he must have been following the wrong person, and gave up, knowing he likely wouldn't spot you again. At least, a man came to the window, stared inside for a moment, shook his head and very likely swore, then turned and stomped away, looking very unhappy. He'll probably feel much better when you and I return at the end of a perfectly innocent evening out."

"You don't think they'll believe I deliberately lost them?"

"There was enough confusion for them to think it was their fault, not yours."

The train pulled into the station, and we scrambled aboard. It shot downtown, throwing me against Alec. I tensed at the contact. I didn't want him to think that me spending this time with him meant anything. It was nothing more than a ruse to allow me to participate in the rebellion. I just hoped he was aware of that and wasn't trying to start our flirtation anew.

It was impossible to speak while the crowded car hurtled through the darkness, but at the next station, he took a pair of goggles out of his pocket and handed them to me. "To go with your very fetching new hat," he said. When I stared at him quizzically, he added, "There will be magisters present, and we don't want to risk too many people from that world knowing about your role with us."

I handed the bowler hat to him so I could slip the brass goggles on and tighten the strap around my head. When I replaced the hat, he smiled. "Now you look like a proper Mechanic."

The train lurched forward again, and soon we were in the main station where most of these gatherings were now held. The passengers jumped off the open passenger car and entered the throng. This was the largest gathering

I'd ever seen in this station, and for once, they weren't all Mechanics.

The Rebel Mechanics were easy to spot because of their distinctive and eccentric clothing style, which combined a variety of formal attire and working wear, usually mismatched and put together in unconventional ways. Women wore corsets outside their blouses, men wore formal waistcoats over flannel undershirts, and most of them wore brass goggles as a way to disguise their faces. All of them had the Mechanics' insignia, a gear on a red ribbon, displayed proudly.

Now, though, there were a number of people—mostly men—wearing more conventional clothing. These people had small keys on blue ribbons pinned to their lapels, a sign that they'd been accepted as trusted members of the rebel magisters' movement. One of them stood near the door with a small jewelbox. Everyone who entered with a magister's key had to test it in the lock. I noticed that all the magisters were coming through that door. They apparently hadn't yet been given access to the railway.

I had a key of my own, but as I also had a Rebel Mechanics insignia, I didn't have to go through the test. I thought it best to hide my magister affiliations, especially if the Mechanics were recommending I disguise myself. We'd already suffered the consequences of Henry's revolutionary activities being betrayed.

As with so many Rebel Mechanics gatherings, this looked more like a party than a political event. A band set up on a raised platform near the engine that powered the railway filled the vast chamber with lively music, and couples whirled around the space in the middle. An elaborate machine full of gears and gadgets dispensed drinks, and there were tables full of an odd variety of foods that must have been donated by—or pilfered from—restaurants all over the city. The people not dressed like Mechanics stood on the fringes of the room. Most of them wore brass goggles to hide their identities, so I couldn't read their faces, but their posture struck me as looking rather uncomfortable.

I wasn't particularly comfortable, myself, with Alec holding onto my arm in a way that struck me as being more about possession than keeping together in the crowd. He'd done his job in getting me here, and I couldn't think of any reason we needed to stay together now that we'd arrived. But I also couldn't think of a good reason to wrench my arm out of his grasp, and telling him to let me go seemed rude, given all that he'd just done to help.

Colin came to my rescue, likely prodded by Lizzie, who'd just whispered something to him. "Why, if it isn't our gal Liberty," he said with a tip of his towering top hat. "And quite fetching you look tonight. That hat is very much your style. May I take your coat?"

He gestured to where a few enterprising children, including Nat the newsboy and Mick, a boy from the slums who'd been taken in by the Mechanics, had set up a coat check. Alec had to release my arm so that I could remove my coat, and Colin whisked me away before Alec could try to resume his claim.

On the way to the coat check, we passed Geoffrey and Philip, who didn't so much as glance at me. I wasn't the only one who noticed. "I doubt anyone who sees you tonight will be able to place you, even if they run into you again elsewhere," Colin remarked.

"I should hope not," I said. That was one danger of more magisters being in the group. There was a greater chance I'd encounter someone who knew me as a governess. My future might depend on the hat and goggles hiding my identity. With my hair loose, rather than in the tight bun I wore as a governess, I looked very different from the way most people usually saw me. I knew my disguise was good when even Nat didn't seem to recognize me. He merely took my coat and handed me a check ticket. I let myself relax slightly. For tonight, I could be Liberty Jones, the girl reporter of the revolution, without anyone knowing me as Verity the governess.

Colin turned to face me and bowed. "Would you do me the honor of a dance?"

Dancing with Colin wasn't exactly a pleasure, since he danced with far more enthusiasm than with rhythm or grace, but he was fun, and I felt safe with him. There were no complicated emotions there, so I took his hand and let him sweep me away.

When the song ended, I noticed Alec moving toward us, and I feared he was going to cut in. Before he had a chance to, another man tapped Colin on the shoulder. Colin glanced at me, seeking my approval, before handing me over. I didn't recognize this man, though with his smoke-tinted brass goggles and hat pulled low over his forehead, that would have been difficult whether or not I knew him. He was a much better dancer than Colin, moving with grace and assurance around the room. I was somewhat disappointed when the band stopped playing.

Someone banged a metal tool against the side of the machine that powered the railway, making a loud ringing sound that brought the assembly to silence. The dancers all came to a halt, and my partner gave me a gallant bow, bending over my hand to kiss it before he slipped away, melting into the crowd.

An amplified voice filled the underground chamber, saying, "Ladies and gentlemen, your attention, please!"

The festive tone of the gathering grew more serious as everyone moved to the middle of the room to hear the speaker. "Why, it's the baron!" I said to myself when I'd drawn close enough to see.

"You know him?" I turned to see Alec standing next to me.

"Yes. I met him in Boston. I'm at least partially responsible for his connection to the Mechanics. I just never expected to see him at a gathering like this."

"Recent events have given all of us some strange bedfellows. Disbanding the Assembly even got the nobles' attention."

"This is it, isn't it?" I said, barely above a breath as my heart thudded inside my chest. "This is when it starts."

"It started a long time ago. But it may become more noticeable now."

Once the gathered crowd had moved in to hear him and had grown quiet, the baron spoke again, using the Mechanics' amplification system. When Henry and I had met the baron in Boston, he'd been noncommittal about actually doing anything, himself, but it seemed that recent events had stirred him to action. "I don't expect most of you to know me," he said, "but I'm a representative to the Colonial Assembly from the Massachusetts colony. I'm only elected by a small percentage of the population, those with wealth and status, but I am elected. The same goes for my colleagues in the Assembly." He gestured to the men who stood to either side of him.

"Now, with the dissolution of the Assembly, the people of the American colonies have no elected representatives. We have no seat in the Parliament of the Empire. We have only a governor, who is appointed by the Crown. This cannot stand!"

The crowd roared at this. Angry shouts echoed in the stone chamber. The baron gestured for quiet, and the roar faded. "I know that most of you have never had a say in any government, so this may mean little to you, but that slender fragment of democracy was the only thing standing between us and tyranny. We will not stand for tyranny."

That brought another roar from the crowd, and I found

myself joining in. When the crowd grew quiet once more, Colin stepped up and took over speaking. "The question for us all now is, what will we do about it?" he said. "Are we ready to go to war? Probably not. We have machines, but we've only begun to build enough to make a difference. We have more people than we once did—and many of them have magic. We have more money than before. If it comes to revolution, we'll never win by fighting a war. We're not ready. But if we let this insult stand, it will only get worse. We have to make a statement, do something, and soon, before they send more troops."

The roar following that statement was even louder. My pulse quickened. What would we do? Would there really be a war?

"We need to be clear what our goal here is," one of the assemblymen said. "Perhaps the best first step is to petition the Queen and Parliament for the restoration of our Assembly." That proposal elicited faint applause.

"Rusty rivets to that!" a voice from the crowd called out. "We want freedom!"

That started a chant of "Freedom! Freedom! Freedom!"

Another assemblyman grabbed the speaking trumpet. "Are we ready to go that far, to fight a war? We don't need to break from the Empire, merely to have representation and a say in our own government. Get the corrupt leadership out, and our condition would improve."

The Mechanics drowned him out with the "Freedom" chant, and he turned sharply, leaving the stage with the other assemblymen behind him. Soon, the baron was the only obvious magister remaining on the stage. Many more magisters—but not all—joined them in walking out.

Once they were gone, the chant died out. "Well, it seems we have work to do in building a coalition," Colin said dryly.

"Being willing to object to the government is a big step for them," the baron said. "You'll not get them agreeing to revolution right away. They'll take persuading, and that's true for the rest of the population, as well. Revolution is a rather radical concept, and most people aren't very radical."

"Then we need to persuade them," Colin said, and I felt his gaze on me.

My heart pounding, I raised my voice to be heard and said, "I'm already seeing people in the magister districts reading our newspaper. They're seeking out information, not taking the government's word. That might give us the opportunity to make our case. Why is revolution the best option, the only real option?"

"That's our Liberty Jones," Colin said, grinning. "And I think we need our Liberty to do what she does best: Write! Then we'll wallpaper the colonies with newspapers and pamphlets. That is, if we can find the money to print them."

A voice from within the crowd shouted, "That will be arranged." I turned to see the lady in black—Elinor, if I was correct—nodding as the man next to her spoke.

"Thanks once again to our benefactor," Colin said,

sweeping his hat off his head and giving her a deep bow. "Now, we need the rest of you lot, Mechanics and magisters alike, to go out there and talk to people. When we get the pamphlets, give them out. Then be ready to take the next step. It might be a good idea to arm yourselves, as well." He gestured, and the band resumed playing. He jumped off the stage and made his way to me.

"Do you think you can write us some pamphlets?" he asked. "You know how to talk to magisters and to Mechanics, and to the people in between."

"I–I believe so," I said. I'd enjoyed my newspaper work but hadn't really considered myself a true writer. Could I do it? I certainly wanted to try.

"Excellent. And would it be possible to have some done two days from now? They don't have to be long, just enough to print on a single sheet."

"I should be able to manage that."

"We'll meet you in the park in the afternoon two days from now. We'll find our usual way to slip by your watchers, but it will be important to make it look good."

I reflected on my schedule for the coming days and nodded. "I should be able to go out after three that day."

"We'll see you then," Colin said, clapping me on the shoulder. "Oh, and I hope you realize we don't want to waste time with any of that home rule or restored Assembly nonsense. We're making the case for nothing short of revolution."

"I got that impression," I said dryly.

"And while we're at it, we want to specify that everyone should have a vote."

"Even women!" Lizzie joined us. "If we're going to bother with freedom, we want freedom for everyone, and we might as well get off to the right start in our new nation."

Colin turned to his sister. "Now, Liz, we don't want to get so radical that people won't listen."

She balled her hands into fists and placed them on her hips as she glared at him. "Do you want the women of the colonies for or against you? You'll need our help to win a revolution, and women have more sway over their husbands' opinions than anyone realizes." Turning to face me, she added, "We're dreaming of a nation where everyone is equal, magisters and ordinary folks, rich and poor, landowners and tenants, and that should include women."

"I agree," I said. "Why should we fight for a nation where we'll have no say? Are you asking me to make the case for a revolution that would leave me out of citizenship?"

Colin raised his hands in surrender. "Hey, I'm not the one making decisions. Write it the way you feel you must."

"Considering the person funding the printing is a woman, I don't think there will be much opposition," I countered. Even more so if I was right about Elinor.

"The important thing is that you write, and make it good. In the meantime, you need to look completely above reproach—nothing that would make them suspect you of being our Lady Liberty."

"That's what I've been trying to do," I said wryly. "And then you invited me to come here. Goodness knows what they think I'm doing tonight after they lost me in the crowd."

"Don't you worry a bit. Alec has it under control, don't you, my friend?"

Alec didn't get a chance to answer before there was a loud bang near the exit. "They're doing sweeps of the neighborhood," a Mechanic bellowed. "We need to disperse carefully. Stay out of the theater. Use the other tunnels, and only a few go at a time. And stop with the music. We'd best be quiet."

"Ah, but where's the fun in that?" Colin said with a wink. More seriously, he turned to Alec and added, "You should get her home. We can't have Liberty Jones getting caught out."

"You don't think they'll find us in here, do you?" I asked.

"Not down here, but I'd still feel better about you not being here."

As Alec took my arm to drag me to retrieve our coats, I noticed Geoffrey, Philip, and some other magisters running for the doors, presumably to magically shield them the way they had the night Henry's gang had helped spirit the machines out of the city. The authorities hadn't found the railroad then, in spite of thoroughly searching the area. I hoped the measures they took tonight would be as effective.

The train cars filled up quickly, and soon we were rocketing through the darkness, away from the station. The crowding eased somewhat after we made stops at a couple of stations, and then it was our stop. I was fairly certain that we weren't heading back to the restaurant from which I'd entered the underground system.

That was confirmed when we came to the top of the stairs, and I found myself in the middle of a cheery Christmas party. The other guests appeared to be people of a similar class to me: professional working men and women, dressed respectably. No one would look at them and suspect them of being radicals, but I recognized several from within my network of contacts.

As we passed through the party, someone handed me my hat—the one that had been borrowed to throw the inspector off my trail. I took off the goggles and the bowler with the lantern in its brim and handed them to one of the guests. As I twisted my hair back into a bun and secured my own hat on my head, someone else pinned a sprig of holly to the lapel of my coat, and yet another person thrust a package wrapped in tissue paper and tied with a ribbon into my hands.

The cold air took my breath away when we stepped outside. I didn't spot any of my usual followers, though it was difficult to tell one man from another, bundled up as everyone was. A light snow was falling, just beginning to dust the ground. Alec held his arm out for me to take, and I tried to act like someone going home from a

Christmas party rather than like a rebel who was mentally composing pamphlets aimed at stirring up revolution and worried about whether her friends had escaped the latest government search for the rebel stronghold.

There didn't seem to be anyone watching the Lyndon home at first glance, but as I turned to say good night to Alec, I thought I spotted movement in the shadows across the street. For a moment, I felt bad for the men forced to lurk outside in this weather. I wondered if they were true believers in the government they served or if they were merely doing their jobs. It was the latter sort of person I hoped to persuade.

"Thank you for an interesting evening," I said to Alec.

"I will see you soon," he replied with a tip of his hat. If he had any intention of doing anything else, Mrs. Talbot, the housekeeper, put an end to it by opening the door.

"I thought I heard someone out here," she said. "Miss Newton, you really must let your gentleman friend go home, and you come inside before you catch your death."

"I was just leaving, ma'am," Alec said.

Mrs. Talbot pulled me inside, shutting the door behind me, then turned to brush snow off my shoulders. "I was worried about you," she said.

"Why? I'm home earlier than I planned."

She dropped her voice to just above a whisper. "I think someone was following you. I happened to look out the window when you left"—I had to force myself not to smile at that, since I doubted there was any "happened" about it—"and I saw a man who'd been standing across the street follow you."

I removed my hat and shook the snow from it. "That's really quite odd. I didn't notice anything. If he was following, he did nothing to accost us."

"I think he came back. At least, there's someone who's been out there all evening. I was tempted to ask Lady Elinor if I should bring him a cup of hot coffee, but she went to bed early with a headache, and I didn't want to disturb her."

I had to bite the inside of my lip to keep from smiling at the thought of where Lady Elinor really was. At least, where I thought she was. I wondered how she'd got out unnoticed and how she planned to get home. In fact, I was tempted to lurk on the stairs to try to catch her.

Mrs. Talbot put an end to that plan. "You go up and get out of your coat, dear, and I'll bring you some hot cocoa to warm you up. Lady Flora got Lady Olive to bed, and it was a trial with the snow falling. I wouldn't be surprised if she was out of bed, watching it."

With Olive up watching the snow, Rollo likely doing the same, but more quietly, and Mrs. Talbot bringing cocoa and watching the watchers outside, waiting up for Elinor would be impossible, and I wasn't sure how Elinor would manage to sneak in, unless the Mechanics dropped her off from an airship, as they'd done for me a couple of times.

As I neared my room, Olive's door opened slightly, and

I heard a soft voice from within say, "Miss Newton, it's snowing!"

"Yes, I noticed, Olive. Now, you should go to bed so you'll be surprised to wake up in the morning and see the world covered in a white blanket. It won't be as much of a surprise if you watch the snow fall."

"Oh! No, it won't!" The door closed abruptly, and a few seconds later I heard the squeak of bedsprings. I thought that Elinor would likely owe me for getting at least one potential witness out of the way.

I was eager to get to work on my writing, but I didn't dare until I was certain Mrs. Talbot was away for the night. I took off my coat and hung it on the back of my chair to dry and set my hat on the corner of my desk. I was removing my boots when Mrs. Talbot arrived, bearing a tray with a pot of cocoa. "Here you are. I'm retiring for the night, but you know to ring if you need anything."

"I'm sure I'll be fine, thank you. The cocoa is just what I need."

When I was certain she was gone for good, I poured myself a cup of cocoa, gathered my writing supplies, and tried to think. I considered how I might write different pamphlets for different audiences. There were middle-class magisters who had power but not the same social status as leaders—the people like those who worked in the magic generation plant. There were people like my family, with education and some social position, but without magical power, so that they were relegated to a lower class regardless of wealth or ability. I thought these groups most likely to be willing to consider the rebel cause if they were properly persuaded.

I didn't know what time it was when I finally forced myself to put away my notes and go to sleep, but I felt I'd barely closed my eyes before it was time to wake and face the day. As I walked to and from Rollo's school in the morning and afternoon, I found myself looking at the people I passed and wondering what argument would most likely persuade them to support a revolution. Did they suffer under the weight of taxes that didn't benefit the colonies? Did they care that they had no real vote in the government that ruled them? Did they chafe at the constraints of the class system?

I looked forward to returning home and turning the children over to the music teacher, who was scheduled for that afternoon. Then I might have a chance to sit down and write. But, alas, it wasn't meant to be. When we neared the house, I saw that a carriage sat in front—a large one with the governor's coat of arms on it.

IN WHICH I MUST AVOID CAROLERS

It wasn't unusual for the governor to visit, as he was the children's grandfather and, now that Henry was a fugitive, their legal guardian, but he tended to arrive when he had news or when he was troubled. What did he want now? Was he going to take custody of the children? It was with much trepidation that I entered the house.

"His excellency the governor is waiting for the children in the family parlor," Mr. Chastain informed me as he helped remove Olive's coat. "Lady Flora is entertaining him. I believe you are expected, as well."

I thanked him and handed over my coat so I could go straight to the parlor instead of to my room. Olive and Rollo ran ahead of me up the stairs, and they were already hugging their grandfather when I entered the room.

The governor was a large, imposing man who usually seemed to occupy more space than his body filled, but today he seemed somewhat diminished. Once he'd finished greeting the children, he took a seat, turning his hat around in his hands, and cleared his throat before saying, "I need your assistance with something. I doubt that you're aware of it, but there's unrest in the colonies. I'm hoping to alleviate that by using the holiday season as an opportunity to show charity and goodwill. You children are my family, and I would like you to join me for these events."

"What sort of events?" Flora asked. Her voice had her customary tone of boredom, but I was sure there was a spark of interest in her eyes. That worried me. These days, I feared she'd use the opportunity to strike a blow for the rebellion.

"Speeches at factories to encourage the workers. That sort of thing." He sounded intensely uncomfortable, which made me wonder just how bad things were for him. "It shouldn't disrupt your schedule too badly."

Much to my surprise, he turned to me and said, "You should join us, of course, Miss Newton. I'll be quite busy, and I'll need your help managing the children." He gave a rough bark of a laugh. "And I'm sure it wouldn't hurt to have a commoner among us."

"I would be happy to help, Your Grace," I said, bowing my head. To be honest, I had very mixed feelings. I hated for him to use me for propaganda to bolster his position, especially while I was occupied with creating propaganda for the opposition. On the other hand, I frequently used my access to him to gather information for the rebels, so I supposed we were even.

He stood. "Excellent. Now, I will go visit my daughter, and I will leave a schedule of events with you, Miss Newton, so you can organize the children's activities around them." He pulled a folded sheet of paper out of his breast pocket and handed it to me.

I was sure that the rebels could do quite a lot with that list. I forced myself to wait until he'd finished his visit to Elinor and had departed the house entirely before I made an excuse to go up to my room. I composed a letter to "Alec," writing a few blandly innocuous lines thanking him for the lovely time at the Christmas party. In the blank space, I used the special ink to copy out the governor's schedule. "He seems concerned," I added. "He must be getting a great deal of criticism. Please don't do anything dangerous at these events, as the children and I will be there, but this would be an opportunity to show some unrest." When the message had vanished, I folded and sealed the letter and put it out for the evening post.

I was surprised to receive a letter from Alec that evening. Since it arrived at the same time my note went out, I knew it wasn't a reply to mine. There was even a chance that it had been posted before the meeting, which made it odd that he hadn't mentioned it. I wasn't flustered at the correspondence from him, since whatever feelings I might once have had for him had abated with his duplicity, but if anyone had been watching me, I was sure I looked like any young lady receiving a missive from a young man she admired.

I opened the letter in the parlor and found that the contents were also written by Alec himself. If the letter had been read by the authorities—which seemed likely, given the looseness of the seal—they would have been bored, and they might have questioned my taste in men. His attempt at wooing was rather lackluster. There was only the slightest hint of flattery. Otherwise, the entire letter was about his studies and his activities. If I'd been at all interested in him, I'd have been very disappointed.

I had to wait until later that evening, after the children were in bed, to see what he really had to say to me. He'd certainly left enough space to add plenty of additional information. When I was sure that the household had settled down for the night and it was unlikely that Olive would come looking for a story or a glass of water, I spritzed the letter with the lavender scent.

As with Lizzie's letter, a second letter soon appeared on the page, and I gasped when I saw it, for it was in Henry's handwriting.

I was glad I was already sitting down, or my legs might have gone out from under me. I started to clutch the letter to my breast, then thought better of it—what if that wiped off the chemical formula that revealed his message?

Instead, I read it very quickly, for fear it might fade.

"My dearest Verity," it said, "I hope this finds you and the family well. I am safe, in a place where they'll never find me because they'd never think to look. I must thank you again for all your efforts on my behalf. I owe you everything and can never begin to repay you. Meeting you was the greatest prize I ever gained in a train robbery. Our efforts on behalf of our cause continue, and in many ways I am able to be more effective where I am now, as I no longer have to pretend or hide my true intentions. The most difficult part of my exile is not being able to see you or the children. I miss all of you very much, and I wish you could convey my regards to the children, but you must not give any sign that you are in communication with me. You may write to me by corresponding with Alec, using the secret method, but it is perhaps best if you limit that to times when it is absolutely necessary. I wish I'd had more time to tell you what you've come to mean to me before we were torn apart. Now I suppose we simply must change the circumstances that keep us apart. Stay strong, Verity, though I don't need tell you that, for you are strong." It was signed, "Your devoted servant and most ardent admirer, H."

It was hardly the most romantic love letter ever written, I thought with a wry smile, but it was so very like Henry. At least, I thought that the last few sentences sounded like they indicated romantic feelings. Alas, he was correct that we had to change our circumstances in order to be together, and that was no more true now that he was an exiled fugitive than it had been when he was a magister nobleman and I was a governess no one else knew had magister blood.

I thought I should probably destroy the letter, but the Lyndon mansion had magically powered central heating, so there was no fireplace in my room, and if I used magic to burn it, others in the house might notice. Instead, I folded it up and hid it in the secret compartment of my desk drawer, where I also kept the stolen letter that was proof of the governor's financial difficulty. If anyone found that, letters from a fugitive wouldn't add that much to my guilt. I had to admit that I was glad of an excuse to keep the letter.

I then set to work on my pamphlets. If I'd needed any additional motivation to meet my deadline, hearing from Henry had provided it. The only hope I had of being with him, possibly even of seeing him again, was revolution. The cause was so large, encompassing part of a continent, but the effects were personal. How many people like us were there, who couldn't have the lives they wanted unless things changed?

That gave me the inspiration for one of my pamphlets, a discussion not of large issues, but rather of small, personal ones: who could marry whom, who could pursue careers, who had the right to tell us how to live our lives, who could deny people with talents the opportunities to use them. I focused the others on those who'd never had representation in the government, including women, and on those working for the government. My eyes were burning with exhaustion by the time I had three documents I was satisfied with and had copied them out in disappearing ink.

I'd thought about telling Flora, at least, that I'd heard from Henry, but it added little to what I'd already conveyed from Colin, and I thought it best that no one else know I was in contact with him. I'd thought I was hiding my feelings well (and worried that the effects of my late night would be evident), but at breakfast the next morning, Elinor said, "You're looking brighter than I've seen you in ages, Verity."

"She got a letter that seemed to be from a young man," Flora teased.

"Ah, yes, your mysterious admirer," Elinor said with a twinkle in her eye. "Might we perhaps one day meet him?"

Little did she know that she knew him quite well. "He isn't in the city now," I said.

"Well, when he returns, you must invite him to tea, at the very least."

"I would have said I wasn't sure he existed, but the letters appear to be proof," Flora said.

Olive whimpered, and her shoulders shook as she bowed her head over her breakfast. "Whatever is the matter, dearest?" Elinor asked.

"Miss Newton can't go away. Uncle Henry already went."

"No one said anything about Miss Newton leaving," Elinor said, patting her shoulder.

"But if she has an admirer, she might get married, and then she'd have to leave us."

"I assure you, I am not getting married anytime soon," I said. And if I did get married to the man I'd choose, I'd be even more a part of the family, though of course I couldn't say that. Flora gave me a sharp glance and raised an eyebrow. She'd been there when Henry had kissed me, but she'd said nothing about our relationship.

Olive perked up immediately at my assurance. "Then you'll be with us for Christmas?"

"I certainly will."

"Oh, good," Elinor said. "I was worried that you might want to spend the holiday with your own family, though that was selfish of me. Of course, you should go if you like. You deserve a holiday."

"There will be no need for me to go to my family. I'd rather be with all of you." After my mother's death, my father and siblings had disowned me, since they'd all been aware that I was not actually my father's daughter. Whoever my father was, he must have been a magister. I'd often wondered who he might be. His relationship with my mother had been illicit in multiple ways, given that she was married and a commoner.

"Hooray!" Olive cheered, waving her empty soup spoon.

"I suppose that means I need to buy you a present," Rollo said.

"You would have bought her a present anyway," Elinor said.

"But someone will have to go with us to go shopping, and Miss Newton is usually the one who takes us," he pointed out.

"I'm sure something can be arranged," Elinor said mildly. "Now, I believe it's time for you to get to school."

I got the younger two bundled up and out the door on time. "Do you think it'll snow again, Miss Newton?" Olive asked, turning her face up to the sky. "The last time wasn't nearly enough, and it's already all gone."

"It's cold enough," Rollo said, answering for me.

"I hope it does!" Olive said, skipping ahead of us for a few steps. "Will there be snow for Christmas?"

"It's too soon to know," I replied. "If the roads are bad, we won't be able to go to your country house."

"That won't be a problem," Rollo said. "There's a railway station nearby, and we have a sleigh to take us to the house."

"Well, that's certainly nice," I said, my tone probably more snappish than was warranted, but the night spent thinking about revolution had affected the way I saw the Lyndon family's wealth.

When we reached the school, I was surprised to see that the boys were clustered in groups, reading something. Then I noticed the boy standing on the corner. He wore a school uniform, so it took me a moment to recognize Nat, who was handing out newspapers to the boys. "Special edition!" he called out. "Learn all about the fantastic machines!"

Rollo didn't even pause to think or ask permission before rushing to grab a paper, and he headed to join his friends, his head down as he read, without saying good-bye to Olive or me.

"Care for a paper, miss?" Nat asked.

I hadn't noticed for certain if my usual followers were behind me, but I had the now-familiar feeling of being watched, so I didn't dare show any familiarity with Nat. It was bad enough that I'd let Rollo take a paper without reprimanding him. Then I realized that Nat was likely to be caught by the authorities if they followed me and noticed him.

"No, thank you," I said brusquely. "You shouldn't be here. This is trespassing." I hoped Nat got the message.

"Can't you tell, I'm a student?" Nat said with a wink. He ran off to follow the other boys into the gates of the school when the bell rang.

"I wanted the newspaper with the machines in it," Olive said plaintively as we walked away.

"Maybe your brother will bring it home for you to look at," I said.

She scoffed. "He never shares."

"Perhaps if you ask nicely he'll be willing to tell you about the machines." It would be more difficult to make him stop.

But I had to wonder what their aim was in recruiting schoolboys. They weren't likely to make a difference in the push for revolution. All I could think was that they were expected to possibly influence their parents or older siblings. Then again, they weren't much younger than I was, and many of them were older than Nat, and we were quite involved.

The schoolboys weren't the only ones being targeted, I soon saw. When Olive and I made our way down a commercial street, a group of young women I recognized from Lizzie's boardinghouse passed us. They handed out fliers to other women they passed, including me. The woman who gave it to me winked quickly, but otherwise showed no sign of recognition.

"What does it say, Miss Newton?" Olive asked, walking on tiptoes to try to read it.

"Votes for women," I read out loud. It seemed that Lizzie was putting out some of her own materials. Her rhetoric was fierier than mine tended to be.

"What does that mean?"

"These ladies apparently believe that everyone should have a vote, even women." The flier went on to mention that no one in the colonies really had a say in our government, but a new nation would be more likely to offer representation to all, even women.

"Well, why not?" Olive asked defiantly. "Boys shouldn't be able to tell us what to do."

I would have liked to read the rest of the flier, but knowing I was likely being watched forced me to wad it up and deposit it in the next rubbish bin I passed. I thought that was what a good girl who was a loyal citizen of the Empire would do.

On the next block, we approached a group of carolers led by a tall, red-haired man. "God rest ye merry gentlemen, let nothing you dismay," Colin sang out in his powerful tenor to the small crowd that had gathered around.

It was the next line that caught my attention: "For our good friend the governor has closed our Assembly." It took some work to make it fit the meter, and it didn't quite rhyme, but it was close enough to the true song that one might not have noticed the difference in passing. Some of the listeners smiled when they caught on, while others turned away in disgust. "To save himself from scandal and quash our liberty."

I veered quickly around the corner before we reached them, hoping that my followers hadn't yet properly made out the lyrics. I didn't want to be the reason that the group got into trouble. I winced as their words seemed to follow us: "Oh tidings of rebels rising up, rebels rise up! Oh tidings of rebels rising up."

It seemed that they were wasting no time in beginning the publicity campaign for the revolution, even before I delivered the pamphlets. At least I hadn't had to make my words rhyme or scan to fit a tune.

"I wanted to listen to the carolers," Olive complained.

"Those aren't proper carolers," I said, my voice loud enough to carry. "I'm sure we can find some better ones. Now, we'd best get home. You have lessons to do. I want to finish this unit before Christmas."

There was a letter for me in the morning mail when

we returned home, an invitation from "Alec" to join him for a ride in the park that afternoon. He would meet me on the drive closest to the house at four. That meant the rendezvous was firmly set. The seal on the letter seemed rather loose to me, so I suspected the authorities also knew where and when I'd be meeting someone. I didn't have the opportunity to check for hidden writing, so I didn't know if there was more to the message. Based on the date on the letter, it should probably have been delivered the day before.

The day seemed to drag for me. When we went out that afternoon to pick Rollo up from school, the follower made no move to hide himself. Even Olive noticed that something was unusual. "Who is that man and why is he following us?" she asked, rather loudly.

"He's making sure we're safe from the rebels," I said.

Though I knew we were likely safe from the rebels I knew, I found that I wasn't entirely dismayed at having authorities nearby as we made our way farther along the route to the school. The rebels were out in force, not just Colin's carolers, but ragged bands running up and down the streets, scattering flyers and newspapers, tying red ribbons to everything in sight, and shouting rebel slogans.

On the way back home, I saw that there were carolers, as well, singing such songs as "O come, all ye rebels, rise up and be triumphant." Police were trying to break up the groups or drive the undesirables out of the wealthy neighborhood, but there were just too many of them. I wasn't sure this was the best tactic for the rebels, as it was hardly a way to make wealthy magisters side with them, but I supposed they made the newspapers and leaflets look less radical, in comparison, and it did mean that no one could claim to be unaware that something was happening.

And it did look as though people were listening. It wasn't just obvious rebels gathering around the carolers and taking newspapers. The actions seemed to be making a difference. I could only hope my own contributions would matter as much.

Rollo watched it all with great enthusiasm. "D'you think a revolution is going to happen, Miss Newton?" he asked.

"I'm sure your grandfather will have everything in hand," I replied, unable to look him directly in the eye.

"But if he closed the Assembly…"

"We don't know what's really happening, so it's best not to speculate," I snapped in my firmest governess voice. At least I felt he'd given our follower the opportunity to hear me denounce rebellion. I hoped that might ease some of their suspicion of me. If the scrutiny continued that afternoon, it might be difficult for me to hand over the text for my pamphlets, especially since they likely knew when I was going out and that I was meeting someone.

The piano teacher was late, which made me even more anxious. A glance out the front window showed that the surveillance was still in place. As soon as the piano teacher arrived, I rushed to my room and sprayed the letter I'd received that morning with the lavender-scented chemical.

Nothing happened. There was no secret message, no alternative meeting time or place, no note from Henry. I tried not to let my shoulders sag in disappointment. Since I was fairly certain my mail had been read, it was good that this particular communication had been almost entirely aboveboard, with nothing to indicate that I was in communication with Henry, no matter how closely they examined it.

With no secret writing, I'd have to take the missive at face value, which meant I didn't have much time before the meeting. I hid the blank-looking sheets between the pages of a book, wrapped it in the paper from the package I'd been given at the party, and tied it with a red ribbon, so that it looked like a gift. I put on my hat, coat, and gloves, picked up the package, and hurried downstairs.

When I opened the front door, I barely stifled a yelp when I found myself face-to-face with two very stern-looking men in dark suits—the men I'd come to think of as Inspector Tall and Inspector Stout. Inspector Stout showed me a badge. "We need to talk to you about Lord Henry Lyndon," he said.

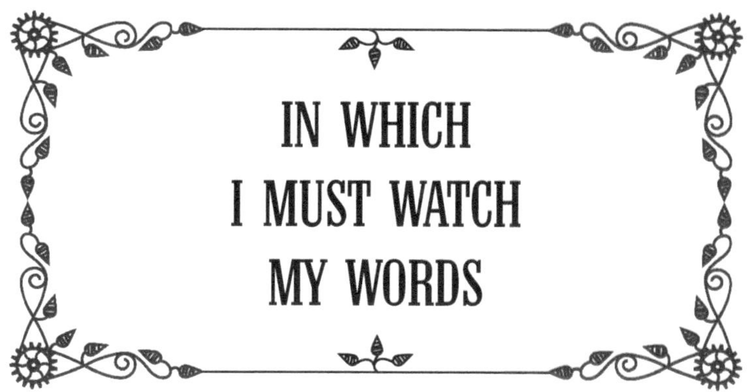

IN WHICH I MUST WATCH MY WORDS

"To-to me?" I stammered.

"Your household," Inspector Stout corrected.

"I'm just the governess, but let me get the butler. He'll take care of you."

I barely turned around before Mr. Chastain had appeared in the foyer. "I didn't hear the bell," he said in his deep voice.

"These gentlemen were on the doorstep when I opened the door to go out," I explained. To the visitors, I said, "This is Mr. Chastain. He'll assist you."

They stepped inside, and I moved around them to continue on my way out the door, but Inspector Tall caught my arm. "Where are you going?" he asked.

"Out. It's my afternoon off, and I have an appointment with a friend."

He raised an eyebrow, and I couldn't help but wonder if he'd been the one to read my mail, so that he knew exactly where I was going and why. Had they timed their visit accordingly? "I'm afraid you won't be going anywhere at the moment," he said. "We need to talk to everyone."

"Will you have a seat in the parlor?" Mr. Chastain boomed, perfectly polite, but with an undercurrent of ice.

I clutched my package to my chest as I joined the men in the parlor. Mrs. Talbot soon arrived, slightly out of breath. I wasn't sure what had signaled her, but she approached the men and said, "I'm Mrs. Talbot, the housekeeper. How may I help you?"

"We don't need you at the moment," the man said.

"I'm afraid I can't allow you to be alone with this young lady. I will stay here as chaperone." I'd always found her to be intimidating, but now I was quite glad of her formidable size and stern temperament. The man blinked once, but he didn't argue with her.

Turning to me, he said, "Have you been in communication with Lord Henry Lyndon?"

Did they know something? Had they possibly found a way to read the secret writing? I'd thought this visit might have been related to my assignation, but it also came the day after I received a letter from Henry. I gave Inspector Tall as direct a gaze as I could manage and said, "I haven't seen him at all." I hoped he didn't notice that I hadn't actually answered his specific question.

"Would you know if he has tried to contact the children?"

"I'm sure I would, as they're always chaperoned. He has not been in communication with the children." Here I felt on much firmer ground, as I could tell the absolute truth while answering him directly.

"I would have to consult their grandfather before I could allow you to speak with the children," Mrs. Talbot put in. "He's their guardian at the moment."

"That won't be necessary," the inspector said. Turning back to me, he added, "You're certain he hasn't communicated with anyone in this house?"

"I'm really just the governess, so I wouldn't know much," I said. "I spend most of my time with the children." A ball of fear had formed in my stomach and was growing. "Has–has he been seen in the city?" I thought anyone would have asked that question. Where *was* Henry, if he was able to get letters to me by way of the Mechanics?

"That's not anything you need to know," he said brusquely. Turning to Mrs. Talbot, he said, "And what about you or the other servants?"

"I've heard nothing," she said with a shrug. "If he's been in contact with the servants, they've not indicated it to me. If you ask me, that one is long gone. He likes the outdoors, always chafed at the city."

I couldn't tell whether or not he believed her. "And her ladyship? I understand that Lady Elinor DeLancey has taken up residence here. I need to speak to her."

"That won't be possible. Lady Elinor is an invalid and is bedridden. It would be improper for her to receive a strange man in her bedroom. And I believe it's safe to say that if she can't leave her bed, she's unlikely to have been in contact with a fugitive."

For a moment, I worried that he'd argue with her. I wished I knew whether he was merely digging around, doing due diligence, or if he was acting on any intelligence. If he'd discovered the secret writing in my letters, then he knew I was lying, and I could be in a great deal of trouble.

While the inspector and Mrs. Talbot glared at each other, I tentatively cleared my throat. "Excuse me, but do you need anything else from me? I have an appointment to keep."

He scowled, and I was fairly certain that he planned to detain me, just because he could, but Mrs. Talbot stepped forward. "A governess has little enough time for herself. Please let the girl go."

"Very well." He gave an abrupt gesture of dismissal.

"Thank you, sir," I said with a slight curtsy before I hurried past him and Mrs. Talbot.

I wasn't quite to the door when he called out, "Wait. What appointment is this?"

I didn't think it unreasonable for me to show some fear by now. In fact, an innocent person who had no idea what was happening would be even more afraid than someone who expected an interrogation. Therefore, I didn't try to fight the tremble in my voice when I turned and said,

"I–I'm meeting a young man I've been seeing. He's going to take me for a drive. And I have a present for him." I held up my package.

He came toward me. "What is it?"

"Nothing much, just a book. We've only recently begun courting. I mentioned I was reading it, and he expressed an interest, so I thought I'd give it to him, and we could discuss it."

He held his hand out for it. I froze. Surely he wouldn't ask to see it if he didn't suspect something very specific.

Mrs. Talbot joined us in the foyer. "Sir, this is an outrage," she said. "The governor will not stand for his family being treated this way."

Inspector Tall never took his eyes off me. "This young lady is staff, not family. I need to inspect that package."

I gulped and handed it over, very glad that I'd been cautious enough to write the pamphlet text in the disappearing ink. "The governor will hear of this, I assure you," Mrs. Talbot said as he pulled the ribbon loose and let the paper fall away. He opened the cover and flipped through a few pages. I held my breath. What would he say about the seemingly blank writing paper pages I'd inserted?

But he didn't get there. Apparently satisfied that it was merely a book, he handed it back to me. I made no effort to stop a tear from trickling down my cheek as I stooped to pick up the paper and ribbon. "Look what you've done to that poor girl," Mrs. Talbot scolded. "Here, dear, let me wrap that up for you again." She was much more deft at wrapping packages than I was, and soon the gift looked as good as new. She whirled on the inspectors, her glare fierce enough to terrify me, even though it wasn't directed at me. "Now, if you're quite through oppressing us, may she go?"

"She is free to go."

"You go, dear, and I will inform Lady Elinor of these events."

Mr. Chastain opened the door for me, giving me a sly wink in the process, and I darted across the street. The combination of fear and relief left me weak, but I didn't have time for a breakdown. I just hoped Alec—or whoever it was who would be meeting me—hadn't feared the worst, given up, and left.

It had begun snowing, only lightly, but there was still a dusting of white coating the world. There was just enough to show my footsteps, and not enough to fill them in quickly, which meant I'd be incredibly easy to follow. Although the inspectors were still inside, I had no doubt that someone else was watching me.

I was only a few minutes late, but I saw no sign of Alec or anyone else from the Mechanics at the specified meeting location. I brushed the snow off a nearby bench and sat, holding my package on my lap. Had he already come and given up on me?

But before I could grow too concerned, a roadster came around the bend, slowing as it approached. I stood, and it stopped right in front of me. Alec was alone in the sporty magical carriage, and he was dressed like a prosperous young businessman. He jumped down and ran around the roadster to help me up into the passenger seat. "Sorry I'm running late," he said. "Snow slows everything down."

"I only just got here, myself," I said once I was seated and the vehicle was in motion.

"There's a rug there, if you want to throw it over your legs," he said. "The open top isn't such a benefit on a day like today."

"The snow's really quite lovely," I replied as I tugged the rug into place.

"Very romantic, I'd say." I couldn't tell if he was playing the role of beau or if he was serious. With Alec, it could easily be both. He leaned a little closer to me and said softly, "I saw that you had company."

"Yes, they were asking about Henry."

"Do they know anything?"

"I couldn't tell."

"I made a loop before coming back to you, and I couldn't be sure whether or not you're being followed."

"Fortunately, I'm not doing anything too suspicious. I just wanted to give you your Christmas gift." I placed the package on the seat between us.

"Oh, you didn't have to get me anything."

"It's not much, but I hope you enjoy it. You'll want to read every page."

"I'm sure I'll love it, if it's from you." He squinted up at the sky. "I think it's snowing harder. I'd better get you home. What do you say to being delivered directly to your door?"

"I think that would be delightful."

Although we hadn't gone too far, it took a few minutes to make it to the next park exit and then return to the mansion. The inspectors' carriage was gone when we pulled up in front, but the place where it had been parked hadn't yet been covered in snow, which suggested that it hadn't been gone long. Alec got out and helped me down, gallantly kissing my hand before he returned to the roadster and drove away. I was glad the inspectors were gone so that I wouldn't have to play the starry-eyed girl when I entered the house. I once might have felt that way about Alec, but my feelings had cooled considerably.

However, I did have to face Flora, who was painting at the window again. "Well, now," she said with a grin when I entered the family parlor. "What's this, Miss Newton? You do have a beau!"

"He's just a friend who likes to play at being gallant," I insisted.

"But he has his own carriage, so he's well-off. Where did you meet him?"

I froze. There was no reasonable explanation for how I knew a young man wealthy enough to have a magical carriage but who wasn't a magister. "We were introduced by a mutual friend," I said, which was true enough. Now, if only she wouldn't ask who that friend was... And she didn't. She returned to her painting, apparently satisfied with my answer. Flora might have more depth than she'd been willing to show, but she still wasn't overly interested in my life.

Mrs. Talbot had apparently notified Elinor of the inspectors' visit while I was out, and Elinor was still seething at dinner. "I've already told Father about their rudeness," she assured me. "While there is some justification for watching this house because of our ties to Henry, there is no excuse for terrorizing a member of our household staff. Searching your package was beyond the pale. I do hope you weren't too traumatized, Miss Newton."

"It was rather frightening," I admitted. Even more so because the package had contained seditious writing. In a way, I felt bad for the inspectors, who would likely be in a great deal of trouble, either for having harassed me or for having missed my wrongdoing entirely. They'd been on the right track, and with that in mind, their actions hadn't been all that wrong.

"You should have called for me," Rollo said. "I'm the head of this household, and I won't let my staff be treated that way."

"You're just a boy," Olive said. "They don't care what title you have."

"They have to listen to a marquis," Rollo insisted.

"Not one who's a mere child," Flora replied. "You should have sent for me. I know how to handle men like that."

"Your grandfather wouldn't have wanted you to be

involved," I said. "Nor would your uncle. There was no harm done, other than to the wrapping on my package, and Mrs. Talbot fixed that."

"I still don't know what they expected to find," Flora said with a sidelong glance at me. "It's as though they believe Henry would be foolish enough to contact any of us, or that we might be hiding him in the attic. You aren't hiding him in the attic, are you, Miss Newton?"

"I don't even know how to get to the attic."

If any inspectors followed us the next morning, either Inspector Tall and Inspector Stout had been replaced or they were being far less obtrusive than they'd been recently, for I saw no sign of them. The rebels were also being quieter. There were no carolers in sight, and no one was passing out newspapers near the school. I wondered whether they'd been arrested, had moved to other parts of town, or were doing something else.

In fact, the whole day was strangely quiet. I would have enjoyed the peace after the previous day's excitement, but I couldn't help but worry that the quiet meant something was wrong. I felt slightly better when I received a note from Alec in the afternoon post, thanking me for the gift. I had the chance to spray it for secret writing just before dinner and found instructions to dress warmly and be ready between eleven and midnight.

That was infuriatingly cryptic. It didn't even tell me

where I should go. Was I to sneak out? Be ready for a knock at the door? Was there to be a riot in the street? I decided to take it at face value. After dinner, I took a nap, setting the clock to wake me just before eleven. I pulled on a second pair of woolen stockings, wound a muffler around my neck, put on my coat and boots, pinned a woolen hat securely to my head, and had my gloves handy. Then I waited.

At about ten after eleven, there was a thump against my window, and I realized what they must be doing. I carried my desk chair to the window, pulled back the curtains, and opened the window to find a rope ladder hanging there. "Oh, you're all quite insane," I muttered to myself as I climbed onto the chair, stepped onto the window ledge, and grabbed the ladder. I was grateful when the ladder began to ascend without me having to climb it. Climbing a rope ladder in the middle of the air was a harrowing experience I didn't want to repeat. It was bad enough riding it as the winch pulled it up to the airship's gondola.

When I reached the gondola, hands reached down to pull me in. I couldn't immediately tell who was on board the small airship, since everyone was bundled up against the cold and they all wore goggles. The man who'd helped me handed me my own pair of goggles, which I quickly fastened over my eyes, fumbling with the buckle on the strap with my gloved fingers. The man stepped up and took over, making quick work of it, though it seemed almost as though he was lingering in my proximity. Was that Alec? But no, he was a bit too tall to be Alec, too quiet to be Colin.

In fact, the other man on board was obviously Colin. A few red curls stuck out from beneath his stocking cap, and he was already talking. "We thought you'd want to be here for this," he said, waving a sheaf of papers he held.

"Are those my pamphlets?" I asked, hurrying to him to see.

"One of them, the one you aimed at workers toiling for the magisters. We're distributing them tonight."

"From an airship?"

"How better to get them into the fort? It'll be like a snowfall, though the flakes are rather larger than normal." He handed me the sheet, which was printed too densely to read in the moonlight. "We already started getting out the one aimed at lower-ranking magisters."

I couldn't help but smile. "That's interesting, considering that next week the governor is visiting the fort and the magic generation plant."

I imagined him raising an eyebrow behind his goggles. "Really? Fancy that. Someone must have let us know about those plans. Our top spy."

I glanced behind us toward the mansion. "Though if they weren't already suspicious of me, surely they will be when they notice me flying away in an airship."

"Turns out, they stop watching the house at eleven. I suppose they assume you're all sound asleep, and they may as well not waste the manpower. Also, we didn't really stop moving, so I'm not sure they'd have realized we picked you up, even if they were watching."

The man who'd helped me board had moved aft to talk to Everett, the airship's pilot, leaving me alone with Colin. "Thank you for bringing me along," I said. "It's good to get out. Are we just going to the fort?"

"If you don't mind, we'll be making some other stops first, distributing pamphlets to Long Island and a few other points."

That wasn't quite what I was asking, but I wasn't sure how to ask if we might be going to wherever Henry was without coming right out and saying it. "As long as you have me home before morning."

From this height, the city looked peaceful under a light dusting of snow. Very few people were out, which I thought was eminently sensible of them in this cold. Even with my extra layers, my feet and fingers were already growing numb. Since I was surrounded by nonmagical people who wouldn't notice, I used a little trick Henry had taught me to magically warm myself.

When we neared the Brooklyn Bridge, we headed out across the water, paralleling the bridge. Once we reached the shoreline, Everett aimed the nose of the ship slightly downward, and Mick, who served as Everett's apprentice, and the other man on board gathered up bundles of pamphlets, leaned over the side, waited until they spotted the target, and dropped the bundles overboard. I heard faint thumps as they landed, and Everett aimed the ship upward again, the engine humming louder for a moment until we steadied at cruising altitude.

We made two more deliveries, including one to a ship docked at the harbor, where they dropped several bundles, then we aimed back toward the city. "Now that we've lightened the load, we can have some fun," Colin said. We approached the East Battery fort on Governor's Island, and Colin handed loose pamphlets to all of us. "Drop them on my signal," Colin said.

I couldn't help but laugh with delight as I sent my own words flying out into the night to blanket the ground below. Once my armload was gone, I ran to the rear of the ship to look back at what appeared from the air to have been a dense snowfall. But it really wasn't snow. It was more like seeds, and I hoped they found fertile ground and bore fruit.

"The next one'll be trickier," Colin said. "They don't post much in the way of guards out here because they think the harbor serves as a decent barrier. They're warier in the West Battery fort, since their security has already been breached."

"I'm not sure increasing the number of guards would have stopped that," I said with a smile that was probably a bit smug. "They still wouldn't stop the laundresses and cleaners from coming in or going out."

"I doubt they yet know that's what happened. But they

might consider an airship to be a threat, so look lively. Where do you think the best drop point is?"

"Most of the barracks are along the rear wall," I said, trying to remember the layout of the fort from my brief visit. "It would really be nice if we could get them through the windows, but that would require the wind cooperating." Or magic, I realized. I could do this, but could I do it in such a way that they wouldn't realize I had anything to do with it?

Or would it really change much of anything if they did know it was me? I'd worried when I first met the Mechanics that they wouldn't accept me if they knew about my magical heritage, but they'd begun working with magisters. They'd accepted Henry. As open and friendly as Colin was, I couldn't imagine him turning his back on me. If anything, he'd think it made me more sympathetic, since the magisters would be even less likely to accept me. For now, though, I thought it best to keep the secret to myself, and I thought I could create a few slight puffs of wind, assuming there were any windows open on a night like this.

As we drew closer to the fort, I noticed that there were one or two windows ajar, with condensation beading on them. All those men crammed into a tight space might have made the air rather more close than was pleasant. When Colin gave the signal, I threw my pamphlets overboard, and then I created a magical gust that swept them toward the open windows. Not all of them made it inside, but

I thought at least a few must have. Henry's escape had ultimately hinged on a single soldier who questioned his orders, so I hoped that enlightening a few more would make a difference.

A shiver went down my spine, and at first I thought it was merely the cold and the excitement, but then I recognized it as magic being performed nearby. I turned to look at the others. Colin and the other man were still flinging pamphlets into the fort, and some of them flew into open windows or into open stable doors. The wind swirled within the walls of the fort, but had magic been involved?

The feeling went away so quickly that I couldn't trace its source, and then it was no longer my biggest concern. A bell began pealing within the fort, and a second later, a shot rang out.

IN WHICH I AM PUT ON DISPLAY

"Everett, get us out of here!" Colin shouted.

"Way ahead of you," the pilot replied. He turned the wheel to steer us away from the fort and angled the engines to propel us upward. "Drop some ballast."

"We don't have many pamphlets left," Colin said.

"Don't drop those!" I said. "They could use those to follow us. He means the rocks."

The other man—who still hadn't spoken, I realized—was already untying some of the sacks of small rocks and sand that were attached around the edge of the gondola. I joined him, letting the bags drop, which allowed the ship to rise higher above the city as we fled the fort.

Quite abruptly, I found myself lying on the floor of the gondola, pressed down by the mystery man, who'd flung me away from the edge of the ship. Before I could protest, he pointed to a small hole in the gondola's wicker side. It was right where I'd just been standing. "Thank you!" I said, my voice shaking. "You saved my life." I just wasn't sure how he'd known to throw me aside like that. He couldn't have heard the shot before the bullet reached us. Perhaps I *had* sensed magic before, and I wasn't the only secret half-breed associated with the movement.

"We've got a problem," Everett called out. "They hit the envelope. It'll take a bigger hole than that to bring us down, but we will lose altitude."

The mystery man was up and already climbing the rigging. Watching him up on the balloon when we were high in the air made me dizzy, so I went back to dropping ballast. We were away from the fort now, but a rifle shot could still reach us. The question was whether we'd be followed. If anyone bothered to pick up and read one of the leaflets we'd dropped, they'd know we were rebels and that our visit wasn't a mere prank.

The next time I looked up at the balloon, there was a patch on it, darker than the mottled gray of the canvas, and the other man was safely back in the gondola. The engine was louder than I'd ever heard it as it pushed us against the wind.

"Will we have enough power to get back?" Colin asked.

"Depends on if they're chasing us," Everett replied.

I looked behind us, watching for anything else in the sky. There was a faint blob in the distance, but I couldn't quite tell if it was one of the military airships coming up from Governor's Island or just a cloud. By now, we were well into the middle of the city. From this height, in the darkness, I couldn't tell if anyone was tracking us on the ground. The ship was colored to be difficult to spot at night.

"There might be an airship coming after us, but it's far away," I said.

"They've got magical engines, so they can move faster than we can," Everett said, "but if they didn't take off until after we left the fort, I don't think they'll be able to catch us. We aren't going to be able to drop you at your house, though. We can't afford to slow down. I want to get back to the hangar."

"Of course," I said, nodding, even though a lump had formed in my throat. How would I get home?

"Don't worry, we'll take care of you," Colin said, patting my shoulder.

I felt a surge of what I was certain was magic, and the ship began moving faster. "Hey, the wind changed!" Everett called out. "That should help." I knew I hadn't done it, but I kept quiet, suspecting our mystery man was keeping his own secret.

Soon, I could no longer see the blob that might have been chasing us. We were over the park now, past the Lyndon mansion. "I might be able to drop you in the park," Everett said. "Would that be easier than trying to get into the city from the hangar?"

"Yes," I said, though it still wouldn't be easy. I was

glad I'd put my house key in my coat pocket, since I hadn't known when the night began what I'd be doing. I might be able to sneak in through the kitchen, but it would be a close call. The kitchen staff began work very early.

"I'll go with you," Colin said. We neared a large hill within the park, and Colin used the winch to lower the ladder. He climbed down and jumped to the ground below, where he held the bottom end of the ladder, keeping it from bucking wildly. I forced myself not to look down as I descended. I could tell that the ship was still moving, and knew Colin must be moving with the ladder. Even so, he kept it steady enough that I never lost my footing. I was enormously grateful when he caught me in his arms and lowered me the rest of the way to the ground.

As soon as I was off the ladder, Mick and the mystery man pulled it up again, and the ship floated away. "Now, to get you home," Colin said. "But we might want to take off the goggles first. Those'll stand out in this neighborhood."

I'd almost forgotten I was still wearing them. I excited the ether around my fingertips to warm them enough to undo the buckle and handed the goggles to Colin. "Who was that other man?" I asked, trying to keep my voice casual. "I don't believe I've met him before, and you never introduced him."

"He's been around. You've probably seen him at some of our events. You just didn't recognize him under all the protective gear."

"Well, he saved my life tonight, so I owe him thanks."

All of us owed him thanks, and the Mechanics might never realize how much.

It was warmer on the ground than it had been in the air with the wind whipping around us, but it was still cold, and it was very dark in the heart of the park. The park was supposed to be closed overnight, so I hoped we didn't run into a watchman. I also wasn't entirely certain where we were.

Colin, though, walked briskly, as though he was totally certain. I could barely keep up with him, but hurrying to maintain that pace warmed me. He held me back and stepped forward to look around before we emerged onto a path. The paths of the park were designed for scenic meandering rather than rapid movement, so I felt like we walked far more than was truly necessary before we reached Fifth Avenue.

Based on the nearest street sign, we had a little more than twenty blocks to go. "It's a pity the subway isn't more convenient," I said.

"We'd walk more getting to a station and then getting from a station than we would just walking. And that's assuming we could find anyone awake to run it. But I might be able to find us some transportation. My favorite roadster lives near here."

"Colin! You can't!"

"I do it all the time, and I'm sure the owner's not using it now. Besides, it'll make for a good diversion to let you get in the house. Now, right this way, milady. Your carriage awaits."

He led me across the street to a row of town houses. They weren't quite as magnificent as the mansions farther down the street, but they were still quite fine. We went around to the alley running behind them, where there was a row of garages.

"You play lookout," he ordered.

"What do I do if someone comes?"

"How good is your damsel in distress? Cry and say you've had trouble. But it shouldn't come to that."

He disappeared into the garage, and a moment later, the large door slid aside. The small roadster I was used to seeing the rebels use rolled out of the garage and Colin jumped out to close the door. "Now, off we go," he said, patting the seat next to him once he was back in the driver's seat.

I climbed on board, and he pulled out onto the street, then onto Fifth Avenue. "That's one good thing about these magical engines," he said. "They're nice and quiet. We'd never be able to pull off a stunt like this with a steam engine. It would wake up the whole neighborhood." He turned to me and grinned. "Do you think we should use that as a selling point? No one can borrow your carriage without you knowing about it."

He pulled down a side street a couple of blocks north of the Lyndon house and turned onto the next avenue heading downtown. He stopped to let me out a block behind the mansion. "Wait a moment or two. If there's anyone watching—and I doubt it at this hour—I'll distract them."

I did as he said, counting slowly to fifty in my head before I hurried across the kitchen yard and used my key to open the back door. The house was blessedly dark and still. I paused to remove my boots, then tiptoed upstairs toward my room.

I was halfway up the stairs when I heard footsteps behind me. I paused on the landing, withdrawing into the shadows, until the black-veiled figure came into view. She looked somewhat less mysterious and imposing while carrying her shoes. Where had she been?

If there ever was a time to bring our secrets out into the open, I decided that it was now. "Oh, hello, Elinor," I whispered. "We both seem to have been out late. Were you distributing pamphlets, too?"

I had to admit to wishing there had been a little more light so I could have seen her reaction. As it was, all I could see was that she'd gone very still. After a moment of silence, she reached out and grabbed my arm in a fierce grip, and then I had no choice but to follow her up the stairs. I couldn't tell if she was afraid or if I was in very serious trouble.

We reached her room, and she shut the door behind us before releasing me and waving a hand to turn on the lights. Then she whirled on me. "You know about me? How long have you known?"

"Only since you came to live here."

"What gave me away?"

"Your walk. So unless you're up and about around

other people who've seen the Lady in Black, you should be safe. Obviously, you've known about me all along, from even before I came to work for the family, since you were on the bus that day. Why haven't *you* said anything to me?"

"While my position isn't quite as precarious as yours, I feel it's safest for as few people as possible to know my secret. It's really too late in the evening for tea, but acquiring warm milk or cocoa would require alerting the kitchen staff or doing more sneaking around than is probably wise at this hour. I have some chamomile, though. That might be nice."

My head was still spinning from the abrupt change of subject as she went over to her dresser and took out a teapot, which she filled in the adjacent bathroom. She boiled the water magically before dropping in a few spoonsful of dried herbs.

"Does Henry know about you?" I asked her as she poured the brew into china cups.

She handed me a cup and gestured for me to take a seat by the ornamental fireplace. "Not that I'm aware of. I've never told him, and he's never said anything that implies that he knows."

After a moment's hesitation, I asked, "Did you know of all his activities?" I wasn't sure if even that was saying too much, revealing a secret he didn't want to share with his brother's sister-in-law.

"You mean the banditry? Yes, I know about it, but I

didn't learn it from him. Well, not directly. I had to piece that together myself, as I'm sure you did."

"He robbed me. That's how I knew."

She'd just taken a sip of tea, so she spluttered when she laughed. "That is absolutely priceless," she said, dabbing at her face and her black dress with a handkerchief. "When did that happen?"

"On the train on my way into the city. And to be more accurate, he didn't actually rob me. He robbed the train I was on. But he had to displace me from my seat to reach the hatch to escape."

"You didn't know who he was?"

"Not at the time. Imagine my surprise when he arrived to interview me for the position and I thought he looked very familiar. I wasn't entirely sure, as he was wearing a mask when he robbed the train, but I recognized his eyes."

She shook her head, smiling. "And you came to work for him anyway. Did you already have rebellious leanings?"

"No. I was desperate. That was why I accepted the ride on the bus, why I took the job. The rebels then found my position useful and recruited me. It was only later that I came to believe that they were right."

Nodding somberly, she said, "And now? You are fully involved?"

I was sure I could trust her, but I was still afraid to tell her absolutely everything. As she'd said, the best secrets were the ones no one knew about. After some hesitation, I said, "I'm fully involved, with both the Rebel Mechanics and with rebel magister groups. I've been spying on your father for the rebels."

"Oh, I knew about that," she said with a dismissive wave. "Why do you think I called you out of that ball and gave you the opportunity to search his office? I believe I tipped you off about a few other things, as well."

I couldn't help but grin. "I admit, I wondered about that. I even worried that you were setting a trap for me, that I would be revealed as a spy if the rebels acted on my information."

"Well, you needn't worry any longer," she said with a grin of her own. "Now we both know that both of us are in it up to our ears. I'd rather keep the children out of it as much as possible."

"Flora knows a little of it," I admitted. "She helped me help Henry escape, so she knows I have rebel connections. She doesn't know anything about you, though."

"Let's keep it that way. But within these walls"—she waved her teacup to the four corners of the room—"we can talk freely, and I would like for us to do so." She gave a huge, deep sigh. "It feels so good to be able to be open with someone, particularly with you, Verity. So, what were *you* doing out tonight? You guessed that I was distributing pamphlets. Were you, as well?"

"Yes. We seemed to be focusing on places the governor will be visiting, so I suspect things won't go very well for him."

"I should feel bad, since he's my father, but he's on

the wrong side of this. I was helping with printing and with getting them out in some of the middle-class magister districts. You did an excellent job on the writing, by the way."

"How long have you known about that?"

"About your journalistic alter ego? I own that newspaper, so of course I knew, from the start. If Father ever dismisses you, or you otherwise find yourself in need of a position, I'll hire you as a full-time reporter, but in the meantime, I'd rather keep you here and contributing when you can. You have access that even I don't have, since people talk in front of you in ways they wouldn't in front of me—that is, if I could tolerate being around people."

"Was it your idea to recruit me as a reporter?"

She shook her head. "Remember, I hadn't met you at that time."

That much was a relief. I'd grown weary of people planning things involving me from behind my back instead of just asking me up front. "Your father really doesn't suspect anything about your activities?"

"Nothing whatsoever," she said with a grin. "Remember, I'm an invalid. He never talks to me about anything of substance, so he has no idea of my views. Actually, I'm afraid he has something of a blind spot about his family. I'm still not sure he entirely believes Henry was guilty of anything."

"Then why didn't he do anything to help him?"

"Appearances, I'm sure. He couldn't afford to put his neck out with all that scandal in the air. It was a no-win proposition. If he intervened on Henry's behalf, it added to the scandal by making him look corrupt. If he didn't, there was the scandal of treason in the family."

"So he was going to quietly make him disappear, instead," I said, a touch of snarl in my voice.

"To be honest, I think he's rather grateful things worked out the way they did. Henry's out of the way, but he's also not in immediate danger. There can't be a trial or any kind of punishment."

"Then why are we being followed and inspected the way we are?"

"Appearances, again. If he tried to make the authorities back down, it would look like he sympathized with Henry or wanted special treatment for his family. They did go too far when they searched your package, though. That gave him a good enough reason to demand that they leave his family and staff alone." She took a sip of tea and smiled. "I'm assuming you were carrying the pamphlet text to your contacts. How did you manage to pull that off?"

"I have ways to hide writing in plain sight. I also get messages in the mail that way."

Her smile broadened. "And have you heard anything interesting that way?"

Once again, I had to wonder how much she really knew and how much she was good at guessing. "I have been in some contact with Henry," I admitted. "I can correspond with him, but it is a method best limited to important messages."

She placed her teacup very decisively on a table and stood. "And now you should probably get to your room before anyone notices you've been up and about. I would appreciate it if you would keep me informed of any news or of your activities."

The hallway was empty, but I didn't relax entirely until I'd reached my own room, which was freezing, since I hadn't latched the window, only pulled it to, and it had blown open. I closed and latched it, shut the drapes, and undressed as quickly as I could before pulling on my flannel nightgown. A glance at the clock told me I had a few hours to sleep. At least I didn't have to get Rollo to school in the morning, since it was Saturday.

When the morning for our outing with the governor arrived early the next week, Elinor was already downstairs when I went to the foyer to meet the children. "You don't mind being paraded around, do you?" she asked softly. "I know you weren't given the option of saying no, but my father is not your employer."

"I don't mind being there for the children," I said. And although I didn't want to help support the governor, I did want to see what happened.

"You are so good to the children," she said with a smile. "I really must commend Henry on his choice of governess." She winced, as though just then realizing that she'd have no opportunity to say anything to Henry. "I can't believe you got Flora interested in current affairs."

"I believe she was always interested. She merely feels more confident about expressing herself now, at least around us."

"True. I suspect she'll sound quite different around her usual friends. But I would appreciate it if you'd curb any impulse she might have to speak out today. The last thing we need is my father thinking that either you or I are a bad influence on her."

Much to my relief, Flora wasn't wearing an obvious Rebel Mechanics symbol when we gathered to await the governor's arrival. She did wear a bright red scarf, and it went well enough with her coat that I couldn't be sure whether it was merely a fashion accessory or a show of rebel solidarity. Rollo was enthusiastic, as he was getting to miss school, and Olive was as bright-eyed and eager as she always was.

The governor arrived a few minutes early, and I was glad I'd gathered the children ahead of time. Elinor hurried up the stairs when the bell rang, since her father was supposed to believe she was an invalid. She shot me a quick smile over her shoulder before she disappeared around the bend of the upper landing. It was the footman who collected us at the door and escorted us to the carriage. The governor's official carriage was quite large, but it was still a tight fit for all of us. I was grateful not to be stuck on the outside seat with the footman.

"You won't have to say anything," the governor told us as the carriage made its way through the city streets. "Just stand beside me and smile. After I speak, there will be envelopes for you to help hand out, and you may thank the recipients for their labor, or if they thank you, you may say 'you're welcome,' but don't make conversation. If they ask questions, the best answer is to say that you don't know. If anything unusual happens, Miss Newton will escort you away, and there will be guards there to protect you."

"What do you mean by 'unusual?'" Flora asked, her face the picture of innocence, though I knew she was baiting her grandfather. "Are the people we're visiting unhappy? Are they likely to begin rioting, or attack us?"

He laughed in a way that was distinctly insincere. "Of course not! But you never know if there might be an outside agitator."

I barely caught myself in time to stop what I'm certain would have been a visible wince. We'd distributed the revolutionary pamphlets with the aim of stirring up agitation.

It took more than an hour to get all the way downtown to the fort, even with other drivers pulling aside to make way for the governor's carriage. This was certainly an occasion on which that underground railway would have proved useful, if the magisters hadn't snubbed it for the prestige of personal carriages. Instead of zooming along under the city, we trundled down the busy streets.

We were met by an honor guard of soldiers and a trumpet fanfare. I wondered if the governor had deliberately planned the first stop of the day to be the one most likely to be friendly to him. Even if our pamphlets had found a receptive audience, I didn't anticipate open revolt or defiance in front of the governor. Our best hope was that the soldiers would think twice if they were ordered to fight against civilians. This was also one place I doubted the Mechanics had been able to infiltrate to stage agitation. We had people on the inside, of course: the laundresses and cleaners who'd helped Henry escape. But they wouldn't be brought out to meet the governor.

The soldiers were lined up in perfectly straight ranks on the Battery in front of the fort, and I couldn't help but shudder at the memory of what had happened the last time British troops lined up here. They'd fired upon slum children they'd seen as a threat, which had sparked riots. Surely the governor remembered that, and if he didn't, I was fairly certain General Montgomery did. I'd seen how he'd reacted to what he'd thought happened, and none of them had any way of knowing that the deaths from that event had been faked.

The general's greeting to the governor was stiff and formal, and I couldn't be sure if that was because of the official occasion or because their relationship had soured. "You remember my grandchildren, of course," the governor said in his booming voice. I tried to make myself invisible behind the children in case the general was one of those rare people who was good at picking faces out of crowds.

There was a reviewing platform just outside the fort, and the general escorted us to it. A young officer stepped forward to hand Flora up onto the platform, and she rewarded him with an icy glare. I got no assistance, but needed none. After all, I'd made it into and out of a flying airship the night before. A few steps were nothing. We were directed to seats on the platform.

"Please enjoy this small demonstration of the discipline and order of the British army," the general said. He waved his hand toward the soldiers, a whistle blew, and the soldiers began marching in complicated formations, directed by short bursts on the whistle.

I soon noticed that we weren't alone. A crowd had gathered around the edges of the Battery—far larger than I'd have expected just from passersby noticing the activity. Suddenly, I realized what the rebels must have planned. They might not have been able to infiltrate the fort, but they were still present.

And they were making their presence known. It started with a few catcalls at the soldiers, but then a voice from within the mob shouted, "Are you going to shoot at us today for watching you?"

The general froze, and the color seemed to leech from his ruddy face down into his red coat. The governor's head swiveled, as though he was searching for the person who'd called out.

"A ruler who fires upon his own people for exercising or demanding their rights is a tyrant!" another voice shouted, and I had to force myself not to react. Those were *my* words, directly out of the pamphlets.

I wasn't the only one reacting. Several soldiers missed turns just then, scrambling the formation, and I knew that *someone* must have read the pamphlets we'd dropped. The general abruptly stood and waved, and the leader on the field blew his whistle in a long burst followed by a short one, bringing the drill to a halt.

The governor made a valiant attempt to salvage the situation, rising and applauding. "Excellent work, men," he shouted. "There's no finer army in the world, which is why the British Empire rules so much of the world. As we like to say, the sun never sets on our Empire, and you men are a big reason why."

The soldiers didn't break discipline to applaud, but there was mocking applause from the crowd. "Yes, you fine, brave men do an excellent job of keeping the peons in line," someone called out, to much laughter. One of the men in the front rank barely suppressed a smile, but most of the others narrowed their eyes. I heard a snicker nearby and turned to see Flora hiding her mouth behind her hand. Rollo glanced between the soldiers, the crowd, and his grandfather, his eyes wide, as though wondering what would happen. Olive appeared unaware of the implications of what was going on. Now that the drilling had stopped and the speeches begun, she seemed bored, swinging her legs and kicking her heels on the chair legs.

I hoped that no one in the crowd did anything to

provoke the soldiers. As long as they were merely shouting, I didn't think the general would allow anything to happen, not after the disaster the last time. But if someone so much as threw a rock, things could spiral out of control very quickly.

"And now, I'd like to offer you a token of my appreciation this holiday season," the governor continued. "If my grandchildren would be so kind as to help me..." He gestured, and the children stood.

We moved to the front of the platform, where the children handed out colorful envelopes while I supervised. The soldiers went through this process as though they were in a drill, stopping with a snap at the end of their file, nodding in thanks, and turning briskly to march away. While they received their gifts, someone in the crowd—I was fairly certain it was Colin's voice, and I knew he wouldn't have been able to resist this event—began singing the rebel versions of Christmas carols, and others joined in. This far away, it wasn't obvious that the words had been changed unless you were listening very carefully. The general smiled and nodded his head in time with the music. I turned to watch the faces of the soldiers. Most of them showed no reaction, but a few smiled and some frowned. I didn't think the army was ready to turn on its rulers, but I hoped some of them were thinking about whom they really served.

That was when it struck me that if it came to revolution, that would mean war, and the rebels would need an army.

Would these men fight with us or against us? It really was vital that we swayed as many of them as possible.

I wasn't sure if the governor noticed the words in the carols, but he was in reasonably good spirits when we returned to the carriage. If he was upset about what the crowd had said, he didn't show it. Perhaps he thought that an envelope with a single small bank note in it would be enough to buy his soldiers' loyalty.

Our next stop was the university, which I knew was a recipe for disaster because it was a hotbed of revolutionary activity. Surely the governor knew that, as well. Or did he hope to sway the students away from rebellion? The one good thing was that if Colin had been stirring up the people around the Battery, he couldn't possibly make it to the university in time to be able to go anywhere near Flora. The subterranean railway only went as low as Eighth Street, so it didn't help in transporting people from the tip of the island.

The students had been assembled in an auditorium, and the governor's secretary, Mr. Barker, a short, heavyset man with a bristling mustache, met us backstage. "Everything is arranged, Your Grace," he said.

"I should hope so," the governor said. "This should go more smoothly than what happened at the fort."

"What happened at the fort?"

"Just a few troublemakers from the slums."

We were escorted onto the stage. The applause when

we entered was respectable, and the governor seemed to puff up a bit at that, as if the sound had revived him after the display earlier. He gestured for silence and motioned for us to take our seats behind him before he began speaking. "By bringing yourselves here to be educated, you're doing the best thing you can do to serve your empire," he began. "You are our future."

Someone in the audience called out, "Then why don't we have a vote?"

He ignored it, going on to say, "I hope your example will inspire my grandchildren here to pursue their education. You see what a priority this is for me, as I've even brought their governess along today."

I forced myself not to cringe. Flora didn't even try to suppress her disgusted reaction. Her grandfather couldn't see her, but all the students saw her aghast expression, and a soft titter rose from the audience. The governor seemed to take that as approval of his joke. "I'm sure she'll make them write a report about today," he added.

That was when a few students stood and walked out. Others joined that first few. The governor stopped speaking and turned to the dean. The two of them had a mumbled conversation, and then the dean shouted to the students, "Be seated! You haven't been dismissed."

"Yes, we have!" a student shouted. "The Assembly was disbanded, so we figure he doesn't want us meeting here, either."

By this time, Flora was biting her lip, and Rollo, who loved the idea of just getting up and walking out of school, was beaming. "Don't get any ideas," I warned him softly.

"Can we go, too, Miss Newton?" Olive asked in a loud whisper that carried easily to the few students who remained in the auditorium. I wanted the stage to open up and swallow me.

That was when the governor said brusquely, "I thank you for your time," and stalked off the stage. I gathered the children to follow him. The dean tried to keep up with him, apologizing the whole way. Finally, the governor stopped, turned to face him, and said, "You seem to have lost control of your students. I suggest you rectify that. I won't have a hotbed of rebellion in the middle of my city." We left Barker and the dean still exchanging angry words.

The atmosphere in the carriage after that was tense. Even Olive was too cowed to speak, lest she set off her grandfather's temper. Flora turned to stare out the window to mask her smile. I mostly kept my eyes focused on my lap so I wouldn't have to make eye contact with anyone. If I looked at Flora, I'd probably grin, but I feared my guilt would show if I looked at the governor. After all, I had a lot to do with the reception he'd had so far today.

We moved on to what the itinerary had referred to as the magic generation facility. It turned out to be the plant that provided the magical power supply to the city, where power from the ether was channeled into storage crystals that could be used to run magical devices. All the employees were magisters, so they were of a higher social standing than most of the soldiers, very few of whom were from the magister class. These were all likely the descendants of great houses, of lines stemming from younger sons who didn't inherit property. They were of a higher class due to their magical heritage, but had to earn a living.

The sense of magic in this place was almost overwhelming. I was glad I'd learned to shield myself, or I likely would have given myself away as having magical blood, myself. As it was, I had to concentrate on maintaining control. The governor and the children appeared to glow, radiating with reflected power, and I hoped I showed no such telltale signs.

The floor of the plant where we went to meet with the workers looked like a library, only without the books. Men in good suits sat at small desks, their hands resting on crystal tubes. When a tube lit up, it dropped into a slot on the desk, and another tube rolled into place. After several tubes, the worker got up and was replaced by another man. It seemed to me to be a terrible way to spend a day, though I supposed it was hardly backbreaking labor.

The work never stopped while the governor spoke. The men who weren't charging the tubes stood and listened, then moved into position when it was their turn. The governor definitely took a different tone with these men than he had with the soldiers, far less patronizing. I suspected he was trying to win over members of the magister class who might have more influence on the upper ranks.

"Your work and dedication are what keeps the colonies going," he told them. "You don't get the credit you deserve, laboring here to give the rest of us the power we need. I want you to know you are appreciated. You make everyone's lives better."

That wasn't entirely true. Magical power was expensive, and so were devices powered by magic. It was out of the reach of most nonmagical people. I'd noticed that for myself when traveling over the city in the airship. I could tell the wealthier neighborhoods by the quality and amount of light. In the poorer parts of the city, it was dark, other than the occasional flicker of candlelight.

Henry believed that plants like this made the magister class lazy. Most magisters never used their own power, relying instead on power supplied by others. He'd made a point of teaching the children to use magic for themselves, and now I could see why. It seemed the utmost in laziness and privilege to have magical power but rely on power from other people. It also struck me that this plant was a very vulnerable point. If it didn't keep power flowing, then magister devices wouldn't work, and most magisters wouldn't know what to do.

I didn't look for familiar faces because the Mechanics didn't have the magic required to fit in, and the rebel magisters I knew were all highly placed noblemen who didn't have to work for a living. It did seem like the workers here would be ideal recruits, though. Surely they had to chafe at being consigned to giving their power for others, merely because of an accident of birth order. Supposedly, my pamphlet targeting magisters had been distributed among the middle class, so at least some of these people should have read it by now.

They didn't seem too disgruntled, though. They were certainly friendlier when they came through the line to be handed their gift envelopes than the soldiers had been. I stood closest to Olive, and most of the men doted on her. "Your sister seems to be making you do all the work," one teased her.

"My sister's working, too," Olive said, gesturing to where Flora was turning on her immense personal charm. "Miss Newton is my governess."

The man frowned, glancing from Olive to Flora to me, then said, "Beg your pardon, miss." I supposed I could see his point. Olive's coloring was more similar to mine than to Flora's, as both Olive and I had brown hair and greenish eyes, while Flora had golden hair and blue eyes. I had an odd feeling for a split second, but before I could dwell upon it long enough to analyze it, I thought I saw someone familiar out of the corner of my eye.

A new shift of workers had come in, and they took their places behind the men currently at the desks. It took me a moment to track the one I'd noticed to his position, and then I had to force myself not to stare, lest I draw attention to him.

I had the strongest suspicion that Henry Lyndon was here in this plant. But surely not, and not today, of all days. Even Henry couldn't be that reckless.

When the man I was watching caught my eye and winked, I had no doubt.

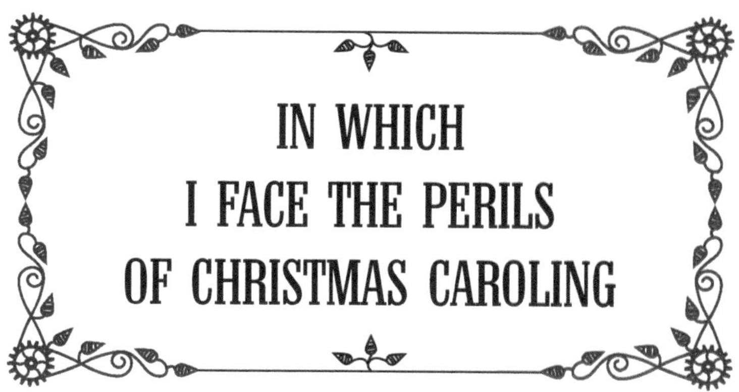

IN WHICH I FACE THE PERILS OF CHRISTMAS CAROLING

I forced myself to look away from Henry, then worried that I'd been too obvious about doing so. What was he doing here? Was he mad? Was this where he was hiding, working in a magical power plant where no one would expect to find a fugitive nobleman, or had he come here specifically for today's event? If the latter, he really was mad to show himself in front of people guaranteed to recognize him.

Although I wanted to watch him, I forced myself to keep my eyes on the children, who didn't seem to have noticed anything amiss. The governor was busy chatting with the manager. I doubted he even saw faces among the workers. They were probably a big blur to him.

A few minutes later, I couldn't resist looking back toward Henry. He was the one sitting at the desk now, his head bent over the magical crystal. It was maddening to be so close to him, yet be unable to speak to him or touch him. I wondered what he would do when he finished his turn and would have to approach us to receive his gift envelope. I didn't think the children would stay quiet if they recognized him, and if the governor saw him, he was doomed.

It turned out that this wasn't to be an issue. The men who'd come forward for their envelopes didn't return to work. Neither did they leave. They linked arms and stood there. As the men at the desks finished their turns, they joined the massed men. One man toward the back called out, "You're taking away our voice! What happened to the Assembly, Governor?" Others joined that cry. I glanced at the governor, whose naturally ruddy face had turned a dark scarlet. He'd tolerated the disrespect earlier in the day, but hearing this from magisters was apparently too much for him.

Another man shouted, "Equal treatment for all! Why should we give you our power?"

From that point, the chant, "It's our power!" rose from the floor, and the men at the desks shoved back their seats and stood, joining in the chant.

The governor waved his hands, motioning for quiet, but the men disregarded him. While the manager's assistant tried to bustle the children and me out of there, the manager shouted at his workers, who all turned their backs and walked out. The manager ran after them.

Flora beamed with glee and Rollo bounced with excitement. I could only imagine the story he'd tell his schoolmates. When the governor joined us in departing, the manager gave up trying to get his employees to return to work and ran alongside the governor. "I don't know what's gotten into them," he said. "They say they won't come back to work unless the Assembly is restored. Their lack of gratitude is appalling."

"How much power do you have stored?" the governor asked.

"A day's supply, depending on usage. The rail lines keep a stockpile, so they should be able to keep running for at least a month. What we collect here mostly goes to residential power. Should we tell people to conserve?"

"No. You should tell your people to get back to work, or you should hire new people. There ought to be plenty of magisters out there who can provide power and who would be willing to do so. See to it."

I would have thought that the governor would cancel the rest of his appointments after the first few had gone so badly, but he apparently didn't want to give the striking magic suppliers the pleasure of affecting him. Or else perhaps he thought that the garment workers we were scheduled to see next would be more appreciative of him. They would be mostly women and entirely nonmagical. This visit could even be considered charity. The poor garment workers would be grateful for the small gifts of money from the great man—or so I imagined his line of thought.

I knew as soon as we entered the garment factory that we were in for trouble. Lizzie pushed a broom in the back of the room. One of the smaller girls running in and out among the machines looked familiar, but I couldn't place her. I didn't know any young girls among the Mechanics, though it was possible she'd been one of the slum children the Mechanics had taken on that ill-fated excursion to the Battery.

Olive pulled on my sleeve. "Miss Newton, there are little girls working here."

"Yes, I'm afraid there are," I said. "They're helping their families have enough money to live."

Her eyes went wide with worry. "Should I be working in a factory?"

"No, you don't have to worry about that." But she did look worried.

Even if I hadn't spotted Lizzie, I'd have known this wouldn't go well when the governor began speaking. His tone was very different from what he'd used to address the magister men or even the soldiers and students. He sounded as if he was talking to children, and I could see the anger flaring up in the women's eyes. He spoke as though he thought they were only there to earn spending money to buy ribbons for their hair, like this job was little more than a way to pass the time until they married or had children.

Flora cleared her throat and murmured, "Grandfather, perhaps you should let me speak. After all, I'm the one who is fond of fashion."

"Don't be silly, Flora," he muttered under his breath.

During that break in his speech, someone at the back of the room—I was fairly certain it was Lizzie—shouted out, "Equal treatment for all! Fair wages for fair work!"

"Yeah, we have to live on this!" another cried out.

"Where'd the money go, gov?" another cried.

"What happened to the Assembly, tyrant?"

"Ladies!" the manager said. "Please! You're being rude to our guest."

"We didn't invite the likes of him," a woman said, spitting on the floor. "Magisters, think they're better than us."

"Liberty!" came a cry from the back of the room—Lizzie, again. The others picked up the chant.

The governor turned and walked away without a word. I gestured for the children to follow. Flora held back, watching the women, and raised a surreptitious fist in solidarity before joining the rest of us. This time, the governor told his footman that he was canceling the rest of his engagements, and when we reached the Lyndon mansion, he dropped us off, not even coming inside with us.

"That was outstanding!" Rollo enthused as we divested ourselves of coats and hats in the front hall. "Who knew so many people were angry at Grandfather?"

"Anyone who pays any attention to current affairs," Flora said haughtily.

"We didn't get to give the ladies their envelopes," Olive said. "They'll be sad."

"I'm sure they have other things to be concerned

about," Flora said before I could reply. "They need better wages and working conditions, not envelopes stuffed with a token pittance."

When the younger two had gone off to the schoolroom to write the essays I'd assigned about their experiences of the day, I said to Flora, "Perhaps it would be best if you didn't talk like that in front of your grandfather—or in front of the younger ones, who might not think to avoid speaking like that to him."

"Why shouldn't we tell him what we think?"

"Because he'll wonder where you learned it, and he may not blame it all on Lord Henry."

She gasped softly, and her mouth froze into a small "O" of shock. "Oh dear, I'm sorry, Miss Newton. I didn't think. That might cost you your position."

"Or it might mean you having to go live with him if he thinks you're hearing these things from your aunt."

"What are they hearing from me?" Elinor asked, coming down the stairs. "You're home earlier than I expected. I had to dive back into bed, though it seems Father didn't come in with you."

"It was a rather eventful morning," I said.

"The magic generators and the garment workers protested while Grandfather was speaking to them," Flora said, her eyes sparkling. "The magic generators even went on strike. And that was after most of the students walked out on his talk. The crowd near the fort wasn't very happy with him, either."

Elinor's reaction was perfectly neutral, betraying no feeling at all. "That seems very odd. I shall have to make sure we have enough power to get us by, though we should be in good stead in this house, as I'm sure Henry taught everyone how to use magic."

Flora laughed. "And to think, I used to protest that I would never need to use my power because there were other people to do that for me. Do you think he knew this was a possibility?"

"I believe this precise circumstance would have been difficult to predict," Elinor said. "Henry probably just wanted you to live up to your potential."

I edged away as they talked, since I wasn't a part of the conversation, but Elinor called me back. "Miss Newton, I'd like to hear your thoughts."

"There's not much more to say." Other than the fact that Henry was somehow in the middle of the magic generation plant, which I intended to share with no one. "There does appear to be some labor unrest. I got the impression that the magic generators are tired of being treated like second-class citizens, even though they are magisters, but I know little of how things like that work in your world. They also mentioned something about the Assembly being dissolved. That would mean the colonists no longer have any elected representatives, if it's true. I haven't heard anything about that, though."

"I suppose you've made assignments based on these events."

"Yes, ma'am. The children are writing essays."

"I'd like to read them. I'm curious to see what they thought. I take it my father was displeased."

"He cut off the rest of his appointments for the day," Flora said. "Do you think this was coordinated, all those protests on the same day?"

"It wouldn't have to be," Elinor said. "They may have merely been taking advantage of the governor's presence. Though it does suggest rather more unrest than anyone in the administration would care to admit to."

That evening, I struggled to find a way to write about the morning's events without giving any indications as to my identity. There weren't many people who'd been at every stop on the governor's tour. I ended up writing from the perspective of someone who witnessed events at the garment factory and had secondhand reports from the magic generation station. People might assume that "Liberty Jones" was one of the seamstresses and had contacts who knew about events elsewhere.

I paused with my pen over the paper. *Would* Liberty Jones have magister contacts? For the most part, she had reported on the governor's actions as an outside observer and an antagonist, or she'd reported more favorably on Mechanics activity. She'd never shown signs of sympathizing with magisters, even if they were allied with the rebel cause.

After mulling it over for some time, I decided to go through with my planned article. We'd targeted magisters with pamphlets calling for revolution, but for that to do any good, the other rebels would have to accept them. Thus far, the only successful joint operation we'd managed had been Henry's escape, and that had been more about him than about uniting under a common cause. The other time we'd tried to get the groups to cooperate, the Mechanics had gone behind the backs of the rebel magisters.

I described the striking magisters as valiantly standing up to their oppressors, who treated them with almost as much disdain as they treated the lower classes. Perhaps that would gain them some sympathy among the Mechanics and other nonmagical rebels. Once I was happy with the article, I wrote a short note to Lizzie, then I copied the article onto that page in the special ink, watching it disappear as I wrote. Sending my articles through the mail this way would delay their publication somewhat, but it looked far less suspicious than anything else I might do, and the close call when handing over the text for the pamphlets had left me rather rattled. I thought it best to avoid too many obvious meetings for the time being.

Next, I wrote a short note to Alec. On the empty parts of that page I used the special ink to write a furious letter to Henry, accusing him of dangerous recklessness and asking what on earth he was thinking, taking such a risk. There had been little point of us freeing him if he was going to walk right back into the lion's den.

Then I had a realization: Had he been here in the city all along? I thought about the mysterious passenger on the airship. I hadn't been able to place him among the Mechanics I knew, but he had been about the right size and shape to be Henry. I'd sensed magic in use. Maybe it hadn't been another secret half-breed like me, but rather a magister in disguise.

I added to my note to Henry, remarking on how nice it had been to work with him in the air. I only wished I could be there to see him react to that. When I was certain both letters looked totally innocent, I sealed them and set them aside to mail. What I really wanted was a face-to-face conversation. Communicating by mail was better than being entirely cut off, but it still wasn't a very satisfactory way to have a serious discussion. It was even more frustrating knowing I had been face-to-face with him, and we hadn't talked. Why couldn't he have said something then?

It was difficult to tell from my perspective if anything had changed. We didn't go out at night, and Elinor and Flora were recharging the household magical devices, so we felt no lack of power. It seemed to me that there were fewer magical carriages on the streets as each day went by, but there was also more snow, so the streets were somewhat treacherous.

As Elinor had mentioned, we were no longer being watched or followed—at least, not so obviously. I thought it best not to let my guard down. While I'd hated knowing I was being followed, it was worse not being entirely sure.

The rebels hadn't let up on their campaign. Copies of

the pamphlets had been plastered everywhere. They were stuck to walls, where they tended not to stay for long in the magister districts. Someone managed to slide them between the pages of government-approved newspapers, apparently even the ones delivered to homes. There were more and more groups of carolers roaming the city, singing the rebel versions of carols and passing out revolutionary pamphlets with covers that made them look like Christmas cards or religious tracts about the meaning of Christmas.

The real difference was that people seemed to be listening. The carolers drew crowds. People read the pamphlets instead of immediately throwing them away. I overheard snatches of conversation in which respectable-looking people discussed the closing of the Assembly and what that meant for the colonies. The plan appeared to be working!

Later that week, as Olive and I walked home after escorting Rollo to school, we came upon a group of carolers. "May we stay and listen, Miss Newton?" Olive asked. I didn't recognize any of them as Mechanics, so there was a slight chance that these were ordinary carolers, and enough of a crowd had formed that we wouldn't be too conspicuous, so I agreed to stay for just one song.

After only a few lines, it became clear that these were rebels. Olive frowned as she listened, then she blurted, "They're not singing it the right way!"

There were some snickers from the listeners, but a few turned to glare. I bent to whisper, "Shh. I don't think these are Christmas carolers. They're singing about something else."

She listened to the rest of the song, her head tilted slightly to the side. "They must be mad at Grandfather, too," she said when the song ended. Fortunately, her remark was drowned out by applause. The carolers began passing out pamphlets, and I tried to tug Olive away, even as she protested, "But I want a Christmas card."

There was a shrill, sharp whistle, the kind police used, and I froze with fear. I couldn't afford to be arrested for being part of a gathering like this. There was too much at stake. Forcing my body to move again, I tugged on Olive's hand. "We need to go home, now!"

But it turned out that the whistle wasn't the police, but rather a lookout. It might as well have been, though. "They're coming! Disperse!" the lookout shouted.

"We really must go, now," I said, yanking sharply on Olive's hand. She resisted at first, but when the rest of the crowd began moving around us, she moved closer to me and stayed tight by my side.

One of my safe shops was nearby, so as soon as we rounded a corner and were no longer in sight of where the carolers had been, I slowed to a more sedate walk and said, "Would you like to get some cakes?"

Olive's face was red, and there were tears running down her face, but she managed a weak smile as she nodded. I stayed on the alert, looking out for signs that we were being followed or that there was any excitement nearby.

Whistles shrieked from around the corner, and I heard a shout or two, but I couldn't tell what was happening.

When we reached the bakery, I stopped and cleaned Olive's face with my handkerchief. "Why did you make us run?" she asked.

"The police were coming."

"But the police are our friends. They protect us."

How could I possibly explain this in terms that Olive could understand, in a way that wouldn't get me in trouble when she inevitably parroted my words to her grandfather? "I told you those weren't proper carolers. You noticed they sang the songs the wrong way, right?" She sniffed and nodded. "Well, the police don't like it when people make fun of the government, and they don't like people gathering to talk about things being wrong. I would get in trouble if we were caught there because I shouldn't have brought you anywhere near people like that. Your grandfather would be very angry. He might even have made me leave."

That started the tears all over again. "You can't go," she gulped between sobs.

"I don't want to go, so that's why I wanted to get away from there."

"Is that what happened to Uncle? Did he listen to people like that?"

Her uncle *was* people like that, but of course I couldn't tell her. "I don't know why they took your uncle away," I said, quite truthfully. I knew Henry had done plenty of illegal and treasonous things, but we'd never learned what the precise charges against him were or what evidence had led to his arrest. "Now, cakes?"

She nodded, sniffing again, and I gave her one more wipe with my handkerchief before straightening and leading her inside. We were seated at a table, enjoying frosted cakes and hot cocoa, when a group of people ran past, followed by several uniformed police officers, who were blowing their whistles for all they were worth. Olive met my eyes, but she said nothing. She clung desperately to me the whole way home.

While she worked on her lessons later that day, she paused, staring thoughtfully into space, then said, "I don't think Grandfather would send you away. He likes you. He never even talked to our other governesses, but he invites you to go on trips with us, and he talks to you. Why are people mad at him?"

That was a delicate topic. "Well, you noticed that there were children working at the garment factory?" She nodded. "There are a lot of very poor people, and a lot of very rich people, and the poor people wonder why the rich people are keeping all the money to themselves, even though poor people are doing a lot of the work. Your grandfather is one of the rich people, and some of the rules his government makes help rich people make more money, but don't help poor people. There are also people who want freedom. They want to be able to say what they want or listen to anyone without worrying that the police will make them go away. The people who make the laws are all in England, and the people in the colonies don't get to choose those people. There were people in the colonies who made laws for us, but your grandfather stopped that. And that's why people are mad."

"Well, it's not fair!" she said. I wasn't sure if she meant that the situation wasn't fair or that it wasn't fair that people disliked her grandfather. She didn't elaborate, and I didn't dare ask her to. I'd tried to keep my answer as neutral as possible while still being truthful. I turned her attention to her schoolwork, focusing on science and mathematics rather than politics.

When we were at lunch that afternoon, I received a letter from Alec. If my reaction was convincingly that of a young woman hearing from an admirer, it was because I hoped the letter hid a message from Henry. I certainly felt like I was reacting accordingly. I felt my face flush, and my hands trembled as I opened the envelope. Flora giggled and winked at me from across the table.

The note was terse enough to leave plenty of blank space, which I hoped meant there was a hidden message. Or perhaps not, as the note read, "I hope you're free tomorrow evening. Some friends of mine are holding a huge Christmas party—the party of the century. It wouldn't be the same without you."

"A love note, Miss Newton?" Flora teased.

"A party invitation."

Elinor, who'd been quietly reading the newspaper, looked up. "You must go, of course." Her tone was so intense that it was almost harsh, like she was making it an order.

I stared at her quizzically, and she met my eyes, holding my glance for a moment, then nodding slightly.

I suspected that the "party of the century" might be something far bigger.

IN WHICH I SET OUT ON A VERY LONG WALK

It was early in the evening before I had the chance to see if there was anything else in Alec's note. The rest of the day was too busy with lessons and supervising the children in independent reading. The weather grew worse, and the cabs had been among the first vehicles to run out of power supplies, so the music teacher had canceled the day's lesson. That meant getting away from the children was nearly impossible. Even if I'd gone up to my room during what was supposed to be my free time, there would have been a risk of Olive wandering by out of boredom. The whole afternoon, I thought of the letter in my desk drawer and what secrets it might hold.

Elinor must have sensed either my impatience or my weariness, for she sent me up to my room to rest before dinner while she conducted her own piano lessons. As long as I heard the sound of the piano drifting up from the parlor below, I knew I was safe from intrusion.

My fingers trembled slightly as I sprayed the page with the lavender-scented formula, then I had to force myself not to cry out when words began to appear in Henry's handwriting. The note was brief and looked as though it had been written in haste.

"Don't be angry at me for not telling you I was back in the city. You would have worried if you'd known, though I suppose I should have known you'd figure it out on the airship. Did you also recognize your dance partner from the Mechanics' meeting?"

I gasped softly as I read. Of course that's who my mysterious partner had been. I really should have recognized him then, for I knew what it was like to dance with him. But at the time, I'd believed it unlikely that he was anywhere near, so I hadn't considered the possibility. I took comfort in the assurance that if I hadn't recognized him, his disguise had been very good.

"But we can discuss all this in person Saturday night," the note went on. "You must come. Liberty Jones will need to make an appearance to her admiring public. This may be when it all starts, and I can't wait to see you. Wear comfortable shoes." It was signed, "Yours ever, H." Below that, Alec's handwriting gave me a time and place to meet my transportation and an assurance that everything had been taken care of.

Public? I thought as I folded the letter and hid it in the secret compartment of my desk. The police were breaking up spontaneous gatherings around the carolers. How could I meet my public? The mention of comfortable shoes suggested a march or demonstration. The location and time for such an event would have to be known in order for people to attend, which would make it all too easy for the authorities to disrupt it. There had to be some sort of trick or plan. Even the Rebel Mechanics weren't bold enough to take that kind of risk.

It was agony getting through the day of the "party." It was a Saturday, so there was no school and there were no lessons to keep me occupied. It was too cold for outdoor activities, with just enough ice to make the paths through the park treacherous and not enough snow for fun. The children were bored and restless, and though I wasn't supposed to be responsible for them on weekends, I played games with Rollo and Olive just to have something to do to pass the time.

When it was time for me to go, I dressed as though I was getting ready for a party, and the children saw me off. I hoped that wherever this meeting was being held was indoors, I thought as I pulled the collar of my coat up around my neck. It was bitterly cold, and snowflakes were swirling in the air. I didn't get the sense that anyone was tailing me, so I followed the instructions that had been hidden on Alec's invitation, turning the corner and heading toward the nearest bus stop.

I paused in the shadows of the side street, listening for sounds around me. There seemed to be some commotion in the distance—a diversion in case I was being watched, perhaps? At any rate, I couldn't see anyone watching my immediate area, so I walked briskly to the rendezvous point Alec had specified.

I thought it seemed a bit darker than usual in this area, but then, I hadn't gone out this way many times after dark. Still, the magic generator strike might have been having an impact. When every streetlamp I passed was dark, I felt my suspicions were confirmed.

I slowed my pace as I neared the designated intersection. I was a few minutes early, and I didn't want to stand around on a street corner for very long. Instead, I kept a watch out for anything that might be approaching that corner.

When I heard a carriage come up behind me, I nearly jumped out of my skin. "Sorry, didn't mean to give you a fright," Philip called out. He was driving a sporty open-topped roadster, with Geoffrey in the passenger seat beside him. "Hop in!" Philip urged.

I climbed into the backseat, and the carriage took off down the street. "You're my ride?" I asked.

"They thought it might look less suspicious for you to meet with us than with lower-class people," Geoffrey said, leaning back to pull a lap rug over my legs. "Scandalous, perhaps, but not necessarily revolutionary."

"This must be a serious meeting if you two are going—magisters as well as Mechanics," I said.

"Not just us. All our circle. And maybe some more," Geoffrey replied. "I believe this is the big one."

"The big one?"

"When we see what support we really have," Geoffrey said. "Between the Assembly being dissolved, the strikes, the protests, and some rather inflammatory propaganda"—he turned and grinned at me—"we should have a lot of new supporters, enough to make a real difference."

"At least, that's what we hope to find out," Philip added. "It's a big march. If enough people join us, the revolution is on. If it's just a few of us, then we'll have to regroup."

"There's a checkpoint ahead," Geoffrey pointed out, and Philip slowed the roadster. "Verity, perhaps you should lie down and cover yourself. I'd rather avoid scandal as well as suspicion."

I heartily agreed with him. I lay down on the backseat and pulled the rug over my whole body. Someone—probably Geoffrey, since Philip was driving—leaned back and arranged the rug, presumably making it look like it was just thrown across the seat. The car stopped, and I heard a muffled conversation in which Philip played his useless young nobleman role to the hilt, making it sound like he and his friend were out for a night of slumming. The officer laughed and sent us on our way. A few minutes later, the rug was pulled aside.

"It's probably safe for you to sit up now," Geoffrey said.

"It was rather warm like that," I replied, though I did

sit up. "I can't believe they still have checkpoints. Didn't they move most of the troops out of town weeks ago?"

"I suspect they'll be back," Philip said. "Things are getting dicey. But this is why we have to act now, before the troops can get here."

"Are we ready for that?" I asked. "We haven't had time to get that many machines built."

"If we've got enough people, we may not need the machines," Geoffrey said.

We neared the part of town where the Mechanics tended to congregate and approached the old theater that served as headquarters, when it wasn't hosting bad variety reviews. "They're having a public rally at the theater?" I asked.

"That's just a starting point," Geoffrey said. "Apparently, we need to pick up a certain Liberty Jones, who I understand is an entirely different person from Verity Newton."

"You know about that?" I asked, trying to remember if I'd told them. They hadn't recognized me at the previous meeting, when I'd been assigned to write the pamphlets, but then I recalled that a few minutes ago, Geoffrey had seemed to know about that.

"Your friends let us know so we could help get Miss Liberty to the meeting."

"And here we are," Philip said, pulling his carriage to a stop. He flipped a few coins at a street urchin lurking nearby. "You get twice that if I come back and find my roadster intact," he told the child. "And if you like, you can sit in the back and wrap up in the rug." The boy didn't waste any time climbing into the carriage.

We walked around the block once, Philip walking in an opposite direction from Geoffrey and me so we could make sure we hadn't been followed. Once we met up again, we approached the theater's entrance. Nat flung the door open for us. "Right this way, lady and gents."

Lizzie met us in the auditorium. "Good, you're here. You weren't followed?"

"Not that we could tell," Philip said.

She turned to me. "You look like a governess."

"I thought you liked the fact that I look respectable," I said.

"That was when we needed you to blend in. Tonight, you're not a governess infiltrating the magisters. You're the firebrand of the movement who'll motivate people to take action."

I laughed, but then I realized she was serious. "Me? Really? Have you spent any time with me? I don't motivate anyone to do anything."

"Your words will be the main reason anyone outside our initial movement joins us. But we do want to keep you in place, so no one must connect Verity Newton, governess to the governor's family, with Liberty Jones. So, let's see what we can do about that. Hat off, pins out of your hair. You'll be less recognizable if you don't look at all like anyone's ever seen you in your other life. You don't wear your hair down among the magisters, do you?"

"No."

"Well, then, all these long curls will surely throw them off the scent." She arranged my hair around my shoulders, and I got a lump in my throat because it reminded me of the way my mother had arranged my hair when I was a child. She fastened a pair of brass goggles around my head, tightening the leather strap, and added a jaunty bowler hat with a bright red hatband adorned with several gears and a bright blue feather. She pinned a large gear tied to a scarlet ribbon onto the lapel of my coat and finished off the ensemble with a red sash draped over my shoulder and tied at my waist.

"What do you think, gentlemen?" she asked, turning me to face Philip and Geoffrey. "Do you recognize Miss Newton, the governess?"

"I'd never have known her if I hadn't watched the transformation, myself," Philip said. That reassured me somewhat.

Others were beginning to join us in the theater. "Why, is that Miss Liberty Jones?" a voice cried out, and I found myself being pulled into an embrace by Colin, who seemed to be dressed as a circus ringmaster, in a bright red tailcoat and striped trousers. "You're looking very rebellious tonight."

"Are we ready to get started?" Lizzie asked her brother.

"Probably about as ready as we'll ever be," he said. "I wonder how many will come out and join us in this weather. Summer's probably a better time for revolutions, but we don't have much choice in the matter. There's no telling what additional damage they could do if we waited for spring." He checked his pocket watch. "And if we want to make our triumphant arrival at Union Square on time, we'd best get started." Turning to Philip and Geoffrey, he asked, "Do you mind joining the parade with your carriage? It's a long march, and we'd like to make it possible for those who can't walk that far to join us."

"I wish you'd told me ahead of time. I could have tied some bunting onto the old girl," Philip said with a grin.

"I'll walk to make room," Geoffrey added.

"We can probably help you with the decorations," Colin said. "We might have a spare red ribbon or two lying about. We're gathering on Broadway."

"I'm not parked too far away," Philip said. He ran out of the theater.

I turned to Colin. "If people know this is happening, won't the authorities also know?"

He shrugged. "We've got to make a public stance at some time so we can gauge our support, and better to do so while not actually doing anything illegal than to take over the Assembly Hall and not have anyone join us. For all the government knows, we're merely going Christmas caroling. In large numbers. With new versions of the songs. My hope is that there will be too many of us to arrest, and after the last time, they won't dare shoot at unarmed civilians."

I was shivering from something other than the cold when we went outside to join the beginnings of the parade. I'd done some very dangerous things in my time with the rebels, from fleeing a riot to joining the destruction of a tea shipment to breaking a prisoner out of the fort, but all of that had been secret. This was the first time for me to do anything openly rebellious, and being in disguise probably wouldn't help me much if I were arrested. I had to hope that Colin was right about there being too many people to arrest.

We were off to a good start, I realized when we joined the group gathering on Broadway. The crowd was a bit larger than I'd seen at any regular Mechanics gathering, and not everyone was dressed in Mechanics-style garb. They'd sent the big engines that could pull an omnibus out of the city, but there were a few engines here, smaller ones just large enough for a few people to ride. There were some odd devices that looked like chariots, with one or two people standing in them, but with no horses pulling them. A few people had velocipedes, there were a number of high-wheeled bicycles, and there were other people-powered vehicles with varying numbers of wheels. It seemed that the engineers of the Mechanics movement didn't just use steam engines. They built all manner of devices. The oddest vehicle was a very small one-man airship that hovered just off the ground. Instead of a true gondola, there was a chair suspended beneath the balloon, with a small engine behind it. Everett sat in the chair, dressed in a red tailcoat and a shiny black top hat. He tipped his hat to me when he saw me, and I nodded in response.

The marchers held flaming torches, lanterns, and small electric lights plugged into mobile storage batteries. Even though these were mostly people who'd been part of the movement all along, it was encouraging to see so many of them out tonight.

The goggles obstructed my peripheral vision, so I was completely blindsided when someone approached me and pulled me into a fierce embrace. It only took me a fraction of a second to know it was Henry. It felt like him, smelled like him. "Oh, my Verity," he breathed into my ear as he held me, and I fought back tears that might have become uncomfortable while wearing goggles as I hugged him back.

When we finally released each other and I could get a good look at him, I couldn't help but burst out laughing. "You've gone native, I see," I said. He was dressed as one of the Mechanics, complete with outlandishly bright waistcoat and bowler hat.

"All part of my clever disguise," he replied with a grin.

"True, no one would look past that outfit to recognize you. But what are you doing in the city? I thought you were safely hiding out in Iroquoia, beyond the reach of the Empire. You didn't explain yourself in your letter."

"I *was* safely away, until things cooled down somewhat, but I wasn't doing much good there. I've been able to make great inroads among the more middle-class magisters. They don't have a lot of money to contribute, but they're sympathetic to the cause, and there are more of them than there are noblemen. They're the ones bringing the city to its knees. They may be able to sap the advantage magic gives the Empire."

"But working at that plant, on the day the governor was visiting? What would you have done if Olive had recognized you? You know how clever she is. She'd have seen past any disguise to spot you."

"Which is why I stayed well away from you. She seemed busy with her task. I can't believe he was so desperate as to trot out the children for public display. At least I never did that while I was their guardian. How are the children?"

"They're well enough, though they miss you. I don't know if you heard, but Elinor moved in so they wouldn't have to go live with their grandfather. She's talking about spending Christmas at the country estate."

"I think being at the country estate now would be very wise. In fact, I wish you were all already out of the city, though we do need you here now."

Now that I'd enjoyed being reunited with him, I stepped back, grabbed his upper arms, and gave him a good shake. "And why didn't you tell me you were here before? All that sneaking around and being mysterious. You could have told me! I know you trust me."

"I do. But I also didn't want to put you in a position where you had to lie about knowing my whereabouts."

I remembered the inspectors' questions and had to swallow the lump that grew in my throat. If I'd known that I'd danced with Henry, I'd have been lying about not having seen him, and I'm not sure I could have convinced the inspectors if I'd known I was lying. "I suppose I'll forgive you, this time," I said with a stern glare that was probably lost behind my goggles, especially in the darkness.

"I'm very glad of that," he said, sliding his arm around my waist. "I'm not sure I could bear you being angry at me."

"Good evening, everyone!" Colin bellowed from his spot on top of one of the engines. "Are we ready to make ourselves heard?"

"Yes!" we all shouted.

"Then off we go!" He waved a red flag, and the procession began moving forward. At first, the walkers had the advantage, since it took the machines a little time to get started, but once the machines had momentum, they moved ahead. Philip waved as he passed us in his roadster, which had been decked out in red ribbons. He had an older lady in the passenger seat, and several children sat in the backseat, tucked under the rug.

"I hope this isn't a disaster," I said to Henry as we walked together, his arm still around me.

"Why would it be?"

"Because the soldiers have a tendency to shoot at civilians who make them nervous."

"I really don't think they'll dare, not this time."

Being surrounded by all of these supporters and the

variety of machines, with Colin singing at the top of his lungs and many of the marchers joining in, it was easy to believe that everything was going to be all right. That hope was bolstered when we reached Union Square and found that there was already a crowd gathered, waiting for the march. These seemed like ordinary citizens, not the more obvious rebels of the movement. "They're here because of you," Henry said.

"They're here because they agreed with me," I argued. "I'm not sure I changed many minds. I just let people know what was happening."

We stopped at the square to officially kick off the march. Colin waved to Henry and me. "Over here!" he called out. We had to work our way through the crowd to reach the engine where he stood. I was surprised to see the baron already there.

Colin pulled the baron up to stand on the engine, so he'd be visible. He gestured for silence, then began to speak. "It's gratifying to see all of you here," the baron began, speaking through a megaphone. "I'm glad to know that we"—he gestured at the rest of us surrounding the engine—"aren't the only ones who desire liberty. Many of my friends here are hiding their identities for their own protection, since what we're doing tonight is considered treason. I stand before you as myself. I am Baron Thaddeus Pierce. I was an elected member of the colonial Assembly, but that body has been disbanded. Now I am a citizen who wants liberty, and I am willing to put my life and my freedom on the line to make that happen. If you are here tonight, you must also be willing to sacrifice in the name of liberty. Are you with me?"

The roar from the crowd was gratifying. Henry's arm around me tightened, drawing me closer to him. I glanced up at him and saw that his jaw was clenched. He was in a similar position to the baron, even if he hid his identity tonight. His entire fate hung in the balance of this movement. He'd never be a free man unless we overthrew the government that considered him a traitor and a fugitive.

"Now, shall we show them what the people of this city—this nation—can do?" Colin shouted. "Let's do some Christmas caroling they won't soon forget."

The whole mob began moving up Broadway. The street was full of people as far as I could see, in either direction. Colin began singing one of his reworded carols, and soon others joined in. As cold as it was, I felt a warm glow. I had Henry beside me, and so many people who were willing to make a stand.

There were even more people waiting at King George Park, where Broadway met Fifth Avenue. Many of them were using magical light, either lanterns powered by magic, or globes of light they'd conjured into their hands. That meant we had magisters among us. I turned to Henry. "Are these the people you recruited?"

"I didn't do much," he said. "I just talked to the people who work generating power for others, and they saw reason in my argument. They might also have read a pamphlet or two."

The baron spoke again to this crowd, then, much to my surprise, he said, "And now I'd like to introduce the young lady who's probably the main reason you're here tonight. Miss Liberty Jones!"

If the crowd hadn't cheered so loudly, the pounding of my heart might have drowned them out. I froze until Henry propelled me forward, right toward Colin, who pulled me up onto the engine so I could be seen. The crowd was even bigger than I'd realized when I was just part of it. I looked out onto a sea of faces and lights that filled the park and the surrounding streets. There had to be at least a thousand people out there, maybe more.

Colin handed me the megaphone, and my mouth went dry. I wasn't prepared to speak. What would I even say? I reminded myself that I'd written the pamphlets, so I had the words. I pretended I was only talking to the children and said, "It's good of you to join us for our little party." The laughter and applause from the crowd encouraged me, so I managed to continue. "I didn't know if anyone was reading my work. All I could do was write what I believed and hope it made sense to someone. All of you being here shows the truth of it, that we want a new nation of our own, that we *deserve* a nation of our own, where all of us can work together and be free!"

The cheering after that was loud, and it was long enough that I could hand the megaphone back to Colin and jump off the engine, back into Henry's arms. He kissed me on the cheek. "Great job, Miss Liberty."

"I hope they don't make me do that again," I said.

Colin rallied the marchers to move onward up Fifth Avenue. By this time, the crowd filled several blocks, packed tightly on the street. One of the steam engines led the way, its whistle blowing every few minutes, and half a dozen more magical carriages had joined the procession. When most of the marchers joined Colin in singing his revolutionary carols, it sounded like a mass choir.

The mood was so cheerful and spirited that it came as quite a surprise when the whole thing came to an abrupt halt. The next whistle that sounded didn't come from the steam engine, and it was followed by a shout of, "Hold it right there."

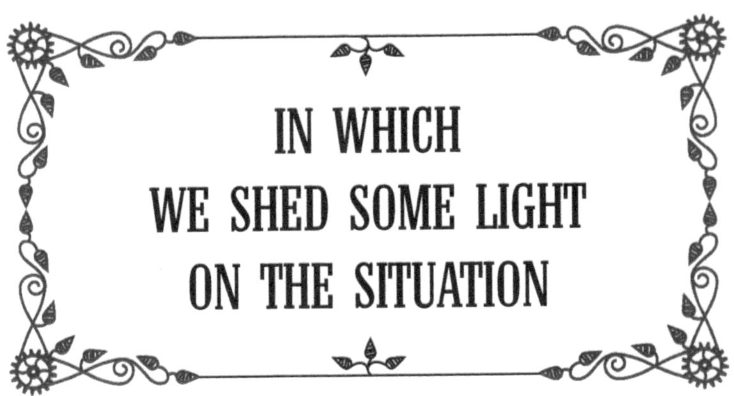

IN WHICH WE SHED SOME LIGHT ON THE SITUATION

I grabbed Henry's arm. "What is it?" I asked.

He rose on tiptoes to see over the crowd, then shook his head. "I can't tell. It sounds like the police."

"The police?" I yelped. "You should get away from here. They'll catch you!"

"I'm safest in the middle of this mob. If I run, they'll notice me and probably come after me. If we stick together, we should be fine."

The steam engine gave a long blast on its whistle. It sounded like a warning. Sure enough, the crowd soon surged forward. There were a few short, sharp whistles, but if there were any other shouts from the police, they were drowned out by the noise of the crowd. Henry hooked his arm through mine, and I tried to stay as close to him as I could as the crowd propelled us onward.

Apparently, the police had tried to set up barricades to keep the march from moving uptown. At least, there were splinters of what might have been barricades in the street about a block ahead of where we'd been when we heard the police whistle. The steam engine, a carriage or two, and hundreds of people had made short work of them. I thought I saw a police helmet among the crowd, but I couldn't tell if the policeman had been swept along by the sea of people, had joined the march, or had lost his helmet to one of the marchers.

Everett raised his small balloon to get a look ahead, then shouted, "We might face trouble on Forty-Second."

I wasn't sure where we currently were. It was hard to tell from the middle of the street. People were leaning out of windows, coming out onto fire escapes, or standing on front stoops to watch the procession as we passed. Anyone who happened to be on a sidewalk when the march came through had to either take refuge in a doorway or get caught up in the crowd. It seemed like quite a few people were joining in as we passed.

The people on bicycles and velocipedes had to dismount because we were moving too slowly for them to remain upright. They pushed their cycles along, trying to move to the front of the march. "Did we count on it being this big?" I asked Henry.

"I don't know what they expected, but this seems rather large."

"Large enough to be threatening?"

"I don't think they'd dare shoot into a crowd this size," he reassured me. "Not unless we give them good reason to do so."

"Is it large enough to support a revolution?"

"It might be. There are also marches in the other colonies tonight. We'll have to see what the turnout was there."

So far, the march was quite orderly. There was no mob-like behavior, no looting or vandalism along the way. The message to give no reason for anyone to be arrested had apparently been taken to heart. It probably helped that we brought more light into these areas than had been there before. Most of the city's street lamps in the nicer areas of town were powered by magic, and they seemed to have run out of power. As we moved deeper into one of the magister neighborhoods, the area around us grew darker, so that our torches, lanterns, and magical light stood out.

It had been in this part of town where I first encountered the Rebel Mechanics. I'd been applying for positions in homes in this neighborhood, with no luck at all, when the Mechanics had appeared with their steam-powered omnibus and had given me a ride uptown. Now the neighborhood was fairly dark, with all the streetlights out and many of the homes unlit. The people who lived here would have been high enough in the social order to rely on others to provide their magical power, though it looked like there were still a few who had either stockpiled or were capable of powering their own devices.

We reached Forty-Second Street, one of the major crosstown thoroughfares. Even at night, the traffic seldom slowed. I wondered what we'd do, but the march didn't lose a step. I thought I heard some horns blaring, bells ringing, and shouting ahead, but by the time we reached the street, the cross traffic had apparently decided it would be easier to wait for us to pass. Marchers shouted and waved to those waiting, and a number of people got off an omnibus to join the march.

I doubted that we would go unimpeded for long. Surely they'd bring out more police or even soldiers. I thought I spotted a few red coats on the side of the street, and if I wasn't mistaken, there were one or two inside the crowd, though I couldn't tell if they were Mechanics dressed for flash, like Everett and Colin, or rogue soldiers.

When we reached the stretch of the avenue that was lined with mansions, the effects of the strike were even more evident. Most of the grand mansions were entirely dark or showed the kind of flickering light behind the windows that implied candles were being used within. "This is why I insisted on teaching the children to use their magic," Henry said. "I hope that's helped."

"Oh, yes," I said. "Elinor and Flora have been recharging the power supply and letting the other two take turns helping." Speaking of Elinor, she'd seemed to know what my invitation had been about. Was she here? I imagined that if she was, she'd be in one of the carriages, hidden from view even while lending her support to the cause.

I was glad Henry had warned me about wearing comfortable shoes by the time we neared the park. I wasn't sure I'd ever walked this far at one time in my life. "At least I'll be close to home at the end of this," I said. "How far are we supposed to go?"

Around that time, the crowd slowed, then stopped. For a moment, we were pressed against the backs of the people ahead of us until those behind us realized that we'd come to a stop. We were outside the first mansion facing Central Park. Unlike many of the other magister residences, this one was ablaze with light. Through the windows, I could see many figures moving about within. A party seemed to be in progress.

Colin boosted himself to stand on the wall separating the mansion's small front garden from the sidewalk. "I think we should sing some Christmas carols for these fine folks," he shouted through his megaphone. He launched into "God rest ye rebel gentlemen," encouraging the crowd to sing along. By this time, we'd heard it often enough to know the words.

I had to wonder why we were singing outside this particular mansion, but then the front door opened and a large man appeared in the doorway, silhouetted against the light from the chandeliers inside. I was fairly certain it was the governor. That explained a lot.

We were too far away and the lighting was too bad for me to be able to see his face when he looked at the sea of people who represented the opposition to his government.

He stood there for a surprisingly long time, not moving. Was he in shock? Did he realize what was happening?

Everett raised his little airship to get a better view. He looked ahead with a spyglass, then turned to look behind us. "Soldiers!" he bellowed. "Lots of them!"

"Hold fast!" Colin ordered. "We outnumber them. They don't have this many troops in the whole city. Don't give them a reason to shoot. Link arms so they can't move us."

I already had my arm linked with Henry's on one side, but I joined to the person on my other side as, all around me, people linked arms, held hands, or put their arms around each other, creating a solid wall of people. We had at least one steam engine on each end of the crowd, and a number of magical carriages flanking the marchers. I tried telling myself that the soldiers would hit magisters first if they did anything, but it was still rather terrifying knowing that soldiers were bearing down on us.

Colin turned to address the governor, sweeping his top hat off his head and giving a deep bow. "Your Excellency," he said. "I present to you the American people. This is who you're oppressing, and this is who you're up against. We're magisters and ordinary folk, rich and poor, from all races and religions. And we want to be free."

"Freedom!" someone in the crowd called out, and it became a chant.

The governor listened for a moment before stepping back inside and closing the door.

"And a merry Christmas to you, too!" Colin called after

him. Turning back to face the marchers, he said, "Now, we should probably disperse peacefully. Let's just turn around and march back down the street. Don't do anything they could arrest you for. Don't threaten the soldiers or police. As you near your home, turn off if it's safe to do so."

The steam engine that had been behind us blew a blast on its whistle. Everett's airship made a large circle over the lower corner of the park, turning around to head downtown. On the street, the crowd began moving. It was the opposite direction from my home, but I went along with the crowd. As Henry had said, we were safer together. If we split off, we'd be easier to capture.

I wondered what the soldiers coming uptown would do when the march reached them. They'd want the crowd away from the magister district, so would they try to stop us or would they let us pass? Stopping this large a crowd would be nearly impossible, and attempting to do so would likely lead to violence, but there was no telling what a frightened soldier might do in this situation.

Everett, our lookout from above, shouted, "They're backing away!" That was encouraging.

Henry tightened his arm around me. "See, we'll be fine. A few rioters, and we'd have been in trouble. A mob this size, there's little short of war they can do against us."

"I thought war was what we wanted," I said.

"Freedom's what we want, and if it takes a war, it takes a war. It would be nice if they'd just agree to back off and leave us be. Maybe this will show them."

A bicyclist went by, perched high above the large front wheel and ringing his bell. He had to weave around the marchers, and he seemed to be struggling to remain upright at the slow pace. His high seat made him easy to spot, even as he moved far ahead to the front of the procession. And then a lot of things happened very quickly.

Everett yelled, "Wait, stop!" just as I saw the cyclist pitch forward over his handlebars. There were shouts and whistles ahead, at least one gunshot, followed by screams as the mass of marchers came back toward us, even as the group from behind us kept coming forward.

At the sound of shots and screams, a wave of red-coated men came running from the armory in the park. Another small group of soldiers came from the mansion the governor was visiting. "Those idiots," Henry muttered, and I wasn't sure whom he meant—the marchers, the soldiers, the cyclist, or perhaps all of them at once.

He tightened his hold on me, and I put my arm around him to ensure that we stayed together. He guided us through the swarm of panicking humanity. I couldn't see above the people around us, but he was tall enough to have a decent vantage point.

It turned out that he was aiming for the next cross street. A number of marchers were fleeing that way, away from the soldiers and the bulk of the march, and we joined them, finally able to move without being pressed against others. The street was still packed with people, but we weren't shoulder to shoulder anymore, so we could run.

The crowd thinned as we crossed the first avenue and people ran up- and downtown. Henry waited until we'd run the next block before turning us uptown. We ran one more block, then slowed to a walk. By this time, my lungs burned, and my chest heaved, my ribs pressing against my stays as I fought to get enough air.

"Goggles off," Henry ordered when we reached a rubbish bin. "And I'm afraid that hat will have to go, as well. It's very fetching, but it makes you look like a Rebel Mechanic, and I suspect that would be a very bad thing at the moment. The sash and emblem, too."

The hat was very nice, but I reluctantly dropped it in the bin, along with the goggles and red sash. Henry likewise removed his goggles. He buttoned his coat up to his neck, hiding his Mechanics-style attire. His hat, which was decorated with gears and red ribbons, also went in the bin. I removed the Mechanics insignia from my lapel and put it in my pocket.

Henry offered me his arm, and we resumed walking, as though we were merely out for an evening stroll. "There went your disguise," I said. It was good to see his face without the goggles hiding it, but that meant others could see him, as well, and we were in a part of the city where he was known.

"Ah, they'll never recognize me without my glasses," he said with a grin. It was true that he didn't look at all like the absentminded young nobleman who moved in the upper levels of society. His coat was shabby, his hair was rumpled, and he didn't wear the spectacles that had been part of his camouflage. Still, anyone who knew him well would know him on sight.

"I can get home from here, I'm sure," I said. "You should get to where you're safe."

"I won't leave you alone in these circumstances," he said. "And besides, I'm probably safer up here than running into all the soldiers, and I'm close enough to an underground entrance."

A shrill whistle made me jump guiltily, and Henry pulled us into the shadow of a doorway just as a group of policemen ran by on the next cross street. I held my breath until they were gone, and we waited a minute more before emerging from our hiding place. At the intersection, we paused to look toward Fifth Avenue. It was hard to tell what was going on. All I could see were masses of people, a carriage or two, and some lights.

We hurried across the street, where I felt very exposed. I couldn't help a soft sigh of relief when we had some buildings between us and whatever was happening. "I feel bad abandoning all of them," I said.

"You're important to the movement, so we need to keep you safe," Henry said. "Liberty Jones would be a real prize, and capturing Verity Newton would mean we'd lose one of our best agents. Most of these people will just be released, if they're even arrested."

"What we need is a diversion, something to get the soldiers and police away long enough to allow our people to escape, like that riot the night of the Battery attack that drew troops away from the fight," I said.

Henry stopped and turned to face me. "What did you have in mind?"

"I don't know," I said with some frustration. "I write. I listen and watch. I don't do the more exciting things. You're the bandit. Haven't you used diversions in your robberies?"

"Not on this scale. We've had to get a few guards out of the way, not a platoon of soldiers." He frowned, biting his lower lip, then turned to survey our surroundings. "Let's see, we probably want to send them this way, possibly uptown a little. That will allow the marchers to get downtown. And it would have to be really spectacular to get their attention and be more important than rounding up peaceful marchers."

"Well, that should be easy enough," I said, unable to hold back a grin.

"And we don't want to actually hurt anyone," he added.

"It would also probably be best if it doesn't seem to be at all related to the march," I said. "We don't want to give them an excuse to blame the rebels."

"Oh, good point, though it does make things more difficult."

"Magic?" I suggested. "Even if we have magisters in the movement, I suspect most of the authorities would still be reluctant to blame magisters for anything that happens."

He patted me on the back. "And you said you didn't know anything about diversions." He looked up the street, frowning in thought. "That might work…"

"What?"

"That's a power juncture over there. It's supposed to be supplying the street lights, which you can see aren't working."

"Thanks to your strike."

"But if we overload it, we could create a rather spectacular light display throughout this entire zone."

"And how would you propose to do that?"

"We connect a few things, then add some power of our own. It'll probably drain the two of us for the next couple of days."

"It's not as though I can use magic at home, anyway," I said with a shrug.

"That's the spirit! Now, let's see what I can cannibalize."

We checked to make sure the way was clear, then hurried to the power junction. I stood watch while Henry used his pocketknife to pry open the casing. "Hmm, yes, it's dead," he said. "No power at all."

He straightened and glanced around. "Aha, there's something I can probably use. You stay here and watch this." He darted off into the darkness toward a carriage parked on the side of the street. It was at an angle that implied it had just stopped rather than being deliberately parked, possibly because it had run out of power. Henry forced open the bonnet, pulled a crystal cylinder out, closed the bonnet, and ran back to me.

"Mind you, this is pure theory, but I'm hoping my theory works," he said as he bent over the power junction.

"It's designed for only so much input, and the lights are meant for sustained use of low power while the carriage needs higher bursts of power. Replace this power supply with the crystal from the carriage, and it should blow out the lights. First, we need to fill it up. Put your hands here, and give it all you've got."

I pulled off my gloves and put my hands next to his on the crystal. I could tell when he started feeding power because the excited ether around us made my whole body tingle. "The power doesn't really have to come from you. You're just a conduit channeling excited ether into the crystal," he instructed.

I tried to visualize what he described. At first, I seemed to be mostly pouring power from myself, but then I had to draw on the ether around me, and that was when it fell into place for me. It wasn't quite as draining, but it still took a great deal of control and concentration. Even in the cold night, sweat beaded on my forehead.

I could barely breathe in proximity to this much magic being used this intensely. My whole body felt like it was on fire, and I wouldn't have been surprised to see my hair standing on end. I wasn't sure how much more I could take before Henry said, "There, that should do it."

The problem was, I didn't know how to stop, and I was too breathless to tell him. He eased the crystal out from under my hands and set it down, then took my hands in his. "Easy, easy," he said softly. I felt the ether around us calm into stillness as he dampened it. "Breathe," he instructed.

"Let go." I forced myself to take a long, deep breath and let it out slowly. With that breath, the last of the magic flowed out of me, and my legs went weak. I collapsed into Henry's arms. He held me tight, his lips brushing my forehead. "You did very well, considering I never taught you that," he said.

"That was…rather more intense than I've ever experienced," I said when I could speak.

"Likewise. I've never done anything like that before, myself. I was improvising based on what I did at the magic plant. Now, do you think you can stand on your own, or should I sit you down?"

"I'm fine," I said. Actually, I felt more than fine, like I'd received a fresh burst of energy. He eased me back onto my feet and held me for a moment until he was sure I was steady before he released me. My hands had grown cold once more, and I pulled my gloves back on.

"And now to see if this works. Do you think you have enough left to give me a little light?"

"Strangely, I feel like I could set the city alight," I said.

"That won't last for long. You'll probably have trouble getting out of bed in the morning."

"I think that would have happened anyway, with all this running." My first attempt at conjuring a light resulted in a blinding flare that I quickly dampened. On the second attempt, I managed to form a small globe. I held it so he could see what he was doing. "I see you're practicing," he said.

"I'm afraid not, not since you've been gone."

"Elinor wouldn't react badly or turn you in."

"I'm fairly certain of that. I just don't really know how to bring it up."

He tightened something, then looked up at me. "You should probably get a little farther from here. I don't know exactly what will happen when I make the final connection."

I thought about arguing with him, insisting that I'd face whatever danger there was alongside him, but I thought better of it. There was no point in futile gestures—by definition. I moved away, making sure I was nowhere near a lamppost, then held my breath as I watched Henry bend once more over the power junction.

I could tell he was doing something with magic, based on the way the ether reacted, but it wasn't like any magic I'd felt before. It was like the ether was being held back and suppressed rather than excited and channeled. Henry put down the crystal, then turned and sprinted toward me, pulling his gloves on as he ran. When he was halfway to me, the ether released.

A split second later, all the streetlamps in this area lit up, burning brighter than I'd ever seen them. It was blinding. When Henry reached me, he caught my hand, and I ran with him, heading uptown. One downside to this scheme was that there would be no hiding in this daylight brightness.

We paused at the next cross street and looked around to see how far the light went. "Good, it's almost to Fifth," Henry muttered. "They'll have to have noticed it."

"But turning the lights on is a good thing, isn't it?" I asked.

"Just wait," he said with a grin, adding somberly, "I hope."

We ran again and it seemed like the lights were growing even brighter. I had to shade my eyes with my free hand. At the same time, I noticed a strange humming sound, and the sense of excited ether made my nerve endings tingle.

When I thought I couldn't bear the sensation anymore, Henry abruptly shoved me down into the service entrance under the front steps of a brownstone, shielding me with his body. The hum grew louder, and suddenly there was a series of explosions. It was like a fireworks display, but louder and more immediate.

When it became silent once more, it was dark again, as every streetlamp in the area seemed to have blown out. I heard distant bells and whistles, heading in our direction.

"Now we'd really better run," Henry said, pulling me out of our hiding place. "They'll be coming this way."

"That was the plan, after all," I pointed out.

We ran uptown, heading for home. Henry started to turn down the next cross street, but we could see lights heading toward us from that direction, with whistles blowing. That meant we had to run back the way we'd come, but there were more lights and whistles as the authorities converged on the site of the explosions.

Henry and I looked at each other. "I thought we were too important to the movement to be captured," I quipped.

"Yes, well, sacrifices must be made for the greater good. But maybe we can convince them that we're innocent people who just happened to be out for a walk when all these crazy things happened."

"Without hats."

"We enjoy the cold weather."

While we bantered, my heart raced. I thought I might be able to talk my way out of the situation, but if they had the slightest idea who Henry was, both of us would be in trouble. When I looked up at him, I could see in his eyes that he'd had the same thought. "Perhaps we should split up," he said.

I wanted to argue with him, even though he was right, but there wasn't much time for that because I could hear the sound of footsteps closing in on us.

Just then, we were both startled by the sound of squealing tires as a magical roadster coming from uptown skidded to a stop next to us. A woman wearing a black lace veil was at the wheel. "Get on board!" she ordered.

IN WHICH I HAVE A STARTLING REVELATION

The carriage was already full of people, but Henry and I jumped onto the running boards and held on for dear life as Elinor turned the carriage around to head uptown again. We tore through the intersection and barreled up the avenue before whipping around the corner at the next cross street. The sound of whistles grew distant behind us, but I wasn't sure if that was because the police had stayed to focus on whatever had happened to the lights or because the wind roaring past my ears drowned them out.

We rounded another corner into an alley and finally slowed somewhat. As we approached a row of garages, Elinor said, "Would you please open door number four? It isn't locked."

Henry jumped off the running board and jogged ahead to pull the door open. Elinor drove the roadster inside, and

Henry closed the door again. The carriage's lamps lit the interior of the garage, and Elinor lit a few other lanterns. "We may as well make ourselves comfortable," she said. "I think it best if we wait here for some time, until we're certain they're no longer looking for anyone. There's an apartment upstairs where you may rest, and the larder is fairly well stocked, if you're hungry, but it's probably best that you use no lights that will show through the windows. We don't want them looking in here."

When the others had all gone upstairs—the mention of a full larder had set them moving—Henry said, "Elinor?"

She pulled the black lace veil back from her face. "Ah, now you've discovered my secret life. I'm sure I don't have to tell you to keep it to yourself." She smiled, moving toward him with outstretched arms. "It's so good to see you again." They embraced briefly, then she grabbed his shoulders and shook him. "What are you thinking, coming back to the city after all it took to get you to safety? And then participating in something like this? Are you *trying* to get caught?" Before he had a chance to respond, she whirled on me. "And you, you let him do this? Why didn't you tell me he was back?"

Henry stepped forward and hugged her again. "Elinor, you should know me well enough to know that this has nothing to do with anything anyone 'lets' me do. Verity couldn't stop me if she tried, and she's given me the same lecture."

She gave him a shaky smile. "Well, I suppose it would

be too much to ask for you to ever behave sensibly. I can only hope that our nieces and nephew inherit the good sense from their mother's side."

"Says the woman who has a secret hidden roadster and who sneaks out in the night to abet a revolution while playing the invalid to society. Fortunately, your sister was the sensible one in your family."

"I spend all day with those children," I said, climbing into the carriage and collapsing onto the backseat. My legs had grown too weary to stand any longer. "Olive's the only one of them I'd call truly sensible. Flora would have led the march tonight if she'd known about it, and probably would have deliberately provoked a confrontation with the soldiers. I'm surprised Rollo hasn't yet run away to join the Rebel Mechanics."

Henry joined me in the seat and put his arm around my shoulders. "I suspect our Olive is a dark horse. She'd be like you, putting on a perfectly respectable, reasonable facade while secretly getting up to all kinds of mischief."

Elinor climbed into the driver's seat and turned to face us, leaning on the seat back. "I certainly hope so," she said with a grin. "If not, then Verity needs to adjust her curriculum."

"How did you find us—and at exactly the right time?" I asked.

"I was on my way uptown with these good people"—she gestured toward the upstairs apartment—"when I felt the magic, and I recognized Henry's style. I had a feeling you were up to something. My initial plan was to offer assistance, but after the explosions, it seemed more likely you'd need to escape."

I patted the seat of the carriage. "So, this is how you come and go."

"Yes, and I'm very glad I found a new garage as soon as I moved down here. Imagine if we'd had to go all the way to the van der Kaamps' barn, where I was keeping it."

"How long have you been doing this?" Henry asked.

"As long as you've been robbing trains."

"I don't suppose you saw whether our diversion did any good," I said, glancing back at the garage door, even though I knew I wouldn't see anything back there.

"I'm afraid not," Elinor said. "I loaded the carriage up with as many people as I could and was in the process of getting them far away when I felt the ether going crazy and turned back to help. I was away from the core of the march by then. But it did seem as though every soldier and policeman in the area was running toward the explosions."

"It won't have kept them for long once they saw there was no real damage," Henry said. "I just hope it was long enough for most of those people to disperse."

"But did you see how many people there were?" Elinor said, her face glowing. "I never dreamed there would be so many. Father will be horrified. It's not the kind of movement he can easily fight."

"What do we do next?" I asked.

"I should think we take over the Assembly Hall and

start our own Assembly," Henry said. "We know we have enough people to support it."

"If they weren't scared by tonight," I said.

"Or tonight might draw us even more supporters, depending on what happened," he argued. "If soldiers hurt anyone during what had been a peaceful march, then we have even more grounds for revolution."

"Even if no one was hurt, we can probably count on the rebels to make it look truly awful," I said, remembering a past incident in which the rebels hadn't been entirely honest. "I'll be able to report on the march itself, and we can get that news out, but someone else will have to report on the aftermath. I probably shouldn't have left when I did."

Henry tightened his arm around me, pulling me against himself. "I didn't give you much choice. I had to get out of there, and I dragged you with me."

"At least my employer knows where I am," I said.

"And you were out with a legitimate reason," Elinor said. "I'm the one who may have trouble getting in, since I'm believed to be an invalid who hasn't left her room all night." She slid out of her seat and stepped onto the running board. "I'll go see what the situation looks like out there."

Henry started to rise. "No, I should go."

She stopped him with a hand on his arm. "I'm the one who looks less suspicious. I can always claim to have been sleepwalking. You're a fugitive." She winked at us before pulling her veil back over her face. "You two enjoy a little privacy, but remember that there are people upstairs."

With that, she hurried to the door, opened it just enough to slip outside, and disappeared into the night, sliding the door shut behind her.

"Ah, alone at last," Henry said, catching the tip of my chin with his finger and turning my face toward his. "I have missed you more than you can ever know, Verity Newton." He tilted my chin up and bent to kiss me. After a quick brush of his lips against mine, he rested his forehead on mine and whispered, "And I perhaps should have said something to you before I was forced to flee the city."

"Well, you were my employer, which made things somewhat awkward," I whispered, feeling suddenly very warm.

"I suppose so," he said. "The employer and the governess is such a cliché. I should have thought about that when I hired you."

"What would that have had to do with you hiring me?"

"Don't you know? It was love at first sight. I knew you were the one for me from the moment you hit me in the head with your bag." I couldn't help but laugh, and he chuckled as well, before saying, "I'm serious! I was tempted to take you with me as a hostage so I wouldn't lose you."

"That wouldn't have worked."

"I know. We didn't really leave the train, so a hostage would have foiled our attempt to blend in with the passengers."

"Not to mention the fact that I wouldn't have been kindly disposed toward someone who abducted me."

"Which was why I thought the better of it. And then

imagine my surprise when I came home, despondent over having lost the girl of my dreams, and found you there in my house. Though that was almost as bad as having you as my hostage, since, as you said, I was your employer and making any kind of advances on you would have been very improper."

"I would think that a greater consideration would be that you're a magister nobleman and I'm a commoner."

He took my hand, lacing his fingers through mine and rubbing his thumb over the back of my hand. I wished we weren't wearing gloves so I could have felt his touch more directly, but it was too cold to remove my gloves, even as warm as his proximity made me. "We both know that isn't quite the problem that it would appear. And besides, it won't matter in our new nation."

I clutched my fingers around his and, heart racing, tilted my head to kiss him. I felt very brazen in doing so, but I feared we might not have many opportunities. He returned the kiss, and when we parted, both of us a little breathless, I laughed softly. "And to think, for quite some time I was convinced that you were interested in some girl in your social set. I caught glimpses of drawings in your sketchbook of a mystery girl. I knew I'd developed feelings for you when I realized how much I despised that girl."

He threw his arm around me and pulled me against him to rest my head on his shoulder. "The girl in my sketchbook was you! I confess to having drawn a few sketches after that night I saw you with your hair loose." He caught one curl in his fingers. "Like tonight."

The garage door rattled, breaking the mood. I sat up abruptly, bumping my head against Henry's chin as I pulled away from him. By the time Elinor entered, we looked as proper as if we'd been chaperoned. "I thought I'd give you two a little warning," she said with a wry grin.

"Is it safe out there?" I asked.

"I wouldn't recommend going anywhere near the site of the fracas, but I think we can get home. Henry, do you know the access points to the underground?"

"I know the one closest to us. Do you know if these people are cleared for that secret?"

"I don't know. I just had my passengers and the people I was able to grab when everything went south, so I don't know them. But I don't think they're familiar with this part of town, so you may be able to confuse them in the darkness and addle them once you get in the tunnels. You should go first and get them downtown. I suspect the Mechanics will have people ready to get everyone home, and I want you out of here, as well."

He stood and climbed out of the roadster, pausing to give me a look over his shoulder before heading up the stairs. Elinor watched him go until he'd disappeared into the apartment before taking the seat he'd just vacated. She said, "After they're gone, you and I can see if we can get home. The excitement actually gives you an excuse for being home so late. If you really were at a Christmas party, you'd have had a hard time getting home. The tricky part will be getting myself in without being noticed."

"I could create a diversion once I'm inside."

She shook her head. "No good. The more excitement, the harder it will be for me to sneak in. It's best if the house is entirely quiet. It's still early for the kitchen staff to be up, so I should be safe. I think it might be best if I sneak in first, and then you enter properly. We can arrange a signal. I'll flash a light from my window when it's safe for you to approach the front door."

Our planning was interrupted by the sound of feet on the stairs as Elinor's passengers and Henry came down. Elinor quickly threw her veil back over her face. An older lady leaned heavily on Henry's arm, and a man in the group carried a sleeping child.

"I would offer to drive you, but I'm afraid that a carriage out right now would draw more notice than individuals on foot," Elinor said, getting out of the roadster.

"I'll be fine if I can lean on this one," the lady said. "And I thank you for getting us safely away from there."

"I only wish I could have done more. Safe journeys, and stay true to the cause."

Henry eased the door open, looked outside for a moment, then gestured for the others to follow. I stared after them, even after the door had shut, and realized that I hadn't had a chance to say good-bye to him.

"You'll see him again soon enough, I'm sure," Elinor said.

I whipped back around to find her smiling at me, her veil pushed back again. "Did you know about us?" I asked.

"I hoped. You may recall that I urged you to dance with him at your first ball. But I would have had to be blind not to notice the two of you tonight."

"You don't disapprove, even though we're from such different classes?"

"You think you're the only one? Why do you think I'm so dedicated to this movement?"

"You?" I asked, sure my eyes must look like they were popping out of my head.

"Mind you, that's not the only reason. I wouldn't have met him if I hadn't already been involved. But it certainly provides motivation if you can't be with the person you love without changing the world."

"Who–who is it?"

"I'd rather keep that to myself for the moment. But he's more brilliant than almost any magister man I've ever met. And he's one of the main reasons I took to my bed. If I'm an invalid, it becomes very difficult to try to arrange a suitable match with someone who would bore me to tears."

"There is something about a rebel man, isn't there?" I said, getting out of the carriage and moving to limber my stiffening legs. "And to think, I'd spent my life expecting to end up as a professor's wife."

"Then you owe us a great debt, I believe," she said with a smile. "It should be safe for us to go now." She waved a hand to turn off all the lanterns inside the garage. "I'll probably need to recharge the old girl, but some other time. Now, let's see if we can get home. I'm ready to get some sleep."

She opened the door, looked out, then gestured for me to come with her. Once we were outside, she shut and locked the door. It seemed very dark now, no street lamps, no lights from nearby windows. There wasn't even any moonlight because of the heavy clouds. I could barely see Elinor in her black clothes with her face covered.

We had to feel our way down the alley toward the street, running our hands along the garages we passed. We paused before entering the street. Everything was totally still and silent. That meant we were less likely to be discovered, but it also made us conspicuous, as there were no other people in the street.

We couldn't move very quickly in the darkness. Instead, we edged along, feeling ahead of us with our feet while guiding ourselves against the walls and fences we passed. There were a couple of times when I almost fell from tripping over a tree root or a bit of uneven pavement. Fortunately, Elinor and I were holding on to each other, and she kept me upright. There were also a few times when her weight fell more heavily on me, and I realized she'd lost her footing. Most of the time, though, she was as surefooted as a cat. I thought I'd have to get her to teach me whatever exercises she did to stay in that kind of condition while pretending to be bedridden.

I wasn't sure how long it took us to make our way to the street that ran alongside the Lyndon mansion. It couldn't have been more than three blocks, but we had to move at a snail's pace. We stopped where we could see the rear of the house, including the kitchen.

"I don't see any lights," I whispered.

"No, it does appear to be quiet," she replied. "We might just survive this little adventure. Now, give me about five minutes, then go around to the front and look for my signal before you come home from your party. Remember to be distressed about how difficult it was to make it home. Your only audience might be the hall boy, so it might not matter, but there's also the chance that Mrs. Talbot has been worried about you and waiting up."

The thought of that made me uneasy. "Henry believes she's a spy for your father."

"What makes him think that?"

"The previous housekeeper left when Henry became guardian of the children, and your father acted as though he was doing Henry a great favor by hiring a housekeeper for him. Of course, she wouldn't be looking out for revolutionary activity, but Henry suspected she was reporting on how he fared with the children."

Elinor laughed and had to clap a hand over her mouth to muffle the noise. "Oh! I should have told him! I selected Mrs. Talbot. I will admit that my father's aim was to have a spy in the house, but I helped him by offering a suggestion, so she's *my* spy. You can rest more easily. But it was probably good that Henry thought he was being watched. That likely kept him from getting into far worse trouble than he did."

With that, she disappeared into the shadows and made her way into the kitchen yard. I saw the kitchen door open and close, then began counting, since I couldn't read my watch. While I counted, I twisted my hair back into a bun, turning myself into a governess once more. When I'd counted a hundred and twenty seconds, I began edging my way toward the corner, keeping one hand on the side of the building.

It was another minute before I reached the end of the building and had to feel for the iron fence railings. I moved more cautiously now, as I was out in the open. But after three more steps, I stopped. There was a carriage parked in front of the house. It looked like the governor's carriage, though I couldn't see if it had the coat of arms on the door. What was he doing here at this time of night?

There was a light in the downstairs parlor window, but the rest of the house was still dark. I wished there were a way I could warn Elinor. This was the one person who not only couldn't catch her coming home so late, but mustn't catch her even being out of bed. She wouldn't be able to claim that she'd merely come down to the kitchen to make a cup of tea without letting on that she wasn't truly an invalid. Although it went against our plan because I hadn't yet seen her signal, I hurried to the front steps. If the governor was distracted by me, it should give Elinor a better chance to sneak up the back stairs.

The front door was unlocked, and I opened it without any pretense at stealth. Unfortunately, the hinges were well-oiled, so it made no sound, in spite of my best efforts. The foyer was still dark, which cast me in shadows from the perspective of the parlor, where the governor paced. Whether it was what little noise I made or my movement, I must have caught his eye. I braced myself to give the explanation I'd prepared, but I didn't expect what he said next: "Elinor? Is that you?"

I stepped forward into the light of the parlor. He frowned and shook his head when he saw me. "Oh, Miss Newton. It's you. Where have you been?"

"I was at a friend's Christmas party, but I had a terrible time trying to get home from near the university. There seems to have been some kind of excitement. The way was blocked for the longest time, and I couldn't even get a cab to take me directly home. I had to walk the last few blocks. But what brings you here at this hour? Is something wrong?"

"I was nearby, and yes, there was some excitement. I merely wanted to make sure everyone here was all right."

I heard feet on the stairs, and turned to see Flora coming down, fastening the belt on her dressing gown. "The hall boy said you were here, Grandfather," she said. "What's the matter?"

"I suppose you were in no danger if no one knew anything was happening," he said. "I'm sorry to have disturbed you."

"What is it?" Flora asked, glancing between the governor and me.

"There was some rebel activity nearby that snarled the city," he explained. "It seems I should have been seeing to Miss Newton's well-being rather than yours, as she was the one inconvenienced, while I seem to have awakened you unnecessarily. Now, my apologies, and I will leave you to get back to bed, or to get to bed, as the case may be."

He put his hat back on and made it to the door before the hall boy could open it for him. Flora stared at the door after he'd gone and raised an eyebrow. "That was odd," she said. "I think it's safe for us to lock the door and let you get some rest, Gary," she said to the hall boy. He nodded and turned the lock before going below stairs. Once he was out of earshot, she asked, "Do you know what he was talking about, Miss Newton?"

"There seems to have been some kind of rebel demonstration that blocked streets. It made it very difficult for me to get home," I said. It was entirely true, though I left out a lot of details.

"How exciting! But you look absolutely frozen. Where did your hat go? I should ring for someone to make you some warm milk."

I patted my head, as though just then realizing my hat had gone missing. My hat, the one I'd begun the evening with, was probably back at the theater. I'd forgotten about it entirely. "There's no need to wake anyone," I said. "I just want to get in bed and try to get some sleep." I was certain that by now Elinor had made it safely to her room, so I headed for the stairs, hoping Flora would get the message.

She didn't. She was wide awake now. "Has a revolution begun? I wonder if there was rioting in the streets."

"I didn't see any rioting," I said. "What I saw was mostly just a lot of people."

"Well, *something* has to have happened if Grandfather was worried enough to stop by here and make sure we were safe. Or does he think that we were like Henry and involved in it?"

Now she was getting a little too close to the truth. Did the governor suspect any of us were involved? Had he really been checking to ensure the household was safe, or had he been making sure we were home? He'd seemed to believe my excuse—or had he? I gave a most unladylike yawn. "Oh, excuse me," I said. "I'm suddenly quite exhausted. It was such an ordeal getting home tonight that I'm entirely spent. Good night, Flora."

This time, she took the cue. "Oh, then I mustn't keep you. I just hope I can get back to sleep," she said. "When Gary knocked on my door in the middle of the night, I feared the worst."

I let her get up the stairs before I turned out the light in the parlor and went up. Alone in the near darkness, I found myself thinking about the governor's reaction to me. He'd mistaken me for Elinor. I recalled that one of the men at the magic plant had thought I was Olive's sister. The governor had always been very kind to me, far beyond what anyone would expect for his grandchildren's governess. Henry had even joked about keeping me nearby as a shield because the governor was nicer and less formidable when I was present. I knew my true father must have been a magister in order for me to have magical powers, and the governor had frequently mentioned meeting my mother and being very fond of her.

As all the pieces came together, I stopped, stunned, three steps from the top of the staircase. Was the governor my father?

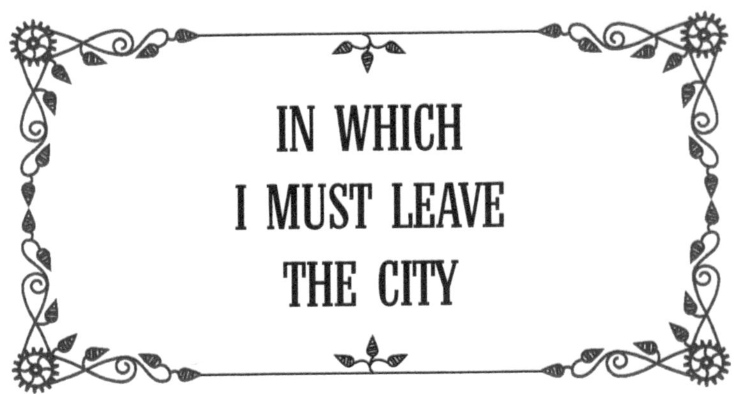

IN WHICH I MUST LEAVE THE CITY

Fortunately, I was so exhausted from the late night and all that walking and running that even this shocking realization didn't keep me awake for long. When I woke late the next morning, every muscle in my body ached, and my legs were so sore I wasn't sure I'd be able to stand. I'd never walked that far in one day, and then there had been all that running.

While I lay there, trying to summon the will to get up, there was a soft knock at my door, and when I said, "Come in," Mary, Elinor's maid, entered with a breakfast tray.

"Lady Elinor heard about your ordeal last night and thought you might enjoy breakfast in bed this morning," she said. "There's no need to worry about getting up for church. The streets are too much of a mess after last night for anyone to go anywhere this morning."

As I forced myself to sit up so she could place the tray across my lap, I asked, "What kind of mess?"

After positioning the tray, she poured a cup of tea. "Well, the weather took a turn for the worse a couple of hours ago, with some freezing rain, so everything's all iced up, and something seems to have happened a few blocks away, between us and the church. They're not letting anyone through."

"Oh my," I said before taking a sip of tea. I barely restrained a sigh at how good it felt. Then I considered Elinor's thoughtfulness toward me. Did she know who I was? Had she known all along that I was her sister? She had mentioned meeting my mother when she was a small child, and Elinor seemed to know everything else.

Mary left me alone with instructions to ring for her if I needed anything else or when I needed her to take the tray away and run me a hot bath. I settled back against my pillows, enjoying the rare luxury of a morning spent in bed, without having to get up to get the children to school or conduct lessons. I could see why Elinor found this way of life appealing.

By the time I finished the breakfast and the pot of tea, I felt better prepared to face the world again, though I did allow myself the indulgence of letting Mary get my bath water ready when she came to retrieve the tray. A long soak in hot water eased my sore muscles enough that merely walking was no longer agony, though I still wasn't moving very quickly. I was still sitting on my bed in my dressing gown, toweling my hair, when there was a knock on my door and I heard Elinor's voice say, "Verity?"

"Yes, come in," I said. When she entered, I couldn't help but stare at her. How had I not seen the resemblance before? We had the same color hair and eyes, and there was a similar shape to our faces. No wonder the governor had mistaken me for her when seeing me in the shadows. Then I had to look away from her because I felt too self-conscious about her being my sister.

"How are you doing this morning?" she asked, sitting on the foot of my bed.

"Sore," I admitted. "Thank you so very much for having Mary tend to me. Breakfast and a bath helped immensely."

"I suspected you'd need it. I know how I felt, and I drove the whole way. I also must thank you for your aid last night. That was some very quick thinking. If you hadn't come in when you did, my father might have resorted to asking to see me."

"Flora came down not long after I arrived, so she might have distracted him just as well as I did."

"Well, whatever it was, I was able to sneak in without being noticed, in spite of him arriving at the worst possible time. Did he say anything interesting?"

"Only that he was concerned because of the nearby excitement. I thought he might have been checking up on us, since he would have known that nothing really happened up here."

"I think some people might have fled in this direction. Perhaps he worried that some fugitive barged in to hide out here."

"You mean, other than us?" I asked, unable to restrain a giggle. She joined me in laughing, and then before I realized what I was saying, I blurted, "He is my father, isn't he? And we're sisters?"

She stopped laughing, but she smiled, and her eyes welled with tears. "How did you find out?"

"I didn't find out so much as piece it together. Last night when I came in, he initially thought I was you, and that made me think."

Nodding, she said, "I don't have definitive proof, but I've known about you for years and was sure when I saw you. If it's any consolation, I believe he really did love your mother. Of course, I was too young at the time to understand what was happening, other than that I saw enough of them together to think she was going to be my new mother, but he's spoken of her often over the years, and he knew about you—and suspected you were his. There was at least some correspondence between them."

"I don't think my mother and her husband were very happy together," I said, "and I don't think it was just because I came along and was very clearly not her husband's daughter. In fact, I think that's how he knew I couldn't have been his. They hadn't been, well, close enough to have another child. I suppose it's nice to know she found some happiness."

"And now you've found a family. I wish you could have known Lily, my other sister, but you have nieces and a nephew."

"Who can't know about me."

"No, not now, but when we change things, it won't matter that you're a half-breed."

"It is a rather extraordinary coincidence that I happened to find a position in the home of my family." I narrowed my eyes at her. "Or was it?"

"I did help Mrs. Talbot vet the applicants for the position, and when I saw your name, I insisted she respond to your inquiry. She doesn't know why, though."

"Does Henry know?"

"If he does, he figured it out for himself and hasn't said anything. He was even younger than I was when it all happened, and at that time, his father was still alive and he wasn't yet living with Lily and Robert, so he was rather distant from affairs on our side of the family. He didn't get to know any of us very well until Robert and Lily took him in."

Although I'd had the revelation the night before, it only now hit me with full force, and I sat there in shock, trying to come to terms with knowing that the man my cause opposed was my father, that the children I taught were my family, and that my current benefactor was my sister.

Elinor leaned forward and took my hand. "What's the matter, dearest? Are you unhappy with this news?"

"I–I don't know what to think. It shouldn't really

change anything, since it has to remain a secret, but it's a great deal to take in."

"It won't have to change anything, though I do hope we can be even closer friends, truly be sisters. When Lily died, it was a great comfort to me knowing that I had another sister somewhere out there, even though I'd never met you. And now, here you are! You're even a kindred spirit to me." She released my hand and leaned over to embrace me. I returned the embrace, feeling a warmth from her that I'd never known with my other sister, who had disowned me at our mother's death, along with the rest of that family.

When we broke apart, I felt so overwhelmed that I had to change the subject. "Do you have any idea if Henry made it back safely?"

"You probably have better ways of communicating with the rebels than I do, at least from this house. I have my sources, but we have to be very careful."

"I'm sure he'll write when he gets a chance, but that means we likely won't learn anything until tomorrow evening's post, at the earliest."

It was sheer torture waiting for word. The official newspapers that we could read openly in the house said nothing of the night's events beyond a small item about "hooligans" disturbing the peace. Rollo's school had closed for the holidays, so I didn't have the excuse of walking him to school to meet up with any of my contacts on Monday. It was far too cold and icy to take a turn in the park. I was stuck inside with the children—with my family—and entirely uninformed of Henry's well-being or the rebels' plans.

I thought I showed admirable restraint when the evening post finally arrived—late—and there was a letter for me. I neither tackled Mr. Chastain to see if I had a letter nor immediately ran with it up to my room. I was sitting with the children in the family parlor, supervising piano practice, when Mr. Chastain delivered the post, and I had to wait until other letters were distributed before I learned that I had a missive. Then I had to calmly and with great decorum open and read it.

The handwriting on the envelope was Lizzie's, so I couldn't even use the excuse of receiving a note from a beau to act flustered. "Oh, good, my friend found my hat," I said as I read. "I will have to meet with her this week to retrieve it."

"We're going to the country on Thursday, so you'll want to get it before then," Elinor said. "You'll need it! I would offer to lend you one of mine, but I go out so seldom that I don't really have many hats."

"We're going Thursday?" I asked. "I thought we weren't leaving until Saturday." I knew that Henry preferred the children to be out of the city before anything happened, but I would have thought Elinor would want to be close to the action. Or did she know something about what was going to happen?

"It's just so dreary in the city, and with Rollo out of

school, I thought a change of scenery would be good for all of us," she said serenely, but she caught my eye, so I suspected there was more to this that she would tell me later.

The rest of Lizzie's note was vague, merely mentioning how successful the party had been and how glad she was that I'd joined them. She and her friends were talking about getting together again the following Friday and hoped I could join them then, as well. I had to force myself not to gasp, grin, or otherwise react. The rebels were definitely planning something.

When I had the chance to check for secret writing, I was relieved to see Henry's handwriting. He assured me that he had made it back to his lodgings safely, as had the rest of the group. Our diversion had allowed the marchers to disperse. Some people had been injured in the melee, but the authorities had captured no one. The mass show of support and the official response had galvanized the movement, so they planned to take immediate action and take over the Assembly Hall, declaring themselves to be a new government for the American nation.

And to think, I would be in the country, I realized, lowering the letter to my lap. Could I tell Elinor that my plans had changed and I would be spending Christmas with friends in the city? On the other hand, how could I miss spending Christmas with my family, even if they didn't know they were my family?

I shook my head. Elinor had a plan, I was sure of it.

She stopped by my room with a pot of cocoa after the children had gone to bed. When she'd poured cups for both of us, she said, "I'm sure you're wondering about the change of plans."

"Yes, particularly since the rebels are making their move on Friday. Did you know?"

"I got word through my channels. I presume you did, as well."

I nodded. "And Henry is safe."

"We'll have the children safely out of the city, but that doesn't mean you have to stay there. I'll make it easy for you to get away."

"You won't be there for the big moment?"

She sighed heavily. "No. I think it best that I'm not, as much as I hate to miss it. I have to think of the children. What the rebels are doing, it won't be easy. It will be a public stand that's terribly risky. Everyone there could end up dead or arrested. It's that serious. I can't in good conscience allow the children to lose another guardian. I must stay out of it. I've supported the movement as much as I can, and I will continue to do so. But in this case, my best contribution is away from the action."

I took a sip of cocoa, relishing the taste of chocolate and the warmth, before I spoke again. "Should I stay behind, as well?"

"You have a bigger role to play. I'm serving the children by ensuring that they have a safe, loving home. You're serving them by making a better future for them.

In the meantime, we'll spend the rest of the week packing to go. It's not that long a journey—less than an hour by train—but if we're to be there for a couple of weeks, we'll need to bring oh so many things. Flora's gowns alone may fill a baggage car. Now, let's make a list of what we'll need to do."

We spent the next hour outlining everything the children would need, drinking cocoa, and laughing. But even as I enjoyed the time, I couldn't stop thinking about what we were putting on the line. I might not be able to go back to my old life as a governess in the Lyndon home after this adventure. Even if our venture proved successful, I would likely be too busy with a revolution to teach lessons and walk Rollo to school, and there probably wouldn't be many balls where I'd be needed as a chaperone.

Later that night, I wrote a reply to Lizzie, sadly declining her invitation for Friday, as the family I served was going to the country for Christmas and I would be out of town. I made arrangements to retrieve my hat from her. In disappearing ink, I told Henry that Elinor was planning for me to get back to the city for the takeover of the Assembly Hall.

I was too busy during the next couple of days to think much about what awaited me. Mrs. Talbot had gone ahead to the country house to prepare it for our arrival, so it was up to Elinor and me to supervise travel preparations. When I'd joined the family on the tour of the colonies the previous month, we'd traveled by airship, which limited what we could pack. We didn't have such restrictions this time, and it seemed to me that we were carrying everything we owned.

I was about to remark on that and suggest that Elinor set limits, but then I realized with a chill down my spine that Elinor was preparing in case we couldn't return to the city. We weren't just going away for the holidays, but possibly for good. The children needed clothing to last them for weeks, if necessary, all favorite possessions, plenty of books, and all their school materials. I noticed that Elinor was also packing up a number of family heirlooms and most of the valuables.

When we loaded up the carriages for the trip to the depot on Thursday morning, I gave the mansion one last, long look. I remembered how overwhelmed I'd felt the first time I saw it. If only I'd known then that I was coming home to my family.

It was the first time I'd been more than a few blocks from the house since the march, having met Lizzie in the park to get my hat, and I stared eagerly out the carriage windows for signs of what had happened. A number of streets were barricaded, and there seemed to be many more soldiers visible. Any groups of more than a few people were quickly dispersed. The mood in the city struck me as tense—or was that merely my imagination, since I knew what was to come?

We were fortunate enough to be traveling on the governor's private railway car, which had been coupled to the rear of the train. It was far more luxurious than any rail car I'd ever seen. It was like traveling in a long, narrow parlor. There were thick carpets underfoot, wooden paneling and brass trim on the walls, and plush velvet seats. It also had its own baggage compartment, so the trunks we hadn't sent ahead were loaded as we boarded.

We didn't have much time to enjoy the luxury, though, for we were barely out of the city when the train stopped and our car was uncoupled, then moved onto a siding and into the Lyndon's private station. There we were met by horse-drawn sleighs to carry us up to the house over the snow, which was thicker and more plentiful than we'd seen in the city.

The house itself sat on top of a steep hill overlooking the river below. The trail leading up from the station wound back and forth as it rose, until we finally reached the crest and the house became visible. It was a sprawling manor built of gray stone, and it seemed to me to be even larger than the mansion in the city, though it was difficult to tell because it was more spread out and not as tall.

I got the impression of extensive gardens, though only the hedges were apparent under the blanket of snow. The sleighs pulled up under a portico to unload their passengers, and Mrs. Talbot met us in the foyer with servants who carried trays of hot cocoa. Although we'd only been out in the cold for the time it took to make it up the hill, I was grateful for the warm beverage.

The interior of the country house wasn't quite as grand

and formal as the mansion in the city. The furnishings seemed sturdier, more timeless, and there was less ornamentation. It struck me as a place designed for the family to live in comfort, while the town house had been designed to impress. I supposed that anyone invited to the country estate would already know the family well enough not to need to be awed by their wealth.

"Go raise the banner to show that the marquis is in residence," Mrs. Talbot instructed one of the footmen. It was easy to forget that Rollo was a titled nobleman, and that this estate and the house in the city were technically his.

"Can I go out and watch the banner go up?" he asked.

"*May* I," I automatically corrected.

"May I?" he said.

"I don't see why not," Elinor said. "But don't track snow into the house. That's not fair to the maids."

"I'll go with you," I said. "I haven't seen anything like this happen before."

"Neither have I," Rollo said as we went outside. "We've only been here once since Father died, and that time, I was still too upset to think of looking at the banner."

Because they were using sleighs for transportation, the drive hadn't been shoveled, so we had to trudge through the snow until we could see the highest peak of the house. I still held my cocoa mug, and it kept my hands a little warmer, though the cocoa was cooling rapidly. I didn't envy the footman who had to go out onto the roof to reach the flagpole.

Rollo had an entirely different attitude. "Do you think Aunt Elinor would let me go up on the roof? I bet you could see all the way back to the city from there."

"It might be dangerous."

"Why d'ya think I want to do it?" he said with a grin. The footman appeared, and Rollo saluted as the footman raised the flag. "Well, now I'm official, I guess," he said. "I still don't really feel like a marquis, though. Not that I'm likely to be one for long."

"What makes you say that?"

"It's pretty obvious that there's going to be a revolution. I don't think we'll have titles on this continent after that."

I couldn't comment on that other than to say, "Shall we go back inside?"

"I suppose so, since neither of my sisters are out here for me to throw snowballs at them."

I patted him on the shoulder, marveling yet again at the thought that he was really my nephew. "I wouldn't recommend trying that. I suspect you'd find that Flora is more adept than she seems, and Olive can be rather ferocious if roused. And they outnumber you."

"Words of wisdom," he said with a grin.

We removed our boots at the entry, so as to not track in snow, and while I was unlacing mine, Mrs. Talbot approached me with an envelope. "This arrived for you in the morning's post, Miss Newton," she said.

"How odd that it beat me here," I said as I took it from her.

"The postal system is quite efficient. Now, shall I show you to your room? Everyone else knows where to go, but you are new here. Your baggage has been taken up already. Leave your boots here. One of the boys will take care of them for you." As if by magic, a maid appeared with slippers for Rollo and me.

I had a room in the same wing as the children, and it didn't seem like a typical governess's room. I'd been assigned a room fit for a member of the family, with a large stone fireplace, four-poster bed, desk, dressing table, and an upholstered chair situated in front of a bowed window that looked out over the river valley. "This is my room?" I asked with some amazement.

"Lady Elinor insisted. There are so few of us here, and we aren't expecting guests, so she saw no reason not to treat you as a member of the family. Now, luncheon will be served in half an hour, if you'd like to rest or change clothes."

I needed a dry skirt that hadn't dragged through snow, but my first priority once Mrs. Talbot left me alone was to get my writing supplies out of my bag and open the letter. It ostensibly was a note from Alec, wishing me a happy Christmas and lamenting that I was out of the city where he wouldn't be able to spend it with me. When I sprayed it with the scented mist, Henry's handwriting appeared, giving terse instructions that "Liberty" be ready that night at eleven by the stables to cover the story of the century.

IN WHICH I RETURN TO THE CITY

I wondered how they'd get me back to the city and what I was supposed to do at eleven. I thought Elinor might know more, but she made no effort to talk to me privately. The afternoon was busy with preparations for Christmas. Elinor sent me with the children and a couple of footmen to cut a Christmas tree from the estate's forests. Rollo packed up one snowball, looked at his sisters, apparently thought better, and hurled the snowball at a tree. I smiled at him, and he shrugged.

Once the tree was back at the house, Elinor supervised the children in trimming it with blown glass and crystal ornaments. She had me sit beside her on the sofa, but with the children present, she couldn't talk to me about the impending revolution. I forced myself not to think about what might happen that night and instead focused on spending that time with my family. Christmas celebrations in my home had never been this joyous. My parents barely spoke to each other and my half-siblings had all grown up and left home while I was still rather young. If they returned home, they only paid attention to me in order to torment me. In later years, we'd observed Christmas merely by attending church. This scene was like something out of a Christmas card, something I'd never believed real people experienced.

As a result, when Elinor pulled me aside after dinner, a grim expression on her face, it was almost a disappointment. As much as I wanted a change, as excited as I was at the prospect of finally taking real action, I also hated to end this idyllic time with the family so soon.

"May I speak to you in my room in an hour?" she asked.

"Of course," I said.

I helped Olive get ready for bed and let her read me a bedtime story. Suddenly struck by the fact that I might not see her again if things didn't go as planned, and that it might be some time before I saw her even if all went well, I gave her a big hug and a kiss on the cheek before I left her room. She surprised me by returning my hug and kiss. "I love you, Miss Newton," she said, and I had to blink away tears.

I paused at the doorway to Rollo's room, but forced myself to move on when I could think of no good excuse for saying my farewells. I didn't even let myself consider saying anything to Flora. She knew enough to suspect that something might be amiss, and then I'd have her trying to leave with me.

I must have still appeared somewhat distraught when I reached Elinor's room at the appointed time, for as soon as she saw me, she pulled me into her arms and patted my back. "Oh, you poor thing," she said. "No sooner do you learn that you're in the midst of family than you have to leave us all behind. But we wouldn't ask you to do this if it weren't important."

She led me over to the small sofa by her fireplace, and we both sat down. "You're not just going to be part of a historic moment."

"I know. Henry said we need Liberty Jones to cover the story of the century."

"Yes, that is part of it. You need to witness events and write the article that will be spread around the world, letting everyone know what happened. Henry will be our sketch artist, providing illustrations. Getting your work from the Assembly Hall to the printer may be dangerous, depending on how events go. But there's more, and I'm afraid I'm the one who volunteered you. In addition to getting the news out, we need someone to bring the official declaration to the governor, and you may stand the greatest chance of anyone to do that and still get away."

"You want *me* to tell the governor about the revolution?"

"You're his daughter, the daughter of the woman who may have been the love of his life. That will make him hesitate to do anything that might harm you. Do you think you can do this?"

I gulped. Being in the midst of rebels would be dangerous, but I'd be among allies. This was going to the heart of our enemy, alone, trusting that any sentiment he held for me would save me. "I have to. You're right, no one else would stand as much of a chance."

"It still won't be easy." Her eyes filled with tears.

"That's not all, right? When I do that, I'll be making my position in the rebellion known. I'll be a fugitive. I won't be able to come home again unless we win." I'd already had a sense that this would be a possibility, but it had depended on what happened. I might still be able to get away undetected, as I had at every other revolutionary activity. In this case, for my mission to succeed, I would have to make myself known. The only way I might possibly return to a normal life would be if my father not only let me get away, but also remained silent about my participation, and I thought that was too much to expect.

"I'm afraid so. That's why I want you to be certain you know what we're asking of you."

"I will do it," I said, as firmly as I could manage when I felt like my entire body was shaking.

"Good. You're to bring whatever you think you need to have with you. A notebook and pencil or pen, of course, but also some things you might need on the run. You can pack a second bag that I will hide for you out here, in case you get a chance to come by. When and where are you supposed to be?"

"At eleven by the stables."

"I can get you there. I'll come to your room at a quarter 'til eleven to take you."

"You don't know what will happen after I'm met, do you? How will I get into the city?"

She shook her head. "No idea. I don't know if they'll bring in the engines for this or keep them out of the city. It would be rather hard to sneak up on the Assembly Hall in a steam engine."

Both of us smiled at the mental image. "I think some of the Mechanics might actually do such a thing," I said. "They haven't really been known for their subtlety."

"Perhaps that comes from having been disregarded for so long." She reached for a folded paper that lay on the table beside her. "Now, I may be able to give you enough of an advantage to get in and possibly even out of Father's home." With a grin, she added, "I am quite the expert at that, and we are fortunate that one of our ancestors was rather fearful after one of the failed uprisings a century ago. He built a number of hiding places and escape routes into the mansion, which I discovered and made use of." She unfolded the paper to show me a diagram of the mansion's secret passages. "This route in through the basement is fairly safe. The entrance is outside the walls, and the passages will take you to the study and to my room."

I leaned over and followed the route she traced with a finger, trying to reconcile what I saw in the diagram with my experiences in that mansion. "There's also access to the roof from the passages," she continued. "I know Henry likes working rooftops, so that might be another good way in—or out." She tapped on the plan. "I've never used the entrance to the passage from the study, but it's beside the fireplace, and if it works like the others, it's the usual pull on a sconce. Honestly, I don't know how someone with the imagination to design secret passages into his home can become so unimaginative when it comes to where the passages are and how they work."

She picked up a key on a ribbon and put the ribbon over my head to hang around my neck. "This will get you into the passages. I wish I had a key to the house I could give you, but one drawback to having played invalid for so long was that I had no reason to have a key to the house if I never left my bed. That was why I had to use the passages for my nighttime excursions." She pointed to a line of marks on the bottom of the page. "I have a telegraph line in my room. When you've completed your mission, if you get a chance, send this message. You do know how it works, don't you?"

"I've seen Alec use it."

"Good. Is there anything else I can tell you that might help?"

"I–I don't know. It's all rather overwhelming. I can't believe this is really happening. Up until now, it's all felt like a game. I believe in the cause, but it seemed like something we talked about and occasionally played at, not anything serious."

"Believe it or not, I feel the same way. But I shouldn't keep you any longer." She glanced at the clock on the mantel. "You've got a couple of hours. I'd suggest that you rest if you can. There's no telling when you might next get the chance to sleep."

Back in my room, choosing what to take proved difficult. I owned very little, and most of my clothing and my books were too bulky to carry on a mission. I tucked my revolutionary documents, including the letter from the governor that was proof of the financial scandal, into a spare pair of stockings and put them and some undergarments into the bottom of a satchel that I could carry over my shoulder. I filled a purse with all the money I had and added that to the satchel, along with my notebook, a pen, an inkpot, a penknife, and several pencils.

Into a larger carpet bag I put my nightgown, as many clothes as I could fit, and a few of my most prized books. That done, there was nothing to do but rest until it was time. I'd have thought that sleep wouldn't be easy under such stressful circumstances, but it had been a full day, so I drifted off soon after I lay down. I felt like I'd barely closed my eyes before there was a soft knock at my door. I was still sitting up, blinking awake, when the door opened and Elinor slipped into my room.

"Let's get you ready," she said. "That dress should do.

I'd recommend a second pair of wool stockings, since you may be outdoors."

Now fully awake, I got up and followed her instructions, putting on extra stockings and a woolen petticoat under the dress I already wore. Elinor handed me a little bundle. "Something to sustain you along the way," she said. I added that to my satchel.

I pulled on my boots, which had been dried and polished after my earlier jaunts in the snow, and Elinor helped me with my coat. When I had my hat and gloves on, she gave me a long, appraising look before nodding and saying, "Well, I suppose I have to send you off."

She picked up the larger bag, opened the door, and glanced up and down the hall before signaling to me. I put the strap of my smaller bag over my shoulder so that it hung across my body and followed her. I was surprised when she went not to the doorway to the servants' stairs, but to the library down the hall. Once she'd closed the door to that room behind us, she pulled on a sconce beside the fireplace, and a panel moved aside. "A secret passage?" I asked. "Does *every* magister house have one?"

"Apparently Henry's grandfather, who built this place, had a strict wife and a taste for horse races and card games. He liked to be able to get in and out without his wife knowing he'd left the house, so he had a passage built into his library. She never opened a book if she could help it, so she assumed he was in here reading all day. I don't know how many homes have them, but we magisters do seem to have a tendency to lead secret lives." She formed a soft globe of magical light and sent it ahead of us down the passage.

We reached a steep spiral staircase so narrow that I could brace myself with my hands on either side as we went down, and I had to do so, for there was no railing. Elinor navigated it with grace and ease, in spite of carrying the heavy bag. At the bottom of the stairs was a long tunnel that I was fairly certain went beyond the walls of the house. We came to a short flight of steps with a door at the top. Elinor dropped the large bag at the foot of the stairs, and when we climbed the stairs and opened the door, I saw that we were just outside the kitchen yard, where we couldn't be easily seen from the house.

Elinor pulled me to her in one last embrace. "Oh, I hate to see you go, little sister. I wish I could go with you. Do you think you can find this spot again?"

I nodded, fighting back tears. "I believe so."

"Then you saw where I dropped your bag. It will be there for you if you have the opportunity to come back here. Now, go and change the world, but be as safe as you can. Give my love to Henry."

"I hope this isn't farewell forever," I said, returning her embrace. "Keep an eye on Flora. She's developed revolutionary tendencies, herself."

"Why do you think I wanted her out of the city at this time? It will be harder for her to run away and join you from out here."

Someone nearby whistled "Yankee Doodle" very softly. This was it. One last hug with Elinor, and then I went out to meet my contact.

At first, I didn't see anyone, but then I made out a shadowy figure just around the corner from the stables. When I drew closer, I recognized Henry and barely stopped myself from crying out in delight. "You?" I whispered when we fell into each other's arms.

"I know this estate better than anyone, so who else? Now, we need to get down the hill."

"To the station?"

"To the river. Do you trust me?"

"Of course I do."

"Good. Because the next few minutes are going to be rather, well, let's just say exhilarating." He picked up an object that had been leaning against the stable wall. "Fortunately, my old sled was still here."

"We're going to sled down that hill?" I recalled how steep it was, how many switchbacks it had taken to get to the house from the station.

"Don't worry, I've done this hundreds of times. I may have to adjust for my current weight and you as a passenger, but I've ridden double on this hill before. You're in good hands."

"You also have a tendency toward reckless endangerment," I reminded him. But I still followed him to the very edge of the hill, where he put down the sled and gestured for me to sit. He sat behind me, his legs on either side of me. His feet rested on a steering bar at the foot of the sled. He pushed off with his hands, then wrapped his arms around me.

We moved slowly at first, picking up speed as we went down the hill. We went at an angle, so we weren't going straight down the steep slope. Under other circumstances, and perhaps in daylight, it might have been exciting. In the darkness, it felt like we were plunging into a bottomless pit. I bit my lip to stop myself from screaming.

"Lean left," Henry ordered into my ear, and I felt him shift his weight. I joined him, and the sled swung around a corner as he straightened one leg to move the steering bar. We continued down the slope, moving at a different angle. The next time, we leaned right. Before I knew it, we were approaching the rail platform. Henry straightened both legs, braking the sled, and we came to a stop just short of the tracks.

Henry released his hold on me and stood, then bent to take my hands and pull me to my feet. My legs were still shaking so badly I wasn't sure they'd have supported me if Henry hadn't put his arm around me to steady me. "We'll have to do that again sometime in better conditions," he said. "It really is quite fun."

"I think the next time might be fun, now that I know what to expect," I said. "I've never been sledding before."

"Then we'll definitely do it again."

"After we change the world."

"Well, now we have additional motivation. Can you walk?"

"I think so." I did feel a little steadier. He glanced up and down the tracks before leading me across them to a jetty where the strangest boat I'd ever seen was docked.

It had a large smokestack in the middle and something that looked like a mill wheel on either side. "A steam-powered boat?" I asked as we walked up the gangplank.

The man who met us on board must have heard me, for he said, "You think the teakettles are only good for land? We can get you to the city almost as fast as the train. Welcome aboard, Miss Liberty." When he smiled, his teeth showed very white against his dark skin. He wore what must have been the coat from a Royal Navy uniform, with epaulettes and braid, but with all the insignia removed. It fit him so well that it had to have belonged to him. At least one military man had changed sides somewhere along the way, it seemed.

"How have I never heard of such a thing?" I said. "Surely people would have talked about a boat powered by steam."

"Let's just say we've been away from Imperial influence. Now, let's get you to the cabin. It's warm in there."

And it was. The cabin was built alongside the smokestack, which warmed the small structure so well that I had to unbutton my coat. There were other people already in there, seated on rows of benches. Some of them were dressed like Mechanics, but there were a few who appeared to be members of Iroquois tribes, and one or two looked like they might be magister landowners, or possibly sons of landowners. We made for a very unlikely group.

The cabin was well-lit, and I thought it a good opportunity to study Elinor's plans. I got her diagram out of my bag and spread it out on my lap.

"What's that?" Henry asked, leaning to read over my shoulder.

"Apparently, the governor's mansion is riddled with secret passages."

"That would explain how Elinor managed to be so active while being an invalid."

"She thought this might be useful for me to get in and out."

He leaned closer. "Very likely. In fact, it improves our chances significantly."

I turned to look at him. "*Our* chances?"

"You don't think I'd let you go alone, do you? And how did you think you were going to get there?"

"I assumed the rebels had a plan."

"I'm that plan. Don't worry, you're in excellent hands. I've made it in and out of that mansion before—and not just as an invited guest. I also grew up visiting the mansion and the area around it. You won't find a better guide, short of Elinor herself."

We spent much of the journey memorizing the passages as well as we could and discussing which routes would likely be best. "I like that we can get in from outside the walls," he said, "or should we save that for escape?"

"You don't think we can get in and out the same way?"

"It seldom works out that well, I'm afraid. I always like to have at least three escape routes planned." He pointed to the diagram. "Here, there's the basement passage, then I know it's possible to climb down from the study window. And, if all else fails, there's the roof."

"That doesn't seem like a way to escape. You'd be trapped there."

"No, look at this—she seems to have marked a way down the wall here, and there's a tree nearby."

"I think I like the basement passage best," I said with a shudder.

He pointed to the code on the bottom. "What's this?"

"She said she has a telegraph connection in her room, and we should send this message after we complete the mission. I don't know what it says."

"Probably just an acknowledgment that the mission was completed. It seems she thought of everything."

I almost said that we could hardly expect her to send her little sister on a dangerous mission without taking care of the details, but then I remembered that he probably didn't know, and I didn't want to discuss it with him in this setting. I wasn't sure I wanted to tell him at all. What would he think?

We made several stops along the way, and the cabin grew full. Henry got up to give his seat to a woman, and I joined him out on the deck. The brisk, cold air felt refreshing after the close confines of the cabin. We stood by the railing, and he put his arm around me. I leaned against him. "In addition to sledding, I would like to take a river excursion under happier conditions," I said.

"That would be nice, wouldn't it?"

All lights on the deck were suddenly put out, and the boat slowed. Several small rowboats were lowered over the side, and a group of men climbed down into them, then began rowing toward the shore. There were no lights visible from the river, so it was difficult to tell exactly where we were. I asked Henry, and he pointed to the top of a steep hill looming over the river. "That's where the governor's manor is," he whispered. "There's a fort nearby. I imagine we're putting people in place there, probably joining others."

"And to think, that's where we'll be soon," I said, trying to envision it.

The boat resumed normal running and relit the lights after we'd drifted downstream for a few minutes. It was some time later before we reached the city itself. The Assembly Hall was at the lower end of the island, so we still had quite a distance to travel. From this vantage point, the city looked serene. The lack of power was obvious. In a reversal from the way things normally were, it was the poorer neighborhoods that still used gaslights that were lit, while the wealthy neighborhoods were darker.

We were still fairly far uptown when the boat pulled

up against a dock and some of the passengers got off. "It's easier to be unobtrusive when we don't arrive in a great mass," Henry explained. We made several more stops, letting off more passengers, before we began to round the southern tip of the island.

We came up behind the West Battery fort, dousing the lights and going silent once more. The crew used long barge poles to guide us to the dock behind the port, and I barely swallowed a yelp of terror when I saw uniformed soldiers meeting us there. But then some of the passengers jumped off onto the dock and greeted the soldiers like allies. "There are about two dozen of us," one of the soldiers said. "Maybe not enough to make a big difference, but it may help when we switch. We won't do so until the clash happens."

One of the rebels handed him a bundle. "Pass these out to your comrades. It'll help us know we can trust you."

"Are you sure you've got enough people here?" one of the soldiers asked.

"There will be more coming," the rebel said.

"We'll signal when we're called out," the soldier said.

"Well, it seems that someone at the fort read our pamphlets," I said to Henry as the rebels finished unloading people and an alarming number of weapons.

We resumed our journey, having to pause for several minutes near a wharf on the lower eastern side of the island while another steamboat unloaded. We pulled into the slip after that boat left. "This is us," Henry said while the crew lowered the gangplank, as though we'd merely reached our station on a train. Most of the remaining passengers disembarked there. Henry went back to the cabin and came out, pulling the strap of a leather school satchel over his head.

"You know how to send up the alarm if you need us," the captain informed the departing rebels. "We're getting a blockade going in the harbor, so we'll be close by." I peered out across the water and noticed the number of dark shapes sitting between us and the larger fort on the nearby island. The boat that had just left joined them.

The area around the dock was already full of people who'd come off the earlier boat. All of us were divided into groups, with at least one magister in each group to provide magical cover, light, or defense, as needed. I was glad that my abilities weren't known, so I could stay with Henry.

When we reached our designated group, someone said, "Why, if it isn't our friend, Miss Newton." I turned to see a ridiculously handsome man wearing a large and ornate Rebel Mechanics emblem on his lapel.

"Hello, Adonis," I said, recognizing him from the Boston branch of the Rebel Mechanics. I supposed Henry had been assigned to that group because he was probably the only magister they were willing to trust. "You've come all the way from Boston for this?"

"This is where the action is, and you might need Athena's little toy." He motioned to the right. I followed his gesture to see a stately woman standing by a wagon with a shrouded object in it. I shuddered at the memory of what that device could do. It interrupted magisters' ability to manipulate the ether, and the sensation was so unpleasant that it not only kept them from using their magic, it also interfered with their ability to do much of anything. "Just in case there are any barriers we need to get past. Athena's also part of the Massachusetts colony's delegation."

We left the seaport in small groups, moving stealthily down the quiet city streets. Our group had to move more slowly because of the device on its hand-pulled wagon. It seemed to me to make a terrible racket on the cobblestone street. I was certain it would draw attention from a watchman or someone who would sound the alarm.

Because I was so tense, I was acutely aware of my surroundings and heard the sound of wheels approaching before the others, who were busy pushing and pulling the device, did. I held up a hand, gesturing for stillness and silence. A carriage was coming around the corner, probably a magical one, since I didn't hear any hoofbeats. The light from its headlamps hit us before the carriage made it around the corner. Henry stepped forward, ready to act.

The carriage was a small, open-topped roadster, and I went weak with relief when I realized that Philip and Geoffrey were the ones driving it, though it wasn't their usual carriage. "Sorry we're a bit behind schedule," Philip said. "Didn't mean to startle you."

"Did you have any trouble getting her out of the garage?" Henry asked.

"Not at all," Philip replied. "It's not too difficult to steal a carriage from an unoccupied house when you have the key." To the Mechanics, he said, "You can hitch your wagon to the rear bumper, and some of you can climb on board, if you like."

The Mechanics followed his instructions in hitching the wagon, but they eyed the carriage with suspicion. "They're on our side, or they wouldn't be here," I snapped, exasperated. I'd have climbed into the vehicle if I hadn't wanted to stay with Henry, and I knew he needed to stay with the rest of the group.

After what felt like a long hesitation, Athena stepped forward and got into the backseat, turning so she could watch the wagon. Adonis joined her, and the carriage moved off. The rest of us followed more slowly, keeping to the shadows and watching for signs of anyone who might hinder us.

Fortunately, we didn't encounter any reason to use Henry's magic. If I hadn't known better, I'd have thought our group were the only people out and about. I didn't even see signs of other rebels. Were their magisters hiding them?

I began noticing other rebels when we were several blocks away from the Assembly Hall. With that many people converging, the surrounding streets and alleys were starting to fill up. There were pushcarts, carriages, and an omnibus or two on nearby streets, ready to be pushed into service as barricades. We stopped where we had a view of the massive Grecian columns at the front of the building.

We caught up with the roadster on the edge of the crowd, and the Mechanics went to work disconnecting the wagon from the carriage. "You remember where to leave her?" Henry asked his friends.

"We do," Geoffrey said. "And we checked on the way down to make sure that area was clear. We'll go there now." Once the wagon with Athena's device was free, Philip drove off.

"I see you arranged for transportation," I remarked to Henry.

"I thought that would be sensible. We won't have that far to go to reach the newspaper, but it will go much faster on wheels than on foot."

A tall man in a top hat with a giant gear pinned to it came toward us. That had to be Colin. Henry and I hurried to meet him. "Is that the thing?" he asked, glancing at the wagon.

"Yes. Is there a magical barrier?" Henry asked.

"All I know is, we can't seem to get through."

Athena joined us. "Then this should take care of it for you," she said in her soft, melodic accent. She hailed from one of the African colonies. "And once you're inside, it will allow us to shut them out. It just won't be pleasant for any magisters while it's working."

Colin smirked and said, "I would say that doesn't

bother me a bit, but that would be rather ungrateful of me, wouldn't it? Looks like we'll need a few strong backs to get it up the stairs." He raised his hand high above his head and waved. Several Mechanics ran toward us and joined the Boston group in pulling the wagon toward the stairs.

Colin turned to me. "Are you ready to record the occasion for us, Liberty Jones?"

"My notebook is ready," I said with a firm nod.

"This is it, then," Colin said, looking uncharacteristically grim. "We've got supplies staged to go in. They're planning on a weeklong siege. Meanwhile, the delegates and witnesses will go, nonmagisters first. Once we're sure the place is secure, the magister delegates can join us before we let the barrier go up again."

Henry nodded in agreement. "Magisters won't be of much use once that thing is going."

Colin continued laying out the plan. "Then we'll fill in the block, surrounding the hall, with barricades on the ends."

"Our allies at the fort are supposed to let us know when any troops leave the fort," Henry said.

"Let's just hope they really are allies," Colin said, then he glanced at me and grinned. "But how could they not be after reading those brilliant pamphlets? And now I suppose it's time."

He ran to the top of the steps in front of the hall, waved a red scarf in the air, and gave a short, sharp whistle that sounded like one of the Mechanics' steam engines. The revolution had begun.

It was torture having to stand back and watch while a swarm of Rebel Mechanics ran up the steps with the device in their midst. Even from a safe distance, I felt it when the device was activated. I was better able to deal with it now that I was accustomed to its effects, but I still had that moment of feeling frozen.

Once the magical barrier dropped, Colin gave a whistle, and about fifty people came running out of the nearby streets and alleys toward the Assembly Hall. At the top of the stairs, bundles and casks were pushed inside the barrier. We headed up the stairs when we had adjusted to the feeling of the device, and other magisters trailed us. My first experience with that device had been paralyzing, so I understood why they weren't moving very quickly.

I glanced over my shoulder when we reached the top of the steps, and I saw more and more people spilling into the street and staying there, creating a human wall, with the pushcarts, carriages, and omnibuses as barricades in front of them. Then we were past the barrier and into the building, and I felt a great sense of relief when Athena deactivated her device.

The crowd of rebels filled the Assembly Hall's central chamber, a great circular space ringed with columns and topped by a dome. During the daytime, the sun coming through the windows above would light the chamber. Tonight, there were lanterns among the crowd and, now that the magical disruptor had been deactivated, a few large balls of magical light hovered over our heads. Baron Pierce climbed up to the podium where the governor presided over meetings and raised his hands, signaling for silence.

I got out my notebook and a pencil, and Henry pulled a sketchpad and pencil out of his satchel. We moved to the front, Colin clearing the way for us, saying, "Make way for Liberty Jones." We sat in the front row of the desks the assemblymen used during their sessions.

The baron studied the assembled crowd of magisters, Mechanics, and other citizens, and cried out, "The governor disbanded the elected Assembly of these colonies." His voice rang through the space, every word precise. "We, the people of the colonies, from north to south, now assemble here to declare our own government, independent of the tyranny of the British Empire. Ladies and gentlemen, I hereby declare the formation of the new nation of America!"

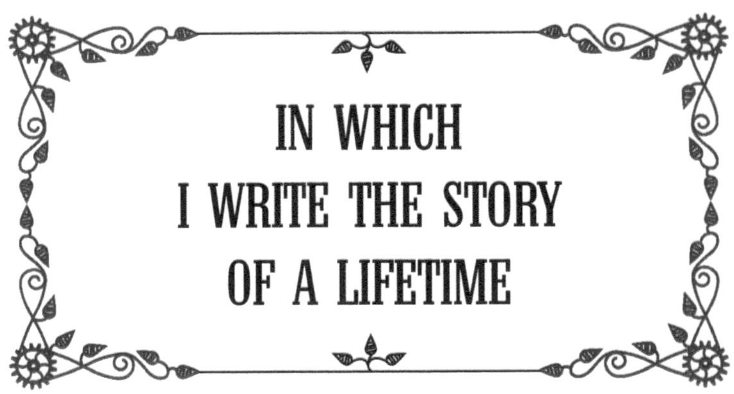

IN WHICH I WRITE THE STORY OF A LIFETIME

I knew I was witnessing history, but there was no time to revel in the moment. I had to record it. I scribbled the words of the baron's speech and made notes on the reaction of the assembled crowd. He read a declaration of independence outlining the reasons the colonies were separating from the Empire, and if I hadn't been so busy taking notes, I'd have been pleased by how much of it echoed the pamphlets I'd written, though in more formal language. The new nation would acknowledge no titles of nobility and make no distinction between magisters and others. People would be free to associate with anyone they chose. All adults, male and female, would have the right to vote, whether or not they owned property.

"Do you accept this declaration?" the baron asked.

"Will the delegates from each of the colonies come forward to state their position and sign this declaration?"

Each group of delegates contained at least one magister—often a former assemblyman from that colony—and someone from one of the other classes. After a short speech expressing their reasons for supporting the declaration, they signed copies of the document.

It was a long, slow process that seemed to take hours. By the time the delegation from Virginia went to the podium, my hand was cramping from taking so many notes. Instead of joining in the applause when the declaration was finalized, I finished my last notes, then stretched my fingers. Glancing over at Henry, I noticed him furiously sketching. There were magical ways to capture images, but I doubted the rebel newspaper had the ability to print them.

While the hall was still ringing with cheers, Colin approached me. "How quickly do you think you can write your article?"

"Half an hour, maybe?"

"It doesn't have to be perfect. It merely needs to capture the moment."

"Yes, and that may take half an hour." I reviewed my notes, shook my hand and stretched my fingers again, then picked up my pen and began writing, trying to shut out the chaos around me. When I finished a draft, I looked up to find Henry standing over me. "Are you ready?"

"I have a draft that will have to do." I put the article

and writing instruments into my bag before putting the strap over my shoulder.

Baron Pierce—I supposed he was Mr. Pierce now—approached us with a cylindrical cardboard tube that had a strap attached to either end. He handed the tube to Henry, who slung it over his shoulder with his satchel. "The newspaper people will want to print a copy of the declaration, and then you'll take it to the governor. We'll put the news out on the ether at noon. I hope you'll have reached the governor by then." Turning to me, he added, "And may God go with you. I hope this isn't a final farewell and that we meet again soon, but I know you're putting yourselves at a great deal of risk with this undertaking."

"We're already outlaws, just from being here," Henry said. "We're not adding much risk by leaving. You're the ones about to be surrounded by enemy forces." He smiled, but his eyes were serious.

A sound like a single loud gunshot startled all of us. We raced to the front windows to see what was happening. A rocket rose into the sky in the near distance, bursting above the lower end of the island. "That must be the signal from the fort that the soldiers are coming," I said to Henry.

"I'm afraid so. This is earlier than we expected the authorities to move in."

"You can hardly fill a whole part of town with people and put up barricades without someone noticing," I said, trying to sound a lot more calm than I felt. How would we get away from here? Were we trapped?

Colin joined us. "We'd better get you out while we still can, and we need to see what Lizzie has for you to deliver. She's reporting on the outside events." To Henry, he added, "Are you armed?"

Henry patted his hip. "And yes, I know how to use it."

"Of course you do. You're a rather successful bandit."

"Who has a bad habit of getting shot," I couldn't resist adding.

Henry gave me a rueful grin. "Well, at least I'm with someone who has experience with that sort of thing."

"You didn't tell me to bring a medical kit." Actually, I should have thought of that, but I hadn't known Henry would be my escort.

"You set up transportation?" Colin asked.

"I made arrangements. The hard part will be getting there."

The two men kept me between them as we left the building. I could tell where the magical barrier was because that was where the wall of people ended. It was a one-way barrier designed to keep people out rather than in, so we were able to pass through without needing to activate Athena's device, much to my relief. "You'll be stuck outside now," I said to Colin.

"Where I'd rather be. I was only in there to escort you two out. There are too many politicians in there for my liking, and I suspect the troops out here will need rallying."

The number of people truly was astonishing. We were only able to get through the mass of humanity on the steps because of Colin shouting, "Make way! Liberty Jones coming through to get the story out!" I was a little astonished when people cheered my passage. I raised a hand to wave, feeling like I was playing a role.

At the foot of the steps, Colin guided us to the left down Wall Street. We froze and ducked when we heard gunfire. Henry pulled me against him, sheltering me under his arm. "They're coming up from the fort, sounds like," Colin said. "We'd better hurry before they can get here."

An omnibus had been pulled across the street just before the next intersection, blocking off the street. On top of and around it were masses of rebels, most of them armed. Even the ones who weren't wearing Rebel Mechanics insignia wore red armbands. Some of the better-dressed people also wore blue ribbons and armbands. A few had wound the red and blue together, in a sign of unity.

"What's the situation?" Colin asked the apparent leader at the barricade. "We've heard gunfire."

"We're surrounded. Not in great force, but they are out there, and more seem to be on the way. We've got police on this end. Come take a look." Colin gestured for Henry and me to stay where we were while he climbed on board the bus to look through the windows.

Colin returned, shaking his head. "There are just a few of them, not a real threat, but that's not the problem. It's a no-man's-land out there between us and them. There's no way you could cross it without being seen. I doubt they'd shoot you two on sight, since you don't exactly look like dangerous rebels, but they'd surely apprehend you."

"We'll have to get out some other way," I said.

"No good," the rebel leader said. "It's like that all around. We could probably take them down, as few as they are, but we've been ordered to avoid bloodshed. They have to shoot first."

"They *are* shooting," I said. "We just heard gunfire."

"That's at the fort," the leader said. "As soon as the troops headed to us, our people were to attack and take the fort. I imagine that'll provide a bit of a diversion soon enough, but it won't help with the police we've got here."

"I have an idea," Henry said, with a gleam in his eye that worried me. "The problem is the no-man's-land, where we'd be clearly visible, right?"

"Can you do an invisibility spell?" Colin asked.

"Not quite. I can blend into shadows a little better than most people can do without magic, and that might be useful, but I don't think even that would allow us to cross that space without being seen. But what if the space weren't there?"

"You mean, attack them?" the leader asked.

"Not really. Just surge forward enough to meet them, even surround them. Eliminate the space, divert their attention, and in the chaos we can be part of the swarm that goes around them. Once we're around the corner, I can blend us into the shadows until we reach our transportation."

"It could work," the leader said. "But us surging at them could be what starts the shooting war."

"There's going to be a war anyway," Colin said. "But the revolution might end if we don't get these two out with the declaration and the news."

The leader turned and sketched out a map in the grime on a bus window. "Here we are, here they are. We'll surge forward all the way across the street to give you cover, but we'll make the most noise over here to draw them away." He pointed to the far side of the map, on the opposite side of the street. "You get around the corner to William Street, then I'd suggest you get off onto the next side street or alley that's passable. We'll try to give you five minutes before we withdraw, but if shooting starts, we may not be able to hold out so long. You'll have to run." He raised his voice and called out, "I need my magpies."

I was surprised to see Philip and Geoffrey join us. They both wore the entwined blue and red armbands. "We need a diversion," Henry said to them. "Something attention-getting, but not dangerous."

"I would suggest that Colin sing," Philip said with a grin, "but you said not dangerous." Even Colin laughed, and I felt some of the tension ease. More seriously, Philip added, "I think I have some ideas."

"Just give us the chance to get away from here," Henry said.

"If you've got the diversion taken care of, I believe we have a plan," Colin said, brushing his hands together with satisfaction. "Now, where's that sister of mine? She's supposed to have a story for you."

"Don't tell me you've been so busy you didn't notice me," Lizzie said from behind him.

He whirled to see her. "And don't you go pretending you've been there all along. I'm not *that* oblivious."

Ignoring him, she came up to me and handed me a folded sheaf of papers. "Here's my story on the standoff, so far. I wish I could report that we've successfully taken the fort, but it's hard to tell from here. Apologies if my handwriting isn't the best. If you think you can make it better as they typeset it, then do so."

I put her article into my bag. "I'm sure it will be fine," I said. "A little rawness will carry the urgency of the situation."

She smiled at me, then abruptly reached out and grabbed me into a big hug. "You take care of yourself, Verity," she said.

"Everyone's acting like we're going on a suicide mission," I said, trying to sound flippant. Though, I supposed, to them, that's what it was. They didn't know why I'd been selected, so they must have thought I was making a great sacrifice.

"I wouldn't trade places with you for anything," she said. "Though I would like to see the governor's face when he reads the declaration."

"I'll do my best to sketch it," Henry said.

"I want to see that sketch, so you'd best get away safely."

When she was gone, Philip clasped Henry's arm. "I left your roadster where we agreed," he said. "Let's just hope it's not surrounded by soldiers."

"Would they really waste men on that?" Henry asked.

"We *are* talking about the colonial government," Geoffrey said dryly. "It doesn't have to make sense." He patted Henry on the shoulder and nodded to me before heading over to where they were to create the diversion.

Colin and the leader went up and down the line, briefing their people. A group of rebels got ready to run through the door on the opposite side of the bus, while others scrambled under the bus or climbed to the roof. The rest massed on either end of their barricade. Henry and I made sure our bags and the case carrying the declaration were secure, then he locked his arm tight around mine so we couldn't be separated. "This will probably be the hardest part of the mission—until maybe the end," he said with an attempt at a grin.

I didn't get a chance to reply before there was a loud noise and bright light, seemingly coming from a window in the building on the opposite side of the street. I couldn't see through the mob to tell how the policemen reacted, but the clump of people we were in surged forward, bearing us with them. We were near the far edge, so we could see the sidewalk and could tell where the intersection began.

We had to fight against the current to move around the corner and up the adjacent street, but suddenly we were in the clear, with the crowd behind us. "Run!" Henry ordered.

We sprinted up the street, still arm in arm. With my free hand, I held up my skirts so my legs wouldn't get tangled in them. My bag bounced against my hip as I ran, and I was sure I'd have bruises there later. The noise behind us was unsettling, with shouts and the occasional bang rising above a dull roar, but I didn't dare look back.

We reached the next intersection and veered around the corner, only to find ourselves face-to-face with an armed man. "Stop right there!" he called out.

"You idiot, we're on your side," Henry shouted as we stopped abruptly. I saw then that the man wore a red armband.

"Oh yeah?" the man challenged.

"I'm Liberty Jones, getting the story out," I snapped, short-tempered in these dire circumstances. I hoped my alter ego had some sway with a rebel. "Now, if you don't mind, I'm in a bit of a hurry if we're to make it to press on time."

Much to my relief, he lowered his weapon and stepped back, letting us go. We resumed running, turning uptown at the next intersection. I wasn't sure how long it had been since we left the barricade, but I thought it might have been time for the rebels to pull back. I hoped they could, that the skirmish they'd started to cover our departure hadn't been what started a real battle. I didn't hear the kind of gunfire that would indicate fighting.

I was running out of breath when Henry slowed to a walk. Ahead of us, I saw his roadster parked at the end of the block, and it didn't appear to be guarded. "Oh, thank goodness," I said, each word coming out between gasps for breath. "I'm not accustomed to so much running."

"There will likely be a great deal of running this morning," Henry said as he helped me into the passenger seat. He handed me his satchel and the declaration before he went around to the other side and took the driver's seat. The carriage moved quietly out onto the street.

Although it was nice to ride instead of running, I now felt very exposed. There was no place for us to hide. The city was beginning to wake, but ours was the only self-propelled magical vehicle in sight. Nothing about us would suggest that we were with the revolutionaries, but we were hardly inconspicuous.

It wasn't a very long drive to the printer, which was housed in a nondescript warehouse behind the offices of the government-approved newspaper. Henry parked down the block, so it wouldn't be quite so obvious where we were going, and we took a roundabout route from the roadster to the printer to ensure we hadn't been followed before Henry knocked on the door.

"Who is it?" a voice from within said.

"Liberty Jones with a story for you," I replied.

The door was flung open, and a large man in shirtsleeves and suspenders greeted me like I was a long-lost family member. "Why, Liberty herself! It's good to meet you in person at last. "I'm Melvin Brewster, the editor. Come in, come in. Have a seat. Would you like some coffee?"

The building he ushered us into was bright, hot, and noisy. The presses made a clanging, thumping sound that shook the floor. The room smelled of hot metal, ink, and sweat. I took the articles out of my bag and handed them to Brewster. "Here's my article about the declaration, as well as Lizzie's story on what's happening outside."

"I've got sketches of the events," Henry added, handing over his sketchbook, "as well as a copy of the declaration."

"You know how to work with them to make plates of the sketches?" Brewster asked Henry.

"Somewhat."

"They're over that way." Henry took his sketches and hurried in the direction Brewster indicated. Brewster turned to me. "I've had a draft of the declaration typeset. Can you check it against the final thing for me? Then we'll make a plate of the signatures. Meanwhile, I'll get these stories typeset."

He sat me down at a long table with a sheet of newsprint. I removed the declaration from its case and unrolled it, careful to keep it away from the damp ink. I had marked the few changes between the printing and the signed document by the time Brewster returned to me. "Hey, you work fast," he said. "Do you want to come work for me, full-time?"

"I don't know how possible that will be after today," I said. "I may become a fugitive. Then again, I might be in need of employment."

He took the declaration off to make a plate of the

signatures, and now that the first phase of my mission was complete, I realized how exhausted I was. I was nodding off, my chin falling to my chest, when a new smell nearby woke me. I opened my eyes to see Nat standing in front of me, holding a plate of bacon, eggs, and toast in one hand and a mug of coffee in the other. "The boss said to bring this to you," he said, setting them on the table in front of me.

"Oh, thank you," I said. "I'm surprised to see you here instead of where the action is."

"The action for a newsboy's about to come," he said, grinning. "The most important newspaper ever is about to come off the press, and I'm gonna get it out there for everyone to read."

Henry joined me, carrying his own plate and cup. "It looks like we're all set," he said, sitting across from me. "Now they just have to run it off the press."

"Then we should probably go," I said.

"We have time for breakfast. We'll need our energy, I'm sure. And I'd like to have a copy or two with us. I'd like to be able to show the governor what the city's reading."

That was enough of an excuse for a delay for me to allow myself to eat breakfast, guilt-free. I'd have thought I was too tense to eat, but I found that I had plenty of appetite. The coffee also helped revive me. I preferred tea, but rebels were boycotting it because of the tea taxes, so I didn't dare ask for it here. That was one benefit I'd miss from maintaining my cover as a proper governess in a magister home.

Brewster returned to us with the declaration in its case and a couple of freshly printed newspapers. Although I was eager to complete our mission, I had to admit that I was sad to see the papers arrive, for it meant we had to leave this place of refuge to face the unknown again.

"I heard that they've barricaded Canal Street," Brewster said. "It's more likely that they're keeping people from getting downtown, so you might be able to bluff your way through heading uptown, looking respectable as you do."

"I'm rather good at bluffing," Henry said.

"You're a fugitive," I reminded Henry. "I'm not sure trying to bluff would be such a good idea."

"I doubt every police officer and soldier would know me on sight," he said. To Brewster he added, "Do you need us to carry any papers uptown for you?"

"I think you stand a better chance of getting through if you aren't carrying bundles of sedition with you," the editor said with a grin. "My boys have their ways, don't you worry. We'll get the news out."

Henry and I hurried to finish our breakfast, then took a moment to tidy ourselves in the newspaper office's washroom, since looking respectable was our best hope of getting through. My hair had begun falling down, thanks to the sledding and all that running, so I repinned it. When Henry joined me, I saw that he had a fresh shave and a neatly knotted necktie. There was nothing rebellious-looking about us.

It was still quite dark when we went outside, but there

was a little more activity in the city, with a few people heading to work, so we stood out less. When we were in the roadster and Henry had started it, he said, "I think we should head to the west side. That might be our best chance of getting farther uptown. We might be able to pretend to know nothing about what's happening, and it gives us a straighter shot to the governor's mansion."

"You know the city better than I do," I replied. "Do you really think we'll be able to just drive up there?"

"I'd like to drive as far as we can, though we may have to improvise along the way. Fortunately, most of the descriptions of me are quite inaccurate. No one seems to know me without my glasses."

I didn't have a better plan, so I didn't try to argue with him. I wouldn't have thought that a nobleman who lived uptown would be so familiar with this part of the city, but he steered expertly through the odd maze of streets. "Did you spend much time around here?" I asked, hoping conversation might distract me from my anxiety.

"A lot of government and financial offices are around here. I needed to know the getaway routes," he said.

Oddly, that made me feel better. He might have been prone to gunshot wounds, but he had survived quite a while as a bandit. "Who knew that banditry would end up being such a useful skill?" I said, clutching my seat as he turned a sharp corner.

He had to slow down when the traffic ahead became congested. "That must be the roadblock," he said.

"I thought Mr. Brewster said they'd only be checking in one direction."

"They might still slow us down. Don't worry. At least, try not to look worried."

Most of the vehicles ahead of us were horse-drawn, so we stood out in our magical roadster, which looked like the sort of thing a wealthy young nobleman would drive for fun. It did seem that the line was moving, while no vehicles came from the other direction. I held my breath when we reached the police officers. Henry opened his mouth as if to speak, ready to spin a story, but they just waved us past. I forced myself not to sigh in relief, at least, not until we were well away.

"That's probably the hardest one we'll face until we get much farther uptown," Henry said. "They'll assume that if we were trouble, we wouldn't have cleared the other roadblocks."

His confidence was contagious, and I began to let myself believe that we might manage to complete our mission. I didn't allow myself to think about what would happen to us afterward. For now, all I considered was succeeding.

Traffic slowed again, coming to a complete standstill after we'd inched forward for half a block. Henry rose in his seat to try to see ahead, then sat down, shaking his head in frustration. "I can't see what it is."

Ahead of us, people were getting out of their wagons and carriages, which wasn't a good sign. "Stay here, but be ready to act," Henry instructed as he got out of the roadster. I gathered my bag, his satchel, and the declaration's case into my lap with their straps around my arms and waited as he jogged ahead and chatted with the driver in front of us. Apparently, he didn't get much of an answer, for he ran farther ahead, until I could no longer see him.

It was several minutes before I saw him again. He came sprinting down the other side of the row of stopped vehicles, and when he was in sight, he beckoned me to him. Puzzled and alarmed, I made sure I had our possessions and got out of the carriage, awkwardly juggling all the bags. He ran to meet me, taking his satchel and the declaration from me as he said, "They've locked down the city below Fourteenth, and they're inspecting vehicles. We'll need to find another way."

IN WHICH I MUST REVEAL THE TRUTH

We ran back a block before turning off down a side street. There we kept close to the buildings, so we wouldn't be visible to anyone glancing down the street. "Remember what I said about improvising," Henry said with an attempt at a smile.

"Where are we?" The sky was beginning to lighten to a soft gray, but the additional light didn't help me get my bearings.

"The western end of Greenwich Village."

"If we could get to the underground railway, we might stand a chance of getting uptown that way."

"The trick will be getting there, if they've locked down the city."

"Ah, but we're in rebel territory here."

"Exactly why it's locked down."

"Yes, but there's more than one way to get there. Most of the shops won't be open yet, but there's a bakery near the square that should be able to help us."

"The square? That would be this way." He took my hand, and we walked briskly—hurrying, but trying not to look like we were being pursued. I hoped that looking respectable and being on foot would keep us from being stopped by any authorities.

I still felt quite lost, but that was probably because Henry didn't take a direct route. Any time we saw people ahead, we veered onto another street. The farther we went, the more difficult it became to avoid everyone. We had to walk more slowly in order to blend in. There seemed to be police on every corner now, but they made no move as long as groups didn't congregate. The moment they saw more than five people gathering, the police moved to break it up.

My heart pounded as we walked right past a police officer. I kept my eyes down on the ground ahead of me and tried to will him to see me as just another young lady heading to work, escorted by a young man who worked as a clerk in the same office.

I didn't know if I'd actually done anything magical or if he was only concerned with keeping any mobs from forming, but the officer paid us no attention. "Verity, I've lost feeling in my fingers," Henry said, and I realized I'd been clutching his hand desperately.

I eased my grip without letting go. "Oh, I'm sorry."

The walls around here had been plastered with Rebel Mechanics posters and other signs with revolutionary slogans and emblems. This was where the previous uprisings had begun, when the rebels were merely making noise. I wondered how long the police would be able to maintain the peace around here once word that the revolution had actually begun started to spread.

We soon saw that was already happening. A grimy newsboy was busily pasting a copy of the newspaper's special edition to a wall ahead of us. Another ran down the street, pulling folded newspapers from inside his oversized coat and handing them to people as he passed.

"Brewster was right about his boys having their ways," Henry said softly. "How did they get up here without being stopped?"

"They're children," I said. "And they probably went one at a time. One child wouldn't be considered a threat."

Henry glanced down the street to where the newsboy who'd been pasting ran on to another block. "That one child might bring down a government."

The trees of the square—bare for winter—became visible ahead. "It's on the other side of the square," I said.

"I think we should avoid that area," Henry said, his voice tense. I saw what he meant: people were gathering there, defying attempts by the police to break up the crowd. As much as we might agree with them, we couldn't afford to be caught up in whatever happened.

We went up a block before heading across town. I'd never been so glad to see a bakery before in my life when I spied the warm light coming through dusty front windows and smelled the scent of freshly baked bread wafting out onto the sidewalk.

Little bells jingled when Henry opened the door for us. I was dismayed to see a broad, red-faced man at the counter rather than the young woman I normally dealt with. "Can I help you?" the man asked.

"I heard you had some particularly good cinnamon buns here," I said, using the code words for the network. "Have you made any yet this morning?"

His eyes grew more serious, though his smile stayed in place, now looking like a mask. "Let me go check in back. Just one moment."

He disappeared through a swinging door. In spite of the breakfast I'd had at the newspaper, the smell of bread made my mouth water. It couldn't have been an hour since we'd eaten, but it already felt like a lifetime ago.

The baker returned, and I had to fight the urge to sigh in relief when a young woman came with him. She saw me and smiled in recognition. Before she could say anything, though, the door opened, and another customer came in. The young woman said to me, "They'll be out of the oven in just a minute, if you'd care to wait, miss," before she turned to serve the other customer.

He ordered several loaves of bread and some extra rolls. "I heard things are happening out there," he said while the baker gathered his order. "You'd be wise to stock up and then stay indoors."

I tried to look properly dismayed. I supposed it would be frightening if you were an ordinary person who didn't know what might happen and who just wanted to go about your everyday life. We were causing a great disruption, and it would likely only get worse.

Finally, the customer left, and the young woman said, "How can we help you?"

"We need to get to the tunnels. Do you have access?"

"Not from here, I'm afraid. But we're about to deliver our daily order to a restaurant that does have access. Do you mind posing as bakers?"

Henry and I glanced at each other. "I believe we might manage that," he said.

"Come with me, then," she said, motioning for us to come around the counter and follow her into the bakery. She fitted us with white smocks to go over our clothes. I took off my hat and put it in my bag so I could tie a kerchief over my hair, while Henry swapped his bowler hat for a white cloth cap. Since my bag was roomier, I tucked his hat in it.

We laid our bags and the declaration's case in the bottom of a wheelbarrow-like cart, which the baker then loaded with bread. He covered the whole load with a white cloth and guided us back to the front of the shop, where he gave us directions to the restaurant. "You know the passwords?" he asked me, and I nodded. "Then good luck.

You should be safe. No one ever pays attention to us, other than to get hungry."

Henry took up the cart's handles, and I helped him get it through the door, then I walked alongside it, steadying the load when he had to steer around piles of grimy snow that had been cleared from the street. We passed a couple of police officers, who didn't give us a second glance. They were too busy hurrying toward the square. Fortunately for us, the gathering was diverting all the authorities, making our passage a little easier.

The restaurant wasn't yet open, but the staff was already there, getting set up for the day. The chef who unlocked the door for us gave us a funny look. "I haven't seen you before," he said.

"There have been unusual circumstances," I said. "And did you order any cinnamon buns this morning?"

He hurried us into the restaurant and shut and locked the door behind us. "You need to get into the tunnels?"

"Yes, please," Henry said.

"Tell me, what's happening? Something's happening, isn't it?"

"We've declared independence for a new nation," Henry said. "Now we have to get that message to the governor."

The chef gestured for his staff members to come unload the bread. While they did that, we shed our baker disguises, which left behind a dusting of flour on our clothes. When we could reach our belongings in the cart, we picked them up and put on our own hats once more. I handed the chef one of the newspaper copies. "This is what happened," I told him. "And we thank you for your help."

"You're lucky you got away from there," he said as he led us to the back of the restaurant. "And I have a feeling I won't be needing that much bread today. In fact, I won't be surprised if they shut us down. But then I suppose I'll be able to feed my family and staff if things get really bad." He opened the door for us and said, "I'm sorry, I don't have a light I can give you. Do you know the way?"

"I do," I said, hoping it was true. I hadn't used this particular entrance before, but I was fairly certain I knew which of the main tunnels it accessed.

"We can manage without a light," Henry said, somehow keeping a straight face. We didn't use our magic until the door had shut behind us. It was too big a risk that the chef wouldn't have been happy with the idea of helping magisters. That was something we'd have to work on in our new nation.

I was greatly relieved when we reached the main tunnel and I recognized where I was. We still had a fairly long walk to reach the station, but at least down here we didn't have to worry about being stopped by the police or by soldiers—and if we did, it would mean things had gone horribly wrong. I only hoped that the railway was still operating. Surely the Mechanics would have left someone behind to maintain their operation.

"You've certainly been busy," Henry remarked as we walked.

"I have my network of contacts," I said. "Remember, it was the laundresses I know who got you out of prison. I think I know half the shopgirls in the city."

"That may be why we succeed. We were worried about fighting the Empire with machines that could beat magic, but the key may be in mobilizing the right people—and those aren't necessarily the people with power. Just think, the greatest Empire on the face of the earth might be toppled by a governess."

"I hardly think I can take all the credit. I came in very late. All I've done is put our sentiments into words and connect the magisters to the Mechanics."

"And that, my dearest Verity, is what may allow us to win."

"If I hadn't been there, they'd have found someone else."

"But that someone else wouldn't have been you." I supposed that was true. How many half-breed daughters of the governor were out there? I knew I should probably tell Henry why I'd been chosen for this mission, but I didn't know quite how to bring it up. I also wasn't sure how he'd take it. I knew he cared about me, and he was good friends with Elinor, so me being the governor's daughter wouldn't necessarily make him turn against me. He also already knew that my parentage was somewhat muddled.

But would the knowledge change anything? I didn't want things to be different between us.

We reached the station and found that the lights were on and the engine running, though there wasn't a car in sight. "We need to go uptown," I told the Mechanic who met us in the station.

"We just sent a load of newspapers uptown, so it'll be maybe half an hour before the car's back. Have a seat."

"A few newsboys was one thing, but how did they get all those newspapers up here when we had to go through so much to get here?" I asked as we sat on one of the wooden benches. It felt good to get off my feet, and I found myself wishing we'd taken a few rolls with us when we left the restaurant.

"He said they had their ways," Henry replied with a shrug.

"Yes, but if they had their ways, couldn't they have helped us?"

"Our presence might have put the newspapers at risk. And, at the time, I'd hoped to make it all the way in the roadster. We didn't plan to end up here."

"This way might be faster in the long run," I said. "There's no traffic to contend with."

"Yes, but we'll still have a long way to go from the last station to the mansion, unless there's another secret railway you haven't told me about yet."

"Maybe we shouldn't go all the way to the last station,"

I said after thinking for a moment. "I doubt Elinor would mind if we used her roadster."

"Brilliant idea, Verity," he said, beaming and throwing his arm around my shoulders to pull me against him. "That might even allow us to approach the mansion."

"They wouldn't recognize it as Elinor's carriage, would they? It's a secret that she has one."

"No, but in that part of the city, anyone who looks prosperous will be much less suspicious-looking."

I forced myself not to constantly check my watch, so it was a pleasant surprise when the pilot car returned, several flatbed cars behind it. The staff in the station got it turned around and reconnected, then filled the flatbed cars with stacks of newspapers. We had to sit on newspapers for the trip, along with a crew of newsboys.

It always astonished me how silent the railway was. Most of the Mechanics' creations were noisy. This one was, as well, since the power was provided by a giant turbine in the main station, but the cars themselves ran on magnetism and electricity provided by the machine, so once we were away from the station, the railway was relatively quiet, aside from the sound of rushing wind as we sped through the tunnels.

I would have liked to go as quickly as possible uptown, but we stopped at every possible station to unload newspapers. Most of the load was gone, though we still had enough to sit on, when we reached our station.

The exit I knew here came up through a florist's shop.

I hoped it would be open this early in the morning—and that my contact here would be at work rather than with the mobs downtown. There was no response to my knock in a particular rhythm on the door leading to that shop, so we hurried back down the tunnel to follow the last load of newspapers out. I thought we'd have been less conspicuous going out into the city through a florist's shop than with a bunch of illegal newspapers, but we didn't seem to have much choice.

This exit turned out to be through the basement stockroom of a small corner grocery store. The newspapers were being taken up through the loading doors in the sidewalk, but we went instead up the stairs into the shop itself. I'd been worried about drawing attention by suddenly appearing from the back, but the shop was such a madhouse that I doubted anyone would notice us. People were frantically clearing the shelves, grabbing any food they could get.

"The news has apparently spread," Henry remarked as he guided us through the mob. We escaped from the shop and hurried around the corner, where we paused to catch our breath.

Henry reached to brush my face with his gloved fingers. "You had some flour on you. How about me?"

I patted at the shoulders of his dark coat, where some flour had settled. "That should do it," I said.

Aside from the panicked buying of groceries, the city seemed much more business-as-usual up here. "One could hardly tell there's a revolution happening," Henry murmured.

"At least they aren't stopping all traffic," I noted as a horse-drawn delivery van went by. "That should make things easier."

"But not for long." I followed his glance to the opposite corner, where a newsboy was doing a brisk business in distributing papers. We watched for a moment, noting the reactions. Some people shouted for joy and ran off excitedly. Others looked terrified. These were the ones who headed straight for the shops.

I took Henry's arm again, and we moved toward the magister district. That was the next place where I expected a checkpoint or roadblock of some kind. They always blocked horse-drawn vehicles from those streets, but would they stop pedestrians, as well, today? Ahead of us, I could see horse-drawn carriages turning before they reached the restricted area, but I didn't see that pedestrians were stopping or turning. I clung more tightly to Henry's arm as we approached the district border and didn't relax my hold until we'd passed it.

"There, that wasn't so bad, was it?" Henry said, as though reading my mind. I noticed the tension ease in him, as well, so he'd been more nervous than he'd let on. "Now, do you remember exactly where Elinor's garage was? We took such a roundabout route away from there, and her driving to get there was so mad that I don't have a good sense of where we were, at all."

"I think I might be able to trace back from the house," I said. "I know about how many blocks we walked in each direction, but shouldn't we try to find it some other way first? We probably don't want to go anywhere near the house, in case it's still being watched. They may be looking for us to head there."

"Is there a point along the way you remember?"

"It was so dark then that nothing looks familiar." I paused, mentally tracing my steps from that night and trying to map my route onto my knowledge of the neighborhood. After checking the nearest street sign, I said, "This way, I think."

When we reached the corner I'd been aiming for, I thought it looked familiar. At least, it was a low half wall with evergreen shrubbery above it. When I saw the uneven patch of sidewalk I'd tripped over that night, I knew I was in the right place. "This is it!" I said. I turned to go back the way Elinor and I had come from, keeping my eyes open for anything I recalled while also paying attention to the way the ground felt beneath my feet.

We were within sight of the alley where I believed the garage to be when a man approached us on the sidewalk. We didn't dare turn down the alley while he could see us, so we kept walking, trying to look like any ordinary couple out for a stroll on a cold December morning with a revolution under way. Well, perhaps we weren't trying to convey that last part, but I feared it was obvious.

We nodded at the man as we passed, but before we'd

taken a few more steps, we heard his voice behind us, calling out, "Henry Lyndon, is that you? I thought you were a wanted man."

Henry flinched, but whispered to me, "Keep walking. Don't react. He's behind us, so pretend you think he's talking to someone else."

The sound of running footsteps approaching us from behind proved that the ploy hadn't worked. The man came around in front of us. "It *is* you, Lyndon, I knew it." He didn't sound pleased to have run across an old friend. If he was pleased about anything, it was his opportunity to bring a fugitive to justice. "What the devil are you doing here? Weren't you arrested for treason?"

"I was arrested, but never charged or tried," Henry said, sounding remarkably calm. Of course, the reason he hadn't been charged or tried was that he'd escaped, but that wasn't public knowledge. I wasn't even sure how this man could have known about the arrest. The governor had kept it very quiet, so only the authorities knew. "I thought it was all cleared up. Now, if you'll excuse me."

The man blocked the sidewalk. He wasn't nearly as tall as Henry, but his shoulders were quite broad. "Wait just a minute," he said. "I don't remember hearing anything about you being cleared. The last notice I saw said that you were still on the top of the wanted list. They've had people watching your house for weeks."

It was just our luck, we'd run into someone who worked

for the government. Now it looked like he wasn't going to let us go without a fight.

"Verity, go," Henry whispered as he unhooked his arm from mine. He took a step away from me and reached inside his coat.

I suddenly realized what he was doing, and if he shot this man, that would make him a fugitive for real, and I wasn't even certain it would count as an act of war. In a blind panic, I summoned all the power I could grab from the surrounding ether and unleashed it at the man, who flew backward, landing about ten feet away on the pavement. He didn't move after that.

"What was that?" Henry asked, grabbing my arm and running with me toward the alley where we believed the garage was.

"I don't know. I just didn't want you to shoot him."

"I wasn't going to shoot him. I was just going to threaten him and leave him tied up somewhere. Believe it or not, I've never actually shot a person before."

I winced. "Oh, dear. Now I've probably fractured his skull."

"At least he likely won't remember encountering us."

"If he's still alive."

Both of us had counted the number of garage doors down the alley on the night of the march and had noted the shape of the windows in the apartment above, so we easily found Elinor's garage. The door was padlocked, and

Henry groaned. "I don't suppose the key she gave you works on this, too."

I examined the lock. "No, it couldn't possibly fit. But don't worry. You just stand so you block the view of me from any of those upper windows behind us." I pulled a couple of pins from my hair. "I got very good at picking locks so I could free you."

This lock was much easier to open than the prison cell had been, and I had it unlocked in seconds. "Impressive," Henry said, raising an eyebrow. He shoved the door aside. "But I would hope Elinor has better security than that. And I hope that whatever she uses doesn't lock us out."

There was a faint shimmer to the air just inside the garage, but we were able to pass through it. The key around my neck seemed to warm slightly as we did so. "Her key did unlock that," I commented.

We got into Elinor's roadster, and before Henry began backing it out, he turned to look at me. "Your part in this is done. You delivered your article. They may not have locked the city down entirely. I can take you to a train station, and you can probably get back to the country estate without anyone realizing you were gone or that you were at all involved. If you just give me Elinor's key and the maps, I can do the rest."

"Do you really think they're letting trains out of the city?"

"From up here? Maybe. Though you might have trouble getting a seat with all the magisters who may soon be fleeing. That's why you should go now, before the word really starts to spread."

I shook my head. "No, it's my mission, too." I didn't know why I was so reluctant to tell him the reason, but it was a fact about myself I was still coming to terms with, so I wasn't ready to share it. I attempted a smile. "Besides, haven't you always wanted me with you when you face him?"

"It's likely to get very dangerous from this point. And difficult. We'll have to get into the mansion, and there's no guarantee that we'll get away. We could spend the whole revolution in prison, and then our whole lives if the revolution fails—that's if they don't execute us."

"I'm aware of that," I snapped. "But trust me, you need me with you. I'm our best chance of this mission succeeding."

"I know you're intrepid, but none of us are *that* essential."

"For this, I might be. I have a better chance of surviving and escaping than you do."

"No offense, Verity, but how can that possibly be? He does seem to approve of you as a governess, but ultimately, that's all you are to him. I've made a career out of escaping from tight situations, and you being with me would decrease my chances of escaping."

I was going to have to tell him, or this argument would never end. "That's not exactly true." I took a deep breath, bracing myself. "You see, I'm his daughter."

IN WHICH I AM REUNITED WITH FAMILY

I wasn't sure how, exactly, I expected him to react, but I didn't anticipate him staring at me for a long moment before roaring in laughter.

"I don't see what's so funny," I said. "Elinor is certain of it, so don't mock me."

"I'm not mocking you," he said when he'd managed to stop laughing. "I'm laughing at myself. I can't believe I didn't see it before. You're the very image of Elinor, and I'll bet that when Olive grows up, she'll look just like you. Now, granted, I've never seen you and Elinor next to each other in good lighting, but I've seen you and Olive together so many times. And there is the way the governor has always seemed so fond of you. He mentions your mother every time he sees you. I should have seen it for myself."

"If it makes you feel better, I didn't figure it out that long ago."

He resumed backing the carriage out of the garage. "Yes, but you can't actually see yourself next to others."

When we were outside, I hopped out to close and lock the door. "I knew my father had to be a magister," I said when I was back in the roadster and we were on our way, "but I never expected it to be that one. Elinor said she always knew something must have happened between him and my mother, and when she was helping review applications for the governess position, she picked mine out. I just don't know why she couldn't have told me sooner."

"Elinor does like her secrets. But it explains why she volunteered you for this mission. He really might be reluctant to do anything to hurt you. Even a hesitation could work to our advantage." He gave me a sidelong glance. "And you might be able to shock him by revealing that you know."

I sighed. "Yes, I suppose so, but it feels rather wrong to do so. I'd be using his feelings as a weapon against him—even more so than I already am. And don't tell me that all's fair in war or that he brought it upon himself by being oppressive."

"Just so long as you keep that in mind."

Henry drove sedately through the magister neighborhood of mansions. Moving so slowly when we had a mission to complete frustrated me, but I knew he was trying to fit in. Tearing furiously through these streets would only make people notice us. This district was still fairly quiet. As Henry had predicted, there seemed to be a few families making hasty exits from the grander mansions. There were lines of carriages in front, with possessions being carried out and loaded onto the carriages.

We reached the upper end of the magister neighborhood and turned west through Harlem, north of the park. It seemed like a normal morning here, and on the last Friday before Christmas, the streets were busy as the shops opened. I grew more and more anxious the slower we had to travel. I knew we didn't have a definite deadline for reaching the governor, other than wanting to reach him before the news went on the ether, but the sooner we got there, the less time he and his people would have to prepare, and the greater the chance that we'd find him still at his mansion.

I noticed a commotion ahead of us and touched Henry's arm to draw his attention to it, in case it was something we needed to avoid. A couple of policemen ran down the sidewalk on the park's border, blowing their whistles furiously. "Relax," Henry told me. "I don't think they're after us."

When we got farther down the street, I saw who they were chasing: a young girl of perhaps eleven, wearing a shabby coat over a faded plaid dress. She ran with her arms crossed over her chest, holding something bulky inside her coat. My first thought was that she must be a shoplifter they'd caught stealing from a store, but then a couple of newspapers fell out from under her coat.

"She's distributing the newspaper!" I told Henry. "We have to help her."

Henry swerved to that side of the street, and I stood up, waving to the newsgirl. "Here! Jump in!" I called out.

She stooped to pick up the papers she'd dropped, darted out into traffic, and dove into the backseat of the roadster. Henry veered away from the park, weaving around wagons and buses, so we could disappear into traffic. I kept watch behind us, but I didn't notice anyone giving chase, and soon I was sure we were completely out of sight of the police who'd been chasing her.

When I felt safe, I turned my attention to the girl, who was just sitting up, still catching her breath. "Boy, you really know how to come to the rescue, Verity," she said.

I stared at her for a long moment, trying to place her, before saying tentatively, "Nat?"

She grinned and pushed her bonnet away from her face—his face? "You are a smart one, aren't you?"

"But you're…"

"A girl. I guess I never told you that 'Nat' was short for Natalie. Most of the time, I'm more likely to be left alone when I'm dressed as a boy. Today, I thought they'd go easier on me if I was a girl. Not too many cops want to be seen beating up a little girl." She snorted. "Shows how much I know. Thanks for the lift, your lordship."

"We don't have lords anymore, haven't you heard?" Henry said. "Is there anyplace you'd like me to take you?"

"Just drop me on the other side of the park. That'll save me some steps."

"Other than being chased by police, how are things going?" Henry asked.

"People sure are interested, I can tell you that much. I know the lady's payin' for the papers to go out for free, but I've made a pretty penny or two today. Not too many people taking my papers are sad to see the news."

"That's good to hear," I said. "It should make it easier to win if most people are behind us."

"You're off to tell the guv'ner?"

"That's our mission," I said.

"How're you gonna get outta there?"

Henry and I exchanged a look. "We probably won't," Henry said. "But we knew that risk. I have a few ideas."

"Maybe I can get you some help."

"That would be nice," I said, though I wasn't sure how much she could do. Then again, this whole affair had hinged on people doing what no one expected them to do.

When we reached Broadway, we dropped off Nat and her newspapers. "Good luck, Verity and Henry!" she said, waving us off. "I'll get you some help!" As we headed uptown, I heard her behind us, shouting, "America declares independence from Britain! Read all about the revolution!"

"Now we're back on track," Henry said. "This is where

I was planning to go in the first place. We merely made a slight detour along the way."

"The scenic route," I said, with an attempt at levity.

He gave me another glance. "How did you feel about what you learned?"

"I was glad, for the most part," I said. "I have a family again. I have a sister and nieces and a nephew. They don't know, of course. I'm not sure I could begin to explain it to them. But *I* know, and it's a comfort. I have to admit, I'm not sure what I think about my father. I haven't seen him since I learned the truth."

"This should be an interesting reunion, then."

We still had a long journey ahead of us, for the governor's mansion was at the very far tip of the island. The area was sparsely populated, almost rural. I thought it was rather apt that the man who ruled the colonies was so removed from most of the citizens, isolated on his estate.

The scruffy farms on the edge of the city gave way to the brick walls and fancy iron gates of the magister noblemen's estates, high on a vantage point that gave them commanding views of the city, the river, and the country beyond the city. I caught a glimpse of turrets and peaked roofs beyond the walls.

There hadn't been much traffic on this road, but what there was began to slow. "Another roadblock?" I mused.

"If news of unrest has made it up here, they may be blocking themselves off from the rabble." He pulled off the main road onto a gravel alley. "And I doubt we'd manage to get through. This is where I'm likely to be recognized. The barn where Elinor said she used to keep her roadster is near here, so we may as well leave it here for her."

"But we're still at least a mile from the governor's manor."

"We'll find another way." He pulled up in front of an old barn in what looked like a cluster of outbuildings on the edge of the estate, possibly where the staff and some tenants lived. "This should be it. Care to pick another lock?"

This lock was a little easier, either because it was larger and older or because I was getting so much practice. Henry drove the carriage inside, gathered our belongings, and locked the door behind us. "Now, we watch for a while," he said. We crouched behind a hedgerow, watching the traffic coming and going. There were no horse-drawn vehicles in this magister district, but a steady stream of large magical carriages came and went. They were commercial vehicles rather than passenger carriages. "Hmm, looks like they're stocking up," Henry said. "Most of these seem to be food deliveries. They're planning to hole up on their estates and hope the unrest doesn't touch them."

One of the vans approached, and Henry said, "Stay here and wait for my signal." Before I could question him or object, he drew his pistol, waited for the van to reach us, jumped up onto the driver's seat, and barked, "Stop now!"

The driver did as he was told, raising his hands. "I don't have any money," he protested. "Just fruits and vegetables."

"I want nothing from you other than a ride. We'll be in the back until after you pass the checkpoint, then you'll let us out. No harm done."

"No harm done," the driver said, his voice shaking.

"I'll have my gun on you from inside, so don't try anything funny."

"No, nothing funny."

"Good. Then this should be a minor inconvenience to you." Henry jumped down and ran to the back, and I left our hiding place to join him, struggling with both bags and the tube. He opened the rear door and helped me up inside a dark space that smelled of earth and onions. Henry made his way forward between crates and knocked on the front wall that was just behind the driver's seat. The van moved forward. "Come up here so we can hide in case they actually search at the checkpoint," Henry said.

I followed his instructions, having to pause and free my skirt a few times when it became snagged on the edge of a crate. "You hijacked him!" I said.

"I was beginning to miss the good old days of banditry," he said with a sigh. "It's nice to see that I haven't lost my touch."

Aside from the musty smell and the darkness, it wasn't a bad way to travel. Before very long, the carriage stopped, and I heard voices outside. Henry and I crouched behind the crates. The driver and whoever was manning the roadblock had a brief conversation about what was being delivered and to whom. A moment later, the inside of the van was flooded with light as the doors opened. Just as quickly, they closed again, and the van moved forward. I let my breath out in a long, slow sigh.

Not long afterward, the van stopped again, and the door opened. "You can come out now," the driver said.

Henry moved toward the door, his gun held ready, and checked outside before beckoning to me. He jumped down and took the bags I passed him, then held a hand out to help me. We were inside the walls of one of the estates. "Thank you for your assistance," Henry said, holstering his weapon.

"Are you with those rebels?" the driver asked, eyeing us suspiciously.

"That we are," Henry said cheerfully. "We're all free people as of today."

"You're making me a lot of money today, though I'm sure it's about to be chaos."

"Just be sure to charge them extra," Henry said with a grin. He turned to me and said, "I know where we are. My brother and I visited here when I was a boy. There's a gate that should get us where we need to go, avoiding that main road."

We both shouldered our bags, then followed a path that wound through the snow-covered gardens and under an arbor twined with vines to the exterior wall. The gate wasn't locked from the inside, and we went through it to find ourselves on a country lane. Ahead of us lay the governor's mansion, looming over the city from its vantage point at the top of a hill. A high stone wall on the other side of the lane circled that estate. We darted across the lane and stayed close against the wall so we wouldn't be visible from the house.

"Our next challenge will be getting inside," Henry said. "I somehow doubt that callers will be admitted past the gate."

"We can try that tunnel that opens on the outside of the wall." I took Elinor's diagram out of my bag, and we leaned over it, our heads together. He looked up and at our surroundings a couple of times, determining our position relative to the map. "It should be this way," he said, pointing down the lane.

Before we went very far, the wall curved away from the lane, and the way became much rockier. It would be more difficult to walk, but we wouldn't be leaving footprints in the snow that could be tracked. Henry took my arm to keep me steady as we climbed the hill, following the wall. As the wall curved around the side of the hill and the river appeared below us, I forced myself not to look down. If I focused on my feet, I felt much safer.

We reached a place where the hill rose sharply from just behind the wall, so the wall seemed to be purely ornamental, a decorative facade to the rock behind it. "The door should be around here," Henry said. "But I don't see anything."

"It's a secret door," I reminded him. I took the key from around my neck and approached the wall. The key grew warmer, and suddenly a keyhole appeared. "There," I said, bending to put the key in the hole. A section of the wall slid aside, revealing a tunnel into the hill. We entered, and the door slid shut behind us, leaving us in darkness.

"We can probably use some magic down here, but we'll have to be careful closer to the house," Henry said, forming a glowing ball above us to light our way.

The tunnel was narrow and damp. We soon reached a steep staircase. Henry sent me up first, and I had to steady myself against the wall with one hand while lifting my skirts out of the way with the other. At the top of the stairs, the tunnel flattened out again for about fifty feet before there was a short flight of stairs with a blank wall at the top.

Henry doused his light, and it took me a few seconds to become accustomed to the darkness. It wasn't totally dark—faint light came from somewhere above us—so we could still see the steps. "Hand me the key," Henry said, pausing at the foot of the stairs. "I think it's best if I open the door to see what's on the other side."

He held the key near the wall, as I had done before, but nothing happened. "They wouldn't have found it and sealed it so soon after Elinor left, would they?" he muttered.

"Perhaps I should try," I said. "It may have something to do with who uses it, and I am family." It had only just then occurred to me that this mansion was part of my heritage. One of my ancestors had built it. I climbed the steps to stand next to Henry. He handed me the key, then placed his hand at the back of my waist to steady me on the slender top step as I held the key near the wall.

As had happened before, a keyhole appeared, and I unlocked the door. This one swung open into yet another passage. Light filtered in from small openings near the ceiling and floor. Henry turned to me and held a finger against his lips. I nodded. If light got through, then sound from the passage might get out.

Henry leaned close, his lips against my ear. "Let's go to the study," he breathed, barely audible even at such close range.

We moved slowly and steadily, trying to make as little noise as possible. One thing in our favor was the fact that there was quite a lot of commotion in the house. There were people shouting and rushing about. We could see their movements in the way their shadows blocked the light coming into the passage.

We reached a ladder in the passage. I was glad to go up first, since it meant Henry was below to catch me if I lost my footing. I couldn't hold up my skirts while climbing, so I had to take care with each step that my foot was clear before I set it on the rung. I was starting to understand why the rebel girls wore such scandalously short dresses, and I vowed to adopt that style if we got away from here to rejoin the rebels. I had to crawl on my hands and knees at the top of the ladder until I was clear of it, which was also challenging in a long skirt. Henry came up quickly enough to be able to lend me a hand standing.

There was a spyhole at the governor's study, and Henry bent to peer through. "He's not there," he whispered. "We should go in and wait for him."

I used the key to open the passage, and we found ourselves in the very room in which I'd verified my theory that Henry was the masked bandit, and where he'd learned about my rebel affiliation. Had that only been a few months ago? The massive desk was more cluttered now than it had been that night. If there were any important communiqués we could take to the rebels, they would be difficult to spot.

But Henry didn't search the desk. He went straight to the cabinet beside it and opened the glass doors, revealing a piece of equipment that had an odd blue glow about it. "What are you doing?" I hissed.

"It's an ether transmitter. I want to see what information he already has." A scroll of paper spooled out of the device, and he bent over it.

While he did that, I tried to brush the dirt off my skirt and scrubbed my face with my handkerchief. I didn't want to face my father under these circumstances while looking like I'd been crawling through tunnels and riding in produce vans. The hem of my skirt was a lost cause after so much walking around in snowy conditions, but I hoped my face was reasonably presentable.

Henry straightened and shut the glass doors. "There's nothing on there specifically about a revolution, just talk of 'social unrest.' He doesn't seem to have sent any messages about it to England. These are just messages from around the colonies about mobs taking over and surrounding government buildings. It doesn't look like he yet knows anything about what's really going on."

I heard heavy footsteps in the hallway outside and moved closer to Henry. "I think he's about to learn," I said softly.

The door opened, but it wasn't the governor. It was Barker, his secretary. When he saw us, he opened his mouth as though to shout an alarm, but froze when Henry drew his pistol and pointed it at him. "You may summon your employer, but I'd request that you do so without raising an alarm," Henry said, sounding like the bandit I'd first met that day on the train.

Barker started to turn away, but Henry shook his head. "No. Don't go anywhere."

"Your Grace? There's something you need to see in your study," Barker called out, his voice shaking slightly.

From down the hallway, I heard the governor's—my father's—voice. "Did something come across the ether?" He reached the study door and Barker stepped aside, moving as though to flee down the hallway. A motion from Henry's pistol persuaded him otherwise.

"Both of you inside, and shut the door," Henry ordered firmly. I was greatly relieved when they did so. I wasn't sure what Henry would have done if they hadn't complied. As he'd said, he'd never actually shot anyone, and I doubted he'd have been able to start with the governor, in spite of their differences.

"What is the meaning of this, Lyndon?" the governor demanded. "And you, Miss Newton, how are you involved? How did you even get in here?"

Now that I looked at him, I recognized features in him that I saw in the mirror. We had the same eyes, and I seemed to have inherited the stubborn set of my chin from him. Strangely, this gave me a boost of confidence in facing him. I took the cylindrical case from over Henry's shoulder, opened it, and handed the rolled-up declaration to the governor, along with a copy of the newspaper that I took from my bag. "The American colonies have declared themselves to be a sovereign nation," I said. "We no longer recognize British rule or the representatives of that rule. We mean you no harm, but you have been stripped of all titles granted by the crown, and we recognize no ancestral titles on these shores. You are free to renounce your allegiance to Britain and become a citizen of this new nation, or you will be allowed to leave. You won't be allowed any authority."

"That is preposterous," he sputtered, but he unrolled and read the document.

"There doesn't have to be bloodshed," Henry added. "You can withdraw your troops and allow a peaceful transfer of power. Our people hold the Assembly Hall, where our representatives from throughout the colonies are meeting. Similar takeovers are happening in all of the individual colonies."

"How did you get caught up in such a scheme, Miss Newton?" the governor asked.

"I looked at what was happening and knew it was the right thing to do," I said. "It's also the only chance I have to live a normal life, openly being who I am. As you should know, Father." I'd been doing so well at remaining calm, but my voice shook on that last word.

He gazed at me, his eyes filling with tears. That wasn't the reaction I'd expected. "So, you realized it," he said.

"Yes. Elinor said you truly loved my mother. I'm glad. I think she was very unhappy in her marriage."

"She was."

"But that leaves me at something of a disadvantage, doesn't it, by the rules of your society? I can't be who I am without rather drastic things happening to me."

"That was never my intent. But I could make arrangements for you, give you the right kind of documents—claim you were adopted by a nonmagister family, but that you're fully magister. That would give you a great many more options in society, as well as allow you to use your abilities."

There might have been a time when I would have been tempted, but now I knew it wouldn't give me what I really wanted. I couldn't help but glance at Henry. Taking the governor's offer would mean giving up on him.

My father must have noticed that glance. "*Him?* Is that what this is all about? Did he get you into this?"

"I was into this movement before I knew he was," I said.

He took a step closer to me, reaching out beseechingly

with one hand. "Miss Newton—Verity—it's not too late for you to save yourself. I can't do anything about Lyndon. He's already wanted for treason. But no one has to know about you. Stay with me and forget this nonsense of a revolution that can't possibly succeed, and I'll send you back to Elinor and the children. You could be with your family. I know they care about you, and you care about them. You're the best teacher I could imagine for them, and I've enjoyed having you as part of my life. I'm giving you a chance here."

I was almost torn. He was offering me something I wanted, more than he could possibly have realized. Much to my surprise, Henry said softly, "Verity, you should take him up on it. You've carried out your mission. You've more than done your part. Now you can go back home to the children and be safe."

I turned to stare at him, aghast. "What?" I blurted. "You want me to give up?"

He gave me a grin I was sure he meant to look cocky, though it struck me as sad. "Mind you, I'm not saying he's right. We're going to win, and we can be together then. But in the meantime, you can be safe with your family."

I studied his face for a long moment, trying to read what he really meant. Was this a ploy, a scheme to give us a chance to escape? If it was, I couldn't see it in his eyes, which looked suspiciously bright. It dawned on me that he really was giving me up for my own safety—and at risk of his own freedom. Without me and the key I wore around my neck, he'd have very little chance of escaping this mansion. He'd be arrested, and I doubted the revolution could move quickly enough to save him before he was transported, or worse. I shook my head slowly. "No."

He nodded. "Go."

During all this, I'd forgotten that we weren't alone in the room. Barker shouted, "Guards!"

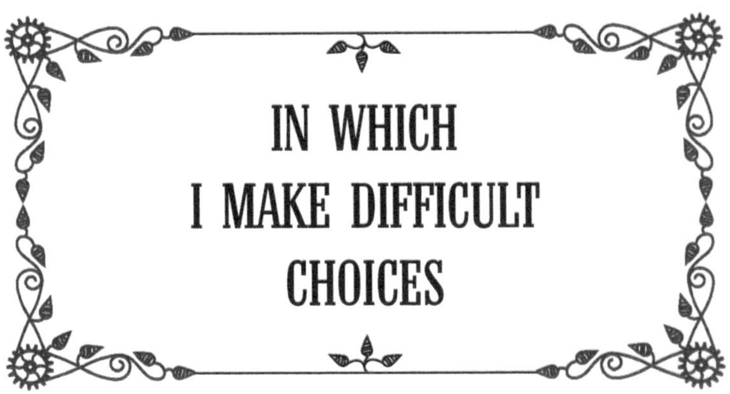

IN WHICH I MAKE DIFFICULT CHOICES

There was no time for making heartwrenching decisions or heartfelt goodbyes. It was time to act. I charged up the ether between myself and the governor, creating a huge ball of glowing, sparking energy. At the same time, I lunged toward Henry, grabbing his arm and bearing him toward the entrance to the secret passageway, pulling on the sconce along the way. The door sensed the key and opened for us. We managed to get inside and shut the door behind us before the glare in the room dissipated.

Inside the passage, both of us went still and held our breaths. "Where did they go?" the governor shouted, and I thought he sounded as distressed as he did angry.

Heavy footsteps sounded, and there were a number of raised voices, all speaking over each other. It seemed like forever until the sound of people searching the study went away. All that time, Henry and I clung to each other in the passage, terrified to make the slightest sound.

Finally, Barker's voice said, "They can't have left the grounds. Search for them!"

Most of the footsteps headed away, but at the same time more footsteps came into the room. "Your Grace, there's something you should see," a voice said.

All the sound moved away from us, and finally Henry and I allowed ourselves to breathe more easily and move. I stood on tiptoes so I could whisper directly into his ear. "Elinor's room?"

He nodded in response, and we began easing our way silently through the passage. Her room was on the same level as the study, but it faced the front of the house rather than the rear, so the passage took us down and around before going back up to the other side of the central hallway. Henry peered through one of the vents to ensure that we were in the right place and that the room was empty before I eased the door open.

"The telegraph will probably be at the window," I whispered. I found the wires hidden alongside the pull for the window shade, coming in the window from above. How Elinor had managed to get the wires to and through the estate without anyone noticing them was a real feat. While I sent the code she'd given me, hoping I was doing so correctly, Henry surveyed the scene outside, looking through a spyglass he took from his bag.

When I was through, he touched my arm and pointed,

handing me the spyglass. I saw a dark mass moving up the main road, toward the estate—a mob of marchers, it looked like. Was this what Nat had done to help us? It was certainly a distraction for everyone in the house. Soldiers ran across the lawn of the estate, toward the gate.

I could also see the fort from there. A blob of red came out of the fort, soldiers heading for the marchers. Henry tugged on my arm, and I didn't need urging to hand him the spyglass and get back to the secret passageway. We needed to get away from here while we could. If those marchers had come to help us, we shouldn't waste their efforts by getting caught in the house.

I would have loved to run, but that was impossible in the dark, narrow passages, especially not when silence was essential. Reaching the tunnel that left the house was a great relief, even though it left us in even more darkness. At least we were less likely to be detected there, and we didn't have to worry about being so quiet.

We reached the end of the tunnel, and I used Elinor's key to unlock the door. Henry opened it a mere crack and looked out before opening it the rest of the way and leading me out. "Now which way?" I asked, still whispering out of what had become a habit.

He looked up and down the wall. "If we could reach them, we might be able to blend in with the marchers, but we'd be rather exposed on the way there. I know a few shortcuts, but it would be risky."

"And there are soldiers heading for the marchers," I pointed out.

"We're probably best off going to the fort. Even if our people haven't taken it, we do have people outside it." Just then, gunfire erupted in the direction of the fort, as if to punctuate what he'd said. "And it sounds like they're taking advantage of the troops leaving to confront the marchers to make a run on the fort. Are you up for managing some rough terrain? We might stand a chance if we move along the edge of these hills."

The honest answer probably would have been "no," since these seemed more like cliffs than hills to me, with the river a long way below, but I didn't feel like I had much of a choice, so I said, "I think so."

"Don't worry, it's not as bad as you'd think. Most of these estates have scenic overlooks and paths leading down to the river."

He held my arm, keeping me steady as we picked our way back to the road. The ground was rocky and uneven, and my boots weren't made for this kind of terrain, so I was grateful for Henry's assistance. On the other side of the road, as he had said, there was a scenic promenade winding its way down the side of the hill. That allowed us to walk on a level surface for some distance, far enough below the hill that we shouldn't be visible from the mansion above us. There were already footprints in the snow on the path, so our passage wouldn't be obvious.

"Why didn't you take the governor's offer?" Henry asked, taking advantage of the relatively easy going to indulge in conversation. "You'd done your part. You could have gone home."

"And leave you to be arrested? You couldn't have made it out without the key and me."

"I'd have come up with something. Remember, I've made it in and out of that room through the window before."

"In broad daylight when they know you're around? I didn't want to take that chance. Now that the governor knows I'm with the rebellion, I doubt I could pull off another prison break, and all my contacts are otherwise occupied at the moment."

He stopped and moved to face me. "You really gave up the chance to go back home and be with the family because you were worried about my safety?" His eyes looked very blue in the morning sunlight as he gazed at me with a sense of wonder.

"It wasn't a difficult decision," I said, feeling my face grow warm. Looking at him was almost too intense for me to bear, but I also couldn't bear to turn away.

"I already owe you so much…" He smiled and shook his head. "You'll have to give me the opportunity to dramatically come to your rescue someday."

"I certainly hope not," I said, turning and resuming my way down the path. "That would mean I'd become as reckless as you. I'd prefer not to need to be rescued."

When the path turned to wind down the hill, we lost our easy footing and had to resume working our way across the hillside. I didn't let myself look down, focusing entirely on the ground beneath my feet, and sometimes my hands. All the while, sounds of nearby gunfire rang through the air, but echoes off hills, the river, and the hills on the opposite shore made it difficult to tell where the sounds came from. Was that fighting at the fort, or were the soldiers attacking the marchers?

It was slow, difficult going, and when we reached a nice, flat rock, we paused to rest. Sitting there, I was forced to look down at the river. While we were hidden from view above, I felt like we were very exposed to anyone who might be looking from the river or from the opposite shore. We were both wearing dark gray clothing that blended into the surroundings, but I still was uneasy enough that I ended the break before I felt fully rested. Fortunately, there were also a great many trees for us to hide among—and cling to—in between the paths and promenades of the estates. I wasn't sure which was worse, the rough terrain that had some cover, or the easy walking that left us exposed.

After a particularly difficult stretch that had me feeling like I might as well have been climbing trees, I was looking forward to the clearing I saw ahead when Henry abruptly stopped and pulled me back. I soon saw why: There were armed sentries patrolling that path and the edge of the estate. "I think this might be the estate next to the fort's property," Henry whispered. "They're probably concerned about the fighting."

"What do we do?"

"Let's try going down."

Heading farther down the steep hill didn't sound at all appealing to me, but neither did getting shot. The trees helped us control our descent, and there were several instances in which I found myself hanging from a branch or tree trunk, my feet not getting any purchase on the ground below. After several minutes of this hair-raising endeavor, we moved forward again to see the situation.

"Blast it!" Henry muttered. I saw what he meant. They'd not only cleared ground for a path, but had removed almost all the trees, probably in an attempt to open up the view of the river from the house above. There was no way to get across from here to the fort without being seen by those sentries.

"Maybe if we go back, we might be able to sneak past one of the other estates onto the main road," Henry suggested. "Or there are some spots where we could get to the riverside without killing ourselves."

Getting back up the hill wasn't quite as terrifying as going down it had been, but it was more strenuous. Henry took us at an angle, so we weren't retracing our steps and were moving away from the sentries even as we went up. He maintained his confident—almost cocky—demeanor, but when I glanced at him without him realizing he was being watched, I could see the worry in his eyes. "I think I know a few ways around here," he said. "My brother married the governor's daughter when I was just a boy, and my parents died not long afterward, so I became a part of their family, and we visited here quite often. I did a lot of exploring to get away from the house. That was before Elinor took to her bed. She knew all the ins and outs around here."

"If we ever get the chance to just sit somewhere and talk, I'd love to hear what she was like," I said, feeling wistful about missing out on having her as an older sister while I was growing up.

"Well, you are now stuck with me, since you chose not to go home. I have a feeling we'll have plenty of time to talk between battles and missions." We emerged from a stretch of woods onto one of the paths. "Now, if I'm not mistaken, this is the estate that's a little more rustic," he said. "If we follow the path up, we might have some cover to reach a road, and we should be past where the marchers were on the main road."

It felt strange to follow the path up, toward the castle-like house that loomed at the top of the hill, when we'd been avoiding moving closer to civilization for the past hour or so. Fortunately, the trees hadn't been entirely cleared from the hillside, and the path meandered through a facsimile of rugged forest. That shielded us from view even as we drew closer to the crenellated turrets of the house, which looked like it had been transplanted from the Scottish Highlands, complete with a ghost or two. I sent a mental blessing to the builder of the place, since his apparent romantic inclinations that kept the land looking somewhat wild gave plenty of cover to fugitives.

Henry abruptly froze, grabbing my arm as a signal for me to do likewise. There was a rustling sound above us, someone or something moving through the dry leaves that covered the ground where the trees above had shielded them from snow. We moved off the path, deeper into the trees. I lifted my skirts so they wouldn't drag in the leaves and make any sound as we moved, and we both stepped carefully and slowly.

We weren't quite as visible off the path as we had been on it, but the underbrush had been cleared in this area, so the trees weren't perfect cover if anyone was looking for us. We hid behind a couple of the larger trees and waited, watching the path. Eventually, a man dressed in the attire of someone who worked outdoors—a groundskeeper, perhaps—came down the path, a shotgun over his shoulder. Was he hunting, guarding the perimeter of his employer's property, or searching for fugitives?

He began whistling, so tunelessly that I couldn't make out what song, which I thought suggested he was merely keeping watch, in light of current events. I doubted he'd make such a racket if he were hunting either animals or people. He disappeared from my view, and I heard the whistling move away from us. Several minutes later, the sound grew louder as he came back up the path. He moved with a casual, loose-limbed ease that suggested he wasn't particularly concerned, merely going through the motions.

We didn't move until he was completely out of sight at what must have been the head of the path.

With that possible avenue of escape cut off due to a guard, we had no choice but to keep going back the way we'd come. I tried not to consider the possibility that all the estates would have guards or other employees keeping a lookout, given that there was fighting at the nearby fort. Or, there had been. Now that I thought about it, it had been some time since I'd last heard gunfire. The battle was over, but who had won?

We came back to a rocky stretch, where few trees managed to cling to the hillside. I'd felt exposed there before, and now that twenty or so yards might as well have been a mile in the middle of the city. If that estate owner was looking out for possible rebels coming to oust his family from their home, there would be little chance of us not being spotted.

"Let's go downhill a bit," Henry suggested, apparently having had a similar thought. While we still had some cover, we went down until the hill dropped off in a sharp cliff. We couldn't go lower and still get across. We were less likely to be seen from the top of the hill than we might have been when we were higher, but we weren't low enough for my comfort. "Do you think you can do this?" Henry asked.

I nodded. I wouldn't like it, but I liked the idea of being shot or captured even less. We went across practically on all fours, which helped us cling to the side of the hill while keeping our heads down. I looked only at where I was putting my hands and feet, avoiding looking at whatever lay at the bottom of the hill or whatever might be coming at us from above. I resisted the urge to cry out in triumph and relief when we reached the shelter of more trees.

"Let's try going up again," Henry said. "There should be a lane near here, and maybe they won't be quite as worried about what's happening at the fort."

"The shooting has stopped," I said.

"All the better."

After going through the woods a few yards, we found a path heading uphill. It was wide, covered in snow, and lined with stones. We kept to the trees until we were in sight of the house. This one was like a French château, with pointed roofs on the square towers at each corner, and a great deal of ornamental ironwork. It was surrounded by formal gardens, but that meant there were high hedges we could hide behind, and I hadn't yet seen anyone with a gun.

We waited a few minutes to see if anyone was patrolling before we ran from the cover of the trees into the gardens. There was a gate in the adjacent wall, if we could get there without being spotted. Even if no one was patrolling, if anyone came outdoors, we looked like very suspicious characters, indeed. My skirt was damp and covered in mud up to my knees, as were Henry's trousers. He had streaks of dirt and mud on his face, and his clothes were torn and dirty. I suspected I looked as bad. If anyone who found us didn't assume we were rebels, they'd think we were vagrants. The question was, had the governor or his people sounded the alarm in the neighborhood about looking for us?

"Hey!" someone shouted.

Henry pushed me toward the trees we'd just left. "Go!" he ordered. He drew his weapon as he followed me. I wanted to weep with frustration. We'd been so close to relative safety. Now we were trapped. We couldn't get to the fort along the hillside. We didn't seem able to get away from the hillside and to the main road. Just before I made it to the trees, I thought I heard something above us, and I looked up. It was the *Liberty*!

The small airship was not too far away, heading toward us. In fact, that seemed to have been what the shout was about. "Henry, look up!" I cried. "We need to make it to that clearing."

Once in the safety of the trees, we didn't worry about being stealthy. We were more worried about getting to where the crew of the ship could see us before it passed by. It was following the river channel, so it had been almost level with the ground at the top of the hill. We burst out from among the trees onto the rocky slope before the airship got there. We took off our hats and waved them, hoping someone would notice us.

They must have, for the airship turned in our direction and the rope ladder lowered. The only place the ship could reasonably reach us was at the top of the hill, on the open grounds of the estate above. The lack of trees there had made our passage treacherous before, but now it provided a way for us to escape.

That was, if we could board the ship before the estate's residents noticed us or the airship coming toward them. The airship seemed very high still, and the ladder was still unwinding as it approached. I heard a shout from behind us, and Henry roughly shoved me to the ground, covering me with his body. There was a lot of noise—footsteps, gunfire, the sound of the ship's engines—and then Henry pulled me up. "Jump!" he urged.

I stood and saw that the ladder was above my head. I had to jump to reach the bottom rung. I hung there for a second, then with all my strength, I pulled up enough to hook my arm around it. Henry soon joined me, doing likewise, and we began to move upward, both from the ladder being winched back into the ship and the ship moving away. Below us, people shouted, and there might have been more gunshots, but some of them came from the ship, and the people below scattered.

If climbing into the ship from my bedroom window had been terrifying, and if climbing on the steep hill over the river had been frightening, dangling this high from the bottom of the ladder was thousands of times worse. I was sure I had a magnificent view, but I couldn't bear to open my eyes.

Eventually, I felt hands reaching down to pull me up and into the airship, and I lay on the floor of the gondola, weak with relief and exhaustion, until I'd stopped shaking. I forced myself to sit up and saw that Mick was standing over me. "We're very fortunate that you came by when you did," I said.

"Well, we got your message."

"My message?" Then I realized, that must have been the message Elinor had given me to send. "But how did you know where we'd be?"

"We were just lookin' out for you. We'd have been there sooner, but we were providin' air support to the marchers on the main road. They've got the governor blocked in. Now we're headin' to the fort."

I turned to Henry, who was a lot slower sitting up than I had been. He groaned softly, and I got a sick feeling of unease. Something was wrong. He reached down to touch his thigh, and brought back a hand covered in blood.

"Can you do anything without getting yourself shot?" I blurted, probably not the most appropriate or caring thing to say under the circumstances, but it was all that came to mind.

I reached under my skirt to rip a length of petticoat to use as a bandage, but even my petticoats were covered in mud. He pressed his hands against the wound on his leg, and blood oozed between his fingers. This was bad, I knew. I didn't think strips of petticoat would do much good.

"There's a way to stop the bleeding," he said as I leaned over him. "I don't think I have the strength or focus to do it myself, though." He glanced at the crew on the ship, and I realized what he meant. I'd have to reveal my magical heritage to the rebels.

Right now, I didn't care. He'd already gone very pale, and his face was beaded in sweat. "Tell me what to do."

"Hands above mine. Try to imagine wrapping the excited ether around my leg."

I did as he directed, feeling the energy flow around and through me as I channeled it to him. There was a faint glow around our joined hands. He gasped softly, and I felt our hands grow very warm, then uncomfortably hot, but I didn't stop until he said, his voice a hoarse whisper, "That should do it."

When I lifted my hands from his leg, I saw that blood no longer pulsed from between his fingers. He was still pale, and his breathing was rapid and shallow. "Will you be all right?" I asked.

"I imagine I'll still need a doctor, but I don't think I'll bleed to death immediately."

Letting out a long, slow breath, I leaned back against the wall of the gondola, sitting next to him. Only then did I look up to find Mick staring at me. "Since when are you a blasted magpie?" he said, loud enough for everyone on the ship to hear.

IN WHICH I VISIT A NEW LAND

Ever since I'd become involved with the Rebel Mechanics, I'd feared how they would respond if they knew about my magister heritage. I'd tried telling myself that once they got to know me, it wouldn't matter. After all, they'd accepted Henry, and he was not only a magister, but a titled nobleman, as well.

The look of dismay and betrayal on Mick's face, and the expressions on the faces of the other men on the ship, suggested otherwise. Perhaps it was the fact that they thought they knew me that made the difference. Liberty Jones was a symbol of the rebellion. If she'd been a magister all along, was that symbol a lie? I could understand if they felt betrayed.

"She's not a magister. She's a half-breed," Henry said, his voice weak but steely. "Do you know what that means in our society? To the authorities, it's worse than having no magic at all. It could get her locked away. She had to keep the secret."

"Even from us?" Mick asked.

"A secret's no good if you tell people," a voice boomed from the rear of the ship. All the men on board turned to look at Everett, the pilot. "Leave the girl alone. What we're fighting for is a land where none of that matters, so it shouldn't matter now. We've got bigger things to deal with. And you'd best get ready to lower that ladder."

"Where are we, and what's happening?" Henry asked.

I didn't much feel like getting up, but I was afraid he'd try, in spite of his condition, so I took the spyglass from his satchel and forced myself to my feet so I could look out over the side of the gondola. "We're coming up to the fort," I said as I peered into the distance. "It looks like there are redcoats surrounding it, so our people must be inside."

"That's right," one of the men on the airship said as he strapped weapons to himself. "We're providing reinforcements, since they can't get through otherwise right now. There's a siege, but better to have us on the inside than on the outside."

The distance between the soldiers outside the fort and the spot behind the walls we were aiming for didn't seem all that far. "You'll be very vulnerable while you're on that ladder," I said with a glance at Henry, whose condition proved the point.

"They can't shoot all of us," the rebel said with a shrug. I didn't think he was right. If those soldiers were decent shots, they could easily pick off every man on that ladder.

Henry tugged on my skirt, and I knelt so I could hear him. "Fog. You can make a fog. Hide them. It's like the light you did with the governor, but without the light." That didn't make a lot of sense, but I thought I knew what he meant.

I gave the spyglass back to him before I straightened and turned to face the rebels. "If you're not too opposed to magic, I may be able to hide you and confuse them. I can't guarantee you'll be entirely safe, but it will make it more difficult for them to hit you."

"You can do that?" Mick asked.

"I believe so. I've only just begun to really learn to use my powers, since I had to keep them secret from magisters, too, but I can try, and that's better than you've got without me trying."

"Do it," one of the rebels said, and the others nodded.

I turned to face the fort, but I had to keep blinking because of the wind in my eyes. "Do you have any goggles you could lend me?" I asked. One of the men took off his goggles and handed them to me. They were still too big even after I tightened the strap, but I could at least keep my eyes open.

I had to take a few deep breaths to relax, and then I concentrated on the ether around the ship, stirring it up between us and the soldiers. The air seemed to thicken, forming into a cloud that completely blocked us. I made sure it extended to the ground. The fog filled in just as the nose of the ship crossed over the wall of the fort.

"Go!" the rebel leader shouted, and the men went over the side, scrambling down the ladder. Everett stopped the engines and let the ship drift. It didn't stop completely, just moved more slowly, so they didn't have a lot of time to get down before we reached the other side of the fort. Mick leaned over the edge to watch, and the moment the last man was down, he cranked the winch to bring up the ladder.

"Can you keep that fog on us for a while?" Everett asked as he restarted the engine and swung the wheel around.

I was already tired, and sustaining that big a work of magic was draining, but I preferred that to being shot down, so I nodded and kept it going as we made a large circle around the fort and headed up the river. Only when we'd passed the governor's mansion did I drop it. I sank down next to Henry on the floor of the gondola, utterly spent.

He put his arm around my shoulders and bent to kiss my temple, above the goggles. "Excellent work. You must have had quite the teacher."

"He was good, but I had to work out a great deal on my own, since he abandoned me last month," I said, reaching up to pull off the goggles. I snuggled against his side, resting my head on his shoulder.

I wasn't aware of falling asleep, but when I woke, I found that someone had covered us with scratchy wool blankets that were probably meant more for covering equipment than people, but they were warm, and for that I was grateful. Henry was still asleep, but I checked his pulse, and it was reasonably steady, if fainter than I would have liked. We were still in the air, but I couldn't tell where we were from my position on the floor of the gondola, and I had no desire to get out from under the warmth of the blankets to find out.

"Where are we going?" I asked Mick, who was running around, checking the rigging.

"To our secret base," Mick said.

"It's safest for you two to be well away from the action for a little while," Everett added. "Elinor's orders."

I gave him a long, appraising look. He knew Elinor, by name? Was Everett her rebel love? She had chosen his project to fund, but then she'd funded a lot of the rebel machines. It seemed I had a lot to learn about my sister. "Did Elinor send you to rescue us?" I asked.

He checked his compass and adjusted course before replying. "We were coming to the fort anyway, but she set up a signal so that if we got it before we left the hangar, we'd look out for you on the way. Good thing, too."

"Yes, very good. I'll have to thank her." If I ever saw her again.

When Henry woke, I shared the food in the bundle Elinor had given me with him. He was still pale, but seemed a little better after the rest, the warmth, and the food. Both of us drifted off to sleep again, waking when the gondola shook with a great thump. We'd landed, coming all the way to the ground. For once, I wouldn't have to go down a ladder hanging in midair to leave the airship.

They brought a litter for carrying Henry off, since his injury kept him from being able to walk. When I stepped out of the gondola, I found myself in an entirely unfamiliar setting. Rows of long, low wooden houses faced a central square, and the people surrounding the ship were a mix of Mechanics and people with brown skin and black hair. A tall man wearing the clothes of a rugged outdoorsman, but with silver earrings, necklaces, and bracelets, approached me. "Miss Liberty Jones, I welcome you to the nation of Iroquoia," he said. "We offer you refuge from the British Empire here."

"Thank you," I said. "But I don't intend to be safe for long. We have a revolution to fight."

A steam whistle sounded behind me, and I turned to see a small steam engine with a gun mounted on top of it approach. Alec saluted me from behind the controls when it stopped. "Hello, Verity," he said, hopping down to meet me. "You're just in time to see our army getting ready."

"Are we going to war?"

"Not immediately, unless the governor said something when you gave him the declaration."

"I don't think he took it seriously."

"So he isn't recognizing the new nation, and you can

bet that he'll be sending for more troops. *Then* we'll go to war. And we'll be ready. The Iroquois Confederacy has made a treaty with the American nation, so they're giving us refuge and are joining us in the fight." He indicated the man who'd greeted me. "This is Joseph, our liaison."

"We don't like them much more than you do," Joseph said.

"We've been building machines for war," Alec said. "Would you like to see what we've been putting together out here?"

"Perhaps later. I've had a very long day. Do you know where they took Henry?"

Alec hid his disappointment well, but not entirely. "Of course. You'll have time here to see everything. I doubt they'll get troops here until spring."

"This way," Joseph said. "We have excellent healers. Henry is in good hands." He led me to one of the nearby buildings, where I found Henry lying in a bed, his injured leg bandaged and propped up on a pillow. His eyes had a slightly glazed look, indicating that they'd given him something for the pain. I sat on the edge of his bed, and he reached to take my hand. "We'll be fine here," he said. "This was where they took me when I first escaped."

"They're getting ready for a war," I replied.

"Of course. You don't think the empire will give up without a fight, do you?"

"I was hoping they might."

He chuckled. "Not likely. But I think they'll be surprised

by what the united force of rebels can do. We'll show them a thing or two, and what they've seen so far is only the beginning."

"If this was only the beginning, what else will we have to do?" I wondered out loud.

"I'm sure we'll rise to the occasion."

"We always do."

SHANNA SWENDSON earned a journalism degree from the University of Texas and used to work in public relations but decided it was more fun to make up the people she wrote about, so now she's a full-time novelist. She's the author of *Rebel Mechanics* and the popular adult romantic-fantasy series Enchanted, Inc. She lives in Irving, Texas, with several hardy houseplants and too many books to fit on the shelves.

www.ingramcontent.com/pod-product-compliance
Lightning Source LLC
Chambersburg PA
CBHW030526310726
48979CB00010B/1822/J
* 9 7 8 1 6 2 0 5 1 2 6 4 7 *